Death by a Whisker

Death by a Whisker

A CAT RESCUE MYSTERY

T. C. LoTempio

CROOKED
LANE

NEW YORK

Copyright © 2018 by T. C. LoTempio

Published in the United States by Crooked Lane Books, an imprint of The Quick Brown Fox & Company LLC.

Crooked Lane Books and its logo are trademarks of The Quick Brown Fox & Company LLC.

Library of Congress Catalog-in-Publication data available upon request.

ISBN (hardcover): 978-1-68331-487-5
ISBN (ePub): 978-1-68331-488-2
ISBN (ePDF): 978-1-68331-489-9

Cover illustration by Rob Fiore
Book design by Jennifer Canzone

Printed in the United States.

www.crookedlanebooks.com

Crooked Lane Books
34 West 27th St., 10th Floor
New York, NY 10001

First Edition: February 2018

10 9 8 7 6 5 4 3 2 1

Two words: You know.
That's all that needs to be said.

Chapter One

I walked into the kitchen and stopped dead when I saw the body, lying squarely in the middle of the floor. "Darn it!" I cried. "Not another one!!"

Melvin the Marvelous Mouse was marvelous no more. Five other Melvins had met similar ends in the past two weeks, although this Melvin's fate had been far worse than his predecessors. Whereas the rest had only suffered deep puncture wounds to the neck and extremities, this Melvin was minus his head, a right paw, and a good bit of his tail. I stooped down and picked up the remains, holding the mouse gingerly by what was left of the tail to avoid getting sticky saliva on my fingers. I heard a slight noise behind me, and I turned to face the killer.

My twenty-two-pound orange and white tomcat lay on his side in front of the screen door, trying to look innocent and failing miserably. "Toby, you rascal," I said sharply. He rolled over onto his back and looked at me with wide eyes the color of shamrocks. "Merow?" he said again.

I crouched beside him on the floor and held out the mangled carcass. "Toby, I don't know what's gotten into you. These things aren't cheap, you know." I dangled what was left of the mouse in front of him. Toby opened his mouth in a bored yawn and looked away. I sighed. "I'm not kidding. If I find another Melvin beheaded à la Anne Boleyn, that's it! No more for you."

Toby twisted his head to look at me. He blinked twice. "Er-owl?"

"Oh, Syd. He knows you don't mean it," came a familiar voice.

I glanced over my shoulder at the speaker, my best friend and roomie, Leila Addams. She was dressed impeccably in pale pink leggings and a matching top in a slightly deeper shade that complemented her auburn hair. I glanced at my own attire, dark denim jeans and white T-shirt with FRIENDLY PAWS ANIMAL SHELTER emblazoned across the chest, and tried not to feel frumpy. "Maybe I haven't in the past, but this time I do," I said in my sternest tone, brushing an errant golden-brown curl out of my face. "Five mice in two weeks? I'm starting to think he's got anger issues."

"Him?" Leila gestured toward the cat, who was now lying on his back, all four paws in the air, looking completely innocent. She let out a soft chuckle. "Maybe he just misses the thrill of the hunt. He was a street cat after all."

That was true. His nickname at the shelter had been "The Wanderer" because he used to sneak out at night and do just that. However, since I'd adopted him, his wandering days had seemed to be over—replaced now with a desire to decapitate every rubber mouse he could lay his paws on.

I knelt on one knee beside the cat and shook my finger at him. "If you don't behave, young man, I'm going to ask Donna Blondell for the name of a good kitty shrink."

Toby's head jerked up at mention of the veterinarian's name, and his eyes narrowed. "Er-erl?" He made a noise deep in his throat, and I figured he was remembering the booster shot Donna had administered. Once the exam was over, though, she'd petted him, told him what a handsome boy he was, and even given him a Melvin the Mouse, so it was kind of hard to tell if he regarded the pretty vet as a friend or a foe. I was betting he was leaning toward the former. In Toby's eyes, anyone who presented him with his favorite toy was his friend for life.

I gave the cat my sternest look, which, to be quite honest, wasn't very stern at all. "I meant what I said, Toby. Destroy another Melvin, and it will be your last."

The cat nuzzled my chin, then laid his head against my chest and started to purr.

Leila eased one hip against the kitchen island. "He certainly knows how to work you," she observed. She moved over to the coffeepot and poured some of the steaming liquid into a mug. "While your cat's in nondestructive mode, let's move on to other topics. Like the shelter event that's—oh my gosh—a week from today! I still can't believe Dudley Simmons agreed to appear."

Dudley Simmons, a former Deer Park native, was a classic "bad boy made good." He'd been expelled from Deer Park High and run away to California when he was fifteen. He'd taken several odd jobs, including working in an animal shelter, and done comedy clubs at night before getting his big break. A movie producer had seen his act and signed him for a cameo role in a film, and the rest, as they say, was history. Now he had a syndicated talk show that was immensely popular and had written several books, but it was his latest, about a rescue cat he'd adopted, that had hit *The New York Times* Best Sellers list a few months ago. Since then, he'd been more in demand than ever. His publicist had informed us that Simmons was booked solid for months in advance, which made his appearance here in Deer Park a real coup.

"Well, the credit for that all goes to Tara," I said. "She pursued him relentlessly. The shelter owes her a huge debt of gratitude."

Tara was Tara Pitsenberger, the manager of Crowden's Bookstore. The major book retailer had recently opened a store in Deer Park, and at the grand opening I'd been surprised to learn that Tara was an old college friend of Donna Blondell's. Donna had immediately filled Tara in on the details of our previous cat café event and I, never one to miss an opportunity, had promptly approached her about holding a similar one at the bookstore. Tara was extremely enthusiastic about the idea, being an animal lover, and had quickly started making inquiries. Two weeks ago, she'd brought us the happy news that Dudley Simmons had agreed to the appearance. "Per Tara, he was sold once he heard it was for the shelter. It appears Dudley is a sucker for rescue cats."

"No wonder," Leila said dryly. "Writing about this has netted him a small fortune. I'm sure he also saw big dollar signs before his eyes at all the potential sales."

"Cynical much?" I teased my friend. "I prefer to think Simmons's heart was just in the right place, instead of being two sizes too small."

Leila clucked her tongue. "That Pollyanna attitude will be your undoing someday," she said with a snicker. "I do marvel, though, at how quickly Tara put all this together."

"I agree. She missed her calling—she should be in marketing, not managing a store," I said. "If I were still at Reid and Renshaw, I'd hire her." I opened the cupboard and took down the canister that held Toby's salmon treats. He looked up at me expectantly, and I tossed a handful into his bowl before turning back to Leila. "I haven't told you the best news yet, because we only found out yesterday. Tara convinced Simmons's publisher, Axiom Books, to donate a percentage of the event's sales to the shelter."

Leila let out a low whistle. "A percentage—wow! That should net the shelter a substantial sum. I bet Kat turned a few cartwheels when she heard that."

"She might have, if she were the athletic type," I said with a chuckle. Katherine McCall, or Kat as I'd nicknamed her when I was three and couldn't pronounce *Katherine* to save my life, was my sister and the director of the Friendly

Paws Animal Shelter in Deer Park, North Carolina. When I'd left my job as director of marketing in a prestigious New York ad agency, she'd immediately urged me to come home and lend a hand at her shelter, which was having financial difficulties. I'd agreed to accept the part-time consultant position, mainly because I was at loose ends career-wise and because, as Dorothy had said to Toto, "There's no place like home."

Leila drained her mug and walked over to put it in the sink. "So, what have you got planned for this lovely Saturday? Or are you working today?"

I shook my head. "I'm not on the schedule, but I was going to take a ride over there anyway. We're expecting some rescues in, plus Harry over at Staples should be bringing the new posters by." I'd had some additional ones made, featuring photos of all the adoptable cats we'd be bringing to the event. I walked over to put my own mug in the sink. "What about you?"

"There's some garden show over in Pottstown that Parker wants me to cover." She glanced at her watch and let out a yelp. "Oh, golly, I'd better get moving too. I have to pick up Betty Stiles. He wants her to take some photos."

As Leila rushed off, I put my own mug in the sink. I glanced down at Toby, who was curled on his cat bed, watching me. "I've got to get going too." I waggled my finger at the cat. "Take it easy on the Melvins, won't you, bud?"

Toby blinked, then stretched full length on the cat bed and wiggled his paws in the air. I chuckled. In the short time I'd been a cat owner, I'd learned that it did no good to give cats any directions—they pretty much did what they wanted.

I let myself in the back door of the shelter just as a tall woman with ash blonde hair was exiting. "Excuse me," the woman murmured as she pushed past me and down the steps into the parking lot. I went inside and was immediately greeted by Maggie Shayne. Maggie not only volunteered, she also worked as our shelter admin, and I knew that Kat regarded the woman as her indispensable right hand. She glanced at the closed door and said, "Did that woman run you over? She came and wanted to fill out an adoption application, but halfway through she suddenly remembered an appointment. I thought her pants were on fire, she got out of here so fast."

I chuckled. "Did she finish the application?"

Maggie frowned. "No, but who knows. I mentioned the shelter event, so maybe she'll show up there. If she remembers, that is. It was right after that she jumped up and left. Anyway"—her lips stretched into a wide grin—"I'm glad you're here. I was going to call you to come down and have a look. Harry delivered the new posters and they are, in a word, fabulous."

I peeled off my jacket and hung it on the rack by the door. "Great. I can't wait to see them."

"Come on. I put 'em in your office."

We walked down the short hallway to the little cubbyhole all the way at the end that served as my office. I still got a little thrill at seeing the plaque on the door: "Sydney McCall, Publicity Director." Once I'd achieved permanent status, I'd wasted no time in fixing up the spot Kat had declared was mine. It was small but cozy, with a desk and a leather chair, and two other chairs in a burgundy and green plaid situated near the desk. Right now, the chairs were teeming with files that I'd been sorting through, and the myriad of papers that I'd left littering the desktop were covered by the stack of large posters that Maggie had placed on top. She walked over, selected the top one, and held it up.

"See," she cried. "Looks great, right?"

Indeed, it did. The background of the poster was a deep navy blue. The lettering was a stark white and proclaimed:

BOOK SIGNING /SHELTER EVENT! COME SPEND "CATURDAY," AUGUST 14, WITH US AND MEET *NY TIMES* BESTSELLING AUTHOR DUDLEY SIMMONS, WHO WILL AUTOGRAPH COPIES OF HIS NEWEST BOOK, *MY CAT AND ME*.

ALSO, COME MEET SOME OF THE RESIDENTS OF FRIENDLY PAWS ANIMAL SHELTER *WHO ARE* UP FOR ADOPTION!

In the center of the poster was a publicity photo of Dudley and his cat, taken from the back of the book jacket.

Scattered all around the edges of the poster were photographs of the various shelter cats that we planned on bringing to the event.

"*Great* isn't a good enough word," I breathed. "It looks mah-velous, dah-ling."

"I have to agree," said a soft voice. "And I just love the 'Caturday' slogan."

I turned around and grinned at my sister, who looked as cool as a glass of lemonade in her yellow checked shirt and matching crop pants. Kat and I are about as alike as night and day. I'm five foot three, curvy, with mousy brown hair that I try to inject some life into with gold highlights. My sister is close to five nine, willowy, and a natural blonde. My sister can be very spontaneous; I, on the other hand, have a definite tendency to overthink situations. One thing we'd always shared, though, was a deep love of animals. I could still recall Kat nursing back to health a tiny robin whose wing had been broken. She'd cried when the bird was well enough to fly away, and I'd cried with her.

"Thanks. I thought it was pretty cute too," I answered. "I'm really excited about this event, Kat. I think it's going to be a real winner."

"I am too. Tara worked a miracle for us."

"Amen to that."

We both lifted our heads as the sounds of barking dogs reached our ears. "Our new rescues sound pretty lively. Let's check 'em out."

We made our way down the long hall toward the kennel area. Although Friendly Paws specialized in cat and kitten rescues, we prided ourselves on being an "equal opportunity" shelter, taking in stray dogs, rabbits, hamsters . . . an occasional parrot—even a garden snake. Kat pushed open the door and we walked inside. Four pups immediately raced to the edge of the large pen, barking and jumping over one another.

"Poor things," Kat said. "They really miss their owner. Irene didn't want to give them up, but after she fell and broke her hip, she had no choice. Now it's up to us to find them good homes."

Irene Brewster, a feisty eighty-four-year-old, had been a big animal lover, although when her Persian cat passed, she'd sworn she'd never get another pet at her age. When her next-door neighbor's husband got a promotion that entailed moving the family to London, the neighbor had asked Irene if she knew anyone who would want to take on her five puppies and three cats. Irene had assured her neighbor she'd find the animals homes, but had ended up keeping them herself. Everything had gone well until two months ago, when she'd tripped going down her cellar stairs and broken her hip. Fortunately, her son had been able to get her admitted into Shadyvale Convalescent Home, which was about three miles away from his home in South Carolina. Irene had been reluctant to leave her animals at first, but reconsidered after her son agreed to take a cat and a pup to live in his one-bedroom condo. He'd read about our previous cat event at Dayna's Café and contacted us about finding homes for the remaining animals.

I walked closer to the enclosure and peered inside. A large Rottweiler puppy looked up at me with limpid eyes while a blonde Cocker Spaniel put his paws up on the side of the pen and gave a loud yip. The other two puppies were playing in the opposite corner of the enclosure.

I looked over my shoulder at Kat. "Are they all purebreds?"

She shook her head. "Only the Rottie and the Cocker. The others look like mixes—one looks like a Cockapoo, and the one in the far corner over there appears to be a Lab and pit bull mix, but he seems quite friendly."

I'd never agreed with the stigma that was attached to the pit bull breed, and thought it highly unfair. In my opinion, dogs had to be trained to be vicious. I started to ask about the cats, when we heard the strident ring of the back doorbell. Kat turned in that direction but stopped when Maggie called out, "I'll get it." We watched the puppies play for a few minutes, and then walked across the hall to the cattery to inspect our other two new arrivals. "This is Princess Fuzzypants," said Kat, pointing to a cage where a beautiful Maine Coon lay, grooming her long red hair.

I bent closer and smiled down at the cat. "You certainly look like a princess," I exclaimed. "You'll have no trouble finding a 'furever home,' I'm sure."

Princess Fuzzypants lifted her head and fixed me with

piercing blue eyes. "Meow," she said. One paw came up and waved in the air. "Meow."

Kat didn't even bother to stifle her grin. "It would appear the Princess agrees with you."

I chuckled and turned my attention to the next cage and the large brown and tan cat that lay inside. "This one's a beauty too," I said. "A ragdoll, right?"

"Yep. Her name's Annie Reilly."

"Interesting name." I wiggled my fingers inside the bars of the cage. The cat sat up and raised her paw.

"Merow." The cat swiped her paw through the slats of the cage at the silver chain around my neck. I jumped back just in time to avoid her snagging it. "She's a lively one," I remarked. "I hope someone with a lot of energy adopts her."

Maggie came bustling back into the cattery. "Tara Pitsenberger is in your office, Kat," she said. "She said she needs to talk to you and Syd right away. I asked her what was wrong, but she said she wanted to tell you personally."

I heard the hurt note in Maggie's voice, and I knew Kat did too. Maggie considered herself the major domo of Friendly Paws and felt that we just couldn't survive without her—which, of course, we couldn't. Kat slipped her arm around Maggie's shoulders and gave her a quick hug. "And of course, you come with us," she told her. "You are my right hand after all."

A beaming Maggie led the way back down the hall to Kat's office. As we entered, Tara rose from the chair in front of the desk. "Have you heard the morning news?" were the first words out of her mouth.

We all shook our heads in unison. "Well." Tara let out a giant breath. "It's Dudley Simmons. He was in an auto accident in LA this morning."

Kat, Maggie, and I all let out a collective gasp. "He's not dead, is he?" Maggie asked bluntly.

"No, he's not dead," Tara said crisply. "He does, however, have four broken ribs, a shattered shoulder, a concussion, and a sprained ankle. I called his publicist as soon as I heard the broadcast," she said. "He said his recovery would take a good three to six months, possibly longer."

"So that means no event next Saturday." Kat said in a matter-of-fact tone. "Well, it is incredibly bad news, but we'll deal with it." She started to pace in front of her desk, something she always did when concentrating. "We can still have the adoption event at the store, if you don't mind. I know it will probably attract less of a crowd, and we'll lose the added revenue we would have gotten from Mr. Simmons's sales, but . . ."

"Hold on. Not so fast, Kat." Tara held up her hand. "All is not lost. I also called a few people I know who work in the publishing industry, and guess what? I found a replacement author!"

"You did!" Kat let out a squeal. "That's amazing, Tara."

"It certainly is," I said. Having worked in the advertisement industry, I knew just how difficult it could be to get a celebrity replacement on such short notice. "I realize we shouldn't be fussy, but . . . is it someone of equal magnitude as Dudley Simmons? Someone who'll be easily recognizable?"

"Absolutely, if you're a fan of television shopping and *Shopping Your Way*, which most people nowadays are." She paused and spread her arms wide. "It's Ulla Townsend."

"Ulla Townsend? Really?" Even I, not a fan of online or television shopping, knew who Ulla Townsend was. She'd been born and raised right here in Deer Park, had gone to college in California, and then started out as a weather girl before graduating to a small cable shopping channel in Houston. It wasn't long before her sharp tongue and acerbic wit had landed her on the nationally popular *Shopping Your Way* show, based out of Charleston, South Carolina. The woman had quite a following. Last I'd heard, she had over one million followers on Twitter and just about as many on Facebook. As my father would have said, "She could sell snow to Eskimos." As a former marketing executive, I could appreciate someone who knew how to utilize strategic thinking. Not only was she a brand champion, but she knew how to hone into the right customer base for whatever product it was that she was selling. And it seemed that no matter what she sold, from clothing to cosmetics, right on down to small tools, people just couldn't resist the appeal of Ulla Townsend. "I know she's a popular shopping channel host, but she wrote a book too?"

Tara nodded. "Her autobiography. It's only been out

two weeks and it's already number two on the New York Times Best Sellers list. Isn't that fantastic?"

"It certainly is," Kat said. "I have to say, Tara, you are definitely a miracle worker. How on earth did you manage to get someone as popular as Ulla Townsend on such short notice?"

Tara's eyes crinkled up as she said, "Well, to be honest, I had sort of an inside track. My cousin is one of the producers of her cable show. As soon as I heard the news about Dudley, I gave Wendy a call. She was more than happy to get the ball rolling." She reached for her tote bag, which she'd tossed on the floor beside her chair. "I've got to get back to the store. Her agent is faxing over some paperwork for us to sign, but I wanted to tell you as soon as possible. I'll be in touch with the details!" With a quick wave and a smile, Tara hurried out the door.

Kat stood for a minute, brows pulled in. "Well, it's not quite what we expected," she said at last. "But maybe it will turn out better in the end. What do you girls think?"

"She is pretty popular," I said. "She'll definitely attract a large crowd."

Kat turned toward Maggie, who'd remained silent ever since Tara had mentioned the host's name. "Mags? What do you think?"

Normally docile, Maggie now whirled around to face Kat. Her eyes were blazing, and her hands shook as she balled them into fists and rested them on her hips.

"What do I think?" she rasped. "I think that anything

that woman's involved with ends up a disaster. I hope you'll forgive me, Kat, but I absolutely refuse to have anything to do with the event if Ulla Townsend is involved."

And with that, Maggie turned on her heel and barreled out of Kat's office, slamming the door behind her.

Chapter Two

After Maggie's dramatic exit, Kat and I just stood there, rooted to the spot, staring first at the closed door and then at each other. I finally found my voice. "Goodness. What was that all about?"

Kat looked mystified. "I have no idea. I've never seen her act like that before."

I rubbed at my forehead. "She's got definite issues with Ulla Townsend, I can tell you that much. It almost sounded like she knew her personally."

"It's possible. They both grew up here in Deer Park, and they're around the same age."

There was a knock on Kat's door, and then Viola Kizis, one of our other volunteers, stuck her head in. "Maggie wanted me to tell you two that she's got a terrible migraine and she won't be able to finish her shift today. But not to worry—I told her that I could fill in."

Kat and I exchanged a quick look, and then Kat said,

"Thanks, Vi. I appreciate that. Maggie was going to help me take Irene's animals over to the clinic, so if you wouldn't mind—"

"No need to bother Vi," I cut in. "I can help you take the animals over."

"Are you sure? I know you were looking forward to having some time off."

I waved my hand. "Of course I'm sure. Anything for the animals. Besides," I added with a grin in Vi's direction, "I have the feeling Vi'd rather stay here and take care of her back."

Vi's eyes narrowed. "How'd you know my sciatica was acting up?"

"Easy. You grimaced a couple of times, plus you keep rubbing at your lower back."

Vi pulled her hands away from her back and clasped them in front of her. "Ever the detective, aren't you?" she said with a smile.

"Yep, that's me." It had been a relatively easy deduction. Vi's sciatica was always acting up in some way, shape, or form, but the lively seventy-year-old rarely let it stop her from doing exactly what she wanted. "So, now that's settled"—I faced my sister and rubbed my hands together—"let's get moving, shall we? Besides, I'm dying to drive the new van."

*   *   *

It was a few minutes before noon when we pulled the shelter van into the parking lot of the Deer Park Animal Clinic.

The lot was deserted save for the white van that had DEER PARK ANIMAL PATROL printed in big red letters across both sides. Our new van, courtesy of a generous donation from one of the shelter's biggest benefactors, Petra Littleton, was almost its twin, except it had FRIENDLY PAWS ANIMAL SHELTER printed across the sides in navy letters. I slid the van in beside it and switched off the ignition. Kat and I clambered out, and we each hefted a carrier out of the back. We were halfway up the back steps when the door opened, and Donna Blondell smiled at us from the doorway.

"I thought that was you guys," she greeted us. "The new van looks great."

Donna was a Deer Park native like Kat and myself, an attractive blonde in her early forties. She described herself as "an animal lover right out of the crib." She'd gotten her degree at the College of Veterinary Medicine at North Carolina State University, graduating at the top of her class. She'd worked for a while in Raleigh and, after her father passed, had taken her inheritance and opened her own practice in Deer Park. Donna's parents had left her fairly well off, which enabled her to do a lot of charity work for people who couldn't otherwise afford to give their pets the best medical care. She also did all the shelter exams and neuters gratis, which was a big boon to us. She gave me a broad smile as she peered inside the carrier I held.

"Ooh, a Ragdoll, right?" Donna wiggled her fingers at the cat through the bars of the carrier. "She's gorgeous."

"Yes, she is. Her name's Annie Reilly."

"That's quite a moniker. There's another cat and the rest are pups, right?"

"Correct. The other cat's a Maine Coon—Princess Fuzzypants. She's got the sweetest face and the most gorgeous long red hair. Then there's a purebred Rottweiler named Lenny, and a Cocker named Jerry, and the mixes are George and Kramer."

Donna started to laugh. "Someone was a Seinfeld fan, huh? Well, let's get the rest of 'em in here. It's Amanda's day off, but she said she'd be glad to come in and lend a hand." Amanda Winfield was the other vet in the clinic, a cheerful, curvy brunette. She'd recently graduated Duke University—cum laude—and Donna had wasted no time in snapping her up for the clinic. We finished hauling in the rest of the carriers, and then Kat asked Donna and Amanda what time we should pick them up.

"Let's see. I've got a surgery scheduled for Laurie Rubin's tomcat Rufus at three, so . . . how about two thirty?"

"Sounds good," I said. "I have to say, I'm surprised to hear about Rufus. Laurie always said she'd never get him neutered."

"Just between us, I think she got tired of everyone accusing him of fathering half the stray kittens in the neighborhood," Donna said with a chuckle. "No matter what prompted her decision, it's the right one. Not only does neutering help control overpopulation, but it also helps eliminate the risk of contracting or spreading disease. In many cases, it also helps to calm the cat down."

"I'm not sure if it was the procedure or just the fact that now he's got a real home, but Toby shows no signs of wanting to wander anymore," I said. "Although he has been displaying a different sort of behavior lately." I told Donna about my cat's aggressive tendencies toward the plastic mouse.

Donna waved her hand dismissively when I was done. "It's probably just a phase he's going through. I wouldn't worry about it, but keep an eye on him. Let me know if he exhibits any other signs of unusual behavior, like biting."

"Will do." I set Kramer's carrier down on the floor and turned to Donna. "Tara came by to see us earlier."

"I know; she dropped by here too. That's great about Ulla Townsend, isn't it? My apartment is filled to the brim with stuff I really didn't need but bought just because she recommended it."

"The fact she's a Deer Park native will be a big publicity draw too," I said. "She said that her cousin is one of Ulla's producers."

"Wendy—yeah, she is. She's been assigned to Ulla's show for, oh, the past year, I think. She's a real go-getter. In addition to her duties as a producer, she also handles publicity for all of Ulla's shows."

"And speaking of publicity, I've got to get new posters made and new press packs sent out." I slid my sister a sidelong glance. "Oh well, so much for my day off."

"I appreciate all your hard work," Kat said. She reached out and gave my arm a pat. "When the event's over, you can have two days off in a row, to make up for it."

I swatted at my sister's arm. "I'll hold you to that, Sis. Don't think that I won't."

"Oh, I know you will." Kat's pretty face suddenly darkened. "I just thought of something. Simmons's publisher was donating a percentage of the day's sales to the shelter. I wonder if Ulla's publisher will do the same?"

"I think Ulla's book is published by Axiom, which was also Simmons's publisher, but I could be wrong," Donna ventured. "You can check with Tara. If it's a different publisher, believe me, she'll fight tooth and nail to get you the same deal." Donna paused and then added, "Tara loves animals, you know. Had a slew of 'em growing up. I think if she had a stronger stomach, she'd have gone into veterinary medicine too, but she faints at the sight of blood. I'm sure a lot of her determination is motivated by wanting to do right by the shelter."

"I'm sure Tara will do her best. In the meantime . . ." I rubbed at my belly. "It's after twelve and my stomach is growling. You know what that means."

Kat's stomach was growling too, so I didn't have to ask her twice. We said our goodbyes, and ten minutes later I was pulling into DuBarry's crowded parking lot. I slid the van into the last available space, and we climbed out and hurried into the building.

Back in the day, DuBarry's had been known as a down-home type of bar/meeting place. Recently, however, it had undergone a radical makeover so that it was now more of a bar/upscale eatery. The main room was wide open, with tables scattered all around. The bar was a shining block of mahogany wood, accentuated by droplights and a long mirror. Padded stools in gold and purple flanked it. The lighting was dim but cozy. Up until a few weeks ago, it had only been open from three PM until two in the morning, but thanks to a new manager, it was now open at eleven-thirty to accommodate the lunch crowd. I thought it was a smart move: their business had more than doubled. The bar did just as brisk a business in the afternoon as it did in the evening, and the lunch menu now included fare designed to appeal to all ages. We walked up the steps eagerly, but our faces fell once we entered the foyer. The dining room looked packed, and there were at least a dozen people waiting for tables. I made my way over to the hostess podium. I recognized the hostess, Marissa Stevens. She'd recently adopted a gray and white cat from our shelter, and she smiled widely as I approached. "Hi, Syd! How are you? How are plans going for the shelter-slash-book-signing event? It's next Saturday, right? I already asked my manager for the day off so I could go."

"They're coming along." Obviously, the news about Simmons and his replacement hadn't already gotten around, and I didn't feel the need to share just yet. "How's Jilly doing?"

Marissa's eyes lit up. "Oh, she's doing fabulous. She's adjusted to her new home. I got her a little cat bed to sleep in, but she likes to jump up on my bed and snuggle on my pillow."

I smiled, thinking that Toby often did the same thing, when he wasn't massacring his toys. "That's wonderful." I gave the crowded foyer a quick glance. "It looks like you guys are really slammed for lunch today."

"Yeah, word got around about our specials today. They're really, really good." Marissa frowned at the list in front of her. "I'd say it's about a half-hour wait, maybe more. Do you want me to put your name down?"

"Yes, please." She jotted my name on a pad, and I made my way back over to Kat. "It's at least a half-hour wait," I informed her. My stomach let out another loud rumble, and I gave my midsection a rub. "Maybe we should head over to Rosie's."

Kat wrinkled her nose at my mention of the popular diner. "It's probably the same there. Rosie's special today is Yankee pot roast, and you know what a crowd that draws."

I made a face. "I guess we could try the Greek deli. I like Miklos's gyros, but I really had my heart set on a DuBarry burger."

"Who doesn't want a DuBarry burger?" said a voice just behind us. Kat and I both whirled around to face Grace Topping, the owner of the millinery shop situated just up the block in what Deer Park residents referred to as "shopper's square." She smoothed a hand over her silver-gray bob and smiled. "I guess the two of you are here for lunch?"

"That was the original plan," I said, inclining my head toward the hostess podium. "It looks like a half-hour wait at least, though, and quite frankly I don't think I can hold out that long." My stomach let out another loud rumble to punctuate my statement, and we all laughed. "I'm surprised to see you here, Grace," I said. "You usually bring your lunch to work, right?"

"Ordinarily, yes, but today I'd planned a little get-together with my cousin. She called last week and said she'd be coming here for a visit."

"Oh, you mean MaeAnn?" I remembered the woman who was Grace's second cousin. Despite the difference in age, they'd always been close, and I knew that when she'd moved to Georgia, Grace had missed having her around.

"None other," she responded with a smile. "MaeAnn was going to meet me here, so I came early and got a table, but she just texted me that she got hung up visiting my Aunt Margery. My aunt rarely gets visitors in the nursing home, so MaeAnn decided to stay in Weddington a few extra days. Anyway, I was just about to give up my table, but if you two would like to substitute, I won't have to," she finished with a broad grin.

I rubbed both hands together. "Say no more, Grace. We'd love to substitute for your cousin."

After I told Marissa she could remove my name from the waiting list, Kat and I followed Grace to a table set far back in the corner. Once we were seated and perusing the specials, Grace leaned forward and asked, "I heard a news bulletin about Dudley Simmons. Such a shame. Are you going to cancel next Saturday's event?"

"Fortunately, no." I explained Tara's connection and

how she'd been able to get Ulla Townsend on such short notice. "So, the event will be going forward after all," I finished.

"Hmm. Well, I'm glad of that, although I am sad about not getting to meet Dudley Simmons. I'm sure you'll get a big crowd with Ulla Townsend, though. The woman is popular."

"You can say that again," Kat put in. "Are you a fan?"

Grace's jaw dropped. "Oh, dear Lord, no. I think the woman is egotistical and conceited."

I didn't even try to smother my grin. "Hey, Grace, don't hold back. Tell us how you *really* feel."

Grace let out a soft chuckle. "Well, I'll probably buy a copy of her book, but only if it will benefit the shelter. A portion of the proceeds are still going there, I hope?"

Kat held up her hand, all fingers crossed. "Ulla has the same publisher as Dudley Simmons, so that's what we're hoping for."

"I don't think you have to worry. I'm sure that even if the publisher balked, Ulla would insist on it. She wouldn't want to look like a piker. The signing is for charity after all." Grace dabbed at her lips with her napkin. "I'm sure I can find someone on my Christmas list to give her book to."

"Why not read it yourself?" I suggested mischievously. "It's supposed to be a real page-turner."

"No thanks." Grace made a face, as I knew she would. When it came to bios, she preferred staid historical figures like Terry Roosevelt. She reached for her water glass, took a long sip, and then said, "Although I've no doubt the book is interesting, to say the least. Ulla probably considers this event a sort of 'triumphant return.' She always said that if and when she came home to Deer Park, it would only be because she'd have made something of herself, and she was right."

I took a sip of my own water before commenting, "So you knew her when she lived here?"

"No, I never met her, but MaeAnn went to school with her. I've heard lots of stories." Grace leaned forward. "When she was growing up here in Deer Park, she was Ulla Beckman. She and her brother, Bart, and their parents lived on the south side of town."

Back in the day, the south side of Deer Park had been classified as the "poor" section. Times had changed, of course, but some people still bore the "south side" stigma. I imagined Ulla was one of them.

"From what I heard, Ulla wasn't a very attractive teenager, and of course her wardrobe was quite limited," Grace went on. "You know how cruel high school kids can be. Graduation day, Ulla stood up in front of all of them and said they'd all rue the day they made fun of her, that one day she'd come back to Deer Park and she'd be somebody. She'd be famous, and they'd all want to know her, but they could kiss her . . . you get the idea."

"Hmm, that was what? Twenty-plus years ago? She's probably forgotten all about that now."

Grace eyed me over the rim of her water glass. "I wouldn't bet on that. MaeAnn always said Ulla was great at nursing grudges." She tapped the edge of her mug with her fingernail. "Ulla was no shrinking violet. She learned to give as good as she got. She pulled a few good pranks on a couple of girls. Some were mean and nasty too. She got away with it then, and it set the tone for the future, I suppose."

Our waitress appeared just then, and conversation came to a halt as we gave our orders. Both Kat and Grace picked one of the specials, chicken a là king over toast points, and I ordered what I'd salivated over all morning: a DuBarry burger, medium rare, with everything but the kitchen sink on it. Once the waitress had gone, Grace looked at us and asked, "How does Maggie feel about Ulla Townsend taking Dudley Simmons's place?"

"Funny you should ask that," I said. "She had a pretty severe reaction. She got all red and said that she was sorry, but she wouldn't have anything to do with the event if Ulla Townsend was part of it."

Grace's head dipped. "I had a feeling she'd react that way."

I didn't bother to hide my surprise. "You did?"

"Absolutely," Grace said. "Maggie and Ulla were in the same class in high school, and they never got along. As a matter of fact, to say they hated each other would be putting it mildly."

Chapter Three

Toby woke me before the alarm went off the next morning. I awakened to find his gold and white face on the pillow next to mine as he gently raised a paw and batted my cheek.

I stifled a yawn. "I'm awake, Tobes," I said groggily before rolling over onto my back. Undaunted, Toby took a swipe at my comforter and let out a loud meow. Translation: "Get up, you lazy slug." I had the distinct impression that if he knew how to rip the comforter off me, he would have done just that. I struggled to a sitting position and looked at him, and he dropped back onto all fours.

"It's still early. Maggie isn't coming in this morning till ten."

My plan, as I'd outlined to Toby before I went to bed last night, was to arrive at the shelter just when Maggie would be getting there. The shelter was open by appointment only on Sunday, and we each took turns with "early duty" on Sunday, meaning someone went there between eight and ten to feed the animals, walk them, play with them, do whatever needed to be done. Maggie's scheduled time was this morning, and she hadn't cancelled as far as I knew.

Toby meowed loudly again, and I figured this time it was part "Get up, Lazybones," and part "I'm hungry—when are you going to feed me?" I swung my feet off the bed and reached for my robe. "Shower first, Fuzzball," I told Toby, who promptly sat back on his haunches and took a pass at his furry face with his paw.

I showered quickly and then went downstairs to make myself a cup of coffee. While it was brewing, I opened the front door and got the morning paper. I carried it into the kitchen and spread it across the table. I'd informed Leila of the change in guest, and she'd promised to put a notice in the Sunday edition, and there it was, right in the bottom corner of page one:

SHOPPING CHANNEL HOST COMES
THROUGH FOR FRIENDLY PAWS

The two paragraphs that followed touched on Simmons's accident and played up how willing Ulla Townsend had been to step in and help out her old hometown's shelter. I wondered idly if Ulla's publicist had been responsible for most of the notice. Well, if Ulla was half as popular as everyone claimed she was, she should sell a lot of books, which would result in revenue for the shelter. I hoped.

After I was well fortified with three cups of coffee, I left the remainder in the pot for Leila when she woke up, said goodbye to Toby, and hopped in my convertible. My first stop was Dayna's Sweets and Treats. The combination café and bakery had originally been known as McCall's when my parents had owned it, and after my dad's death, Kat and I had sold it to Dayna Harper, an attractive African American woman. Dayna had helped us out with our very first shelter event, which we'd held at her shop, and she'd promised to provide treats for the book signing as well. As soon as I walked through the glass door, I was hit by an overwhelming bout of nostalgia. Dayna had kept things pretty much the same as my father had, from the wide counter with its high-backed stools to the glass cases that displayed dozens of her homemade, mouthwatering treats. Dayna herself was behind the counter, and she waved as I made my way over to her.

"Kinda early on a Sunday for you, isn't it?" she asked in her singsong voice. "Or is today your early day at the shelter?"

"No, not my early day—it's Maggie's. I thought I might go over and lend her a hand, though, and take something sweet while I'm at it."

"Well, girl, you came to the right place for something sweet." Her gaze wandered to the large display case. "I'm trying out some new pastries for the event next week. How about a Dabby Dough?"

I slid onto one of the leather-covered stools and rested my elbows on the wide Formica counter. "Sounds interesting. What's in it?"

"I made it from leftover apple pie dough. They're filled with a mixture of cinnamon and sugar and butter, then rolled, sliced, and baked. Then there's this other one." She pointed to another pastry next to the Dabby Doughs.

"That looks good," I said. "What's that one called?"

"It's a Moorkop, a Dutch cream-puff pastry. They came out pretty good too, if I do say so myself." Dayna went over to the case, selected one of each, put them on a plate, and held it out to me. "Go on, try 'em," she said with a wink. "You can be one of my official tasters. Free of charge."

I surveyed the Moorkop. The top of the cream puff was glazed with dark chocolate, and it was capped with a dollop of whipped cream. A tiny sliver of pineapple sat at its base. Dayna handed me a fork, and I sliced the puff in half, letting the whipped-cream insides ooze out. I popped half into my mouth and made a little moan of pleasure. "Ooh. So. Good."

Dayna beamed. "I thought you'd like it. Now try the Dabby."

The Dabby was excellent too. I'm not ashamed to say I finished both. "I'll take two of each to go," I said, whipping out my wallet. "And I insist on paying for them," I added. I knew Dayna was often much too generous for her own good. It sometimes amazed me that the store managed to turn a profit, what with all the free samples she liked to give away.

Dayna shrugged. "Suit yourself." As she rang up my purchase, she asked, "So, are you looking forward to Saturday? Now that Ulla Townsend's part of the event, it wouldn't surprise me if Crowden's got a banner crowd of people Saturday. I know some folks from neighboring towns are planning to attend."

I hadn't considered that possibility. I made a mental note to double-check with Tara about security for the event, then paid for the pastries and promised Dayna to stop in again before the big day.

"I'm planning on handing out some leaflets and flyers for my shop too," she told me as she handed me the white and pink pastry box. "After all, there's no telling how much extra business this event could attract."

"That's true. Aren't you glad you agreed to provide the treats, gratis?"

"I'm glad you pointed out I could take the deduction from my income tax as a charitable donation," Dayna said with a broad wink. "This event could prove profitable for both our businesses."

The door opened and Leila sailed in. "Well, fancy seeing you here," she drawled. Turning to Dayna she said with a smile, "Coffee, extra-large, please. The dregs my roomie left me this morning just didn't cut it."

As Dayna moved off to get the coffee, I gave Leila's outfit a once-over. She was wearing a low-cut floral sundress, with a white lace shrug around her shoulders, and strappy white sandals. "Nice outfit. Going to church?"

She flushed. "Ah, no. Actually I'm heading over to Raleigh. They've got an antique street fair going on."

I looked pointedly at the dress. "By yourself?"

Leila shifted her weight from one foot to the other. "No," she said at last. "Jim's taking me."

"Jim Wantrobski? Again?" I couldn't resist a grin. Jim was a reporter/photographer on the *Deer Park Herald*. It was no secret he had a huge crush on Leila, who was always quick to disavow any interest in dating him. However, this was the third time now in the past two weeks they'd gone somewhere together that wasn't work related.

The man in question walked through the sweet shop door just then. "Hey there," he said cheerily. "I got your text. I just have to drop some photos off at the office, and I'll meet you outside here in ten minutes."

Dayna returned to the counter, bearing two large Styrofoam cups of coffee. She handed one to Leila and one to Jim. "I got your text too," she said with a wink. "It's extra strong, the way you like it."

Jim took a quick sip of the coffee, gave Leila a peck on the cheek, and then, with a wave to Dayna and myself, vanished out the door. I gave my bestie a playful poke in the ribs. "I see why you like him. He's very accommodating."

Leila pulled a face at me. "Very funny. And speaking of accommodating males, I heard you had dinner with Will twice last week."

I sighed. "They were more like run-ins. We haven't been on an actual date in weeks. Will's been putting in a lot of overtime since Bennington left." Will Worthington, my current boyfriend, was a homicide detective on the Deer Park police force. His partner, Henry Bennington, had recently taken a position with the Broward County Homicide Department. Since Bennington had given both Kat and myself a hard time during a recent murder investigation, I had to admit I wasn't sorry at all to see him go. "Will's practically living at the station, what with Randy Michaelson and Trent Duggan both out on medical leave. He and Charlie Callahan have been picking up the slack."

"Who's Charlie Callahan?"

"He just transferred here from Macon. I haven't met him yet, but Diane gave me the lowdown." Diane Ryan, one of our volunteers, was also the admin down at the station. Diane loved her job, but she loved to gossip more. "He graduated from the police academy top of his class, worked second lead on some high-profile cases. Plus, he's the nephew of Mayor Bascomb."

"Which means he's in the running for Bennington's slot too," said Leila. She shook her head. "Captain Connolly is fair, but he can be a political animal, especially in an election year. It'll be interesting to see how this plays out." She took a quick sip of her coffee, and then said, "It's time to 'fess up, Syd. Has Will's kissing technique improved since high school?"

"Where's that coming from?" I certainly wasn't about to admit that so far the opportunity for Will to kiss me hadn't presented itself. Our few dates had always been interrupted at the most inopportune moments. "I might ask you the same thing? What sort of a kisser is Jim?"

She winked at me. "Better than I thought." She jumped as her cell phone let out a loud beep. Whipping it out of her pocket, she looked at the screen and shook her head. "He needs to work on his timing, though. He's outside. But our discussion isn't over," she said as she started for the door. "I still want an answer to my question."

"Funny," I murmured as the door closed behind her. "So do I."

I drove right to the shelter and parked a few spaces away from the rear entrance. I noticed Maggie's Volvo parked under the elm tree, and the lights were on in the cattery, a sign that she was already at work. I let myself in, balancing my tote and the pastry box, and called out, "Hello! Maggie, are you here?" Receiving no answer, I set the tote and pastry box down in the breakroom and made my way to the cattery. No one was there, but I saw a thin sliver of light emanating from under the door across the hall marked PLAY-ROOM. I rapped on the door gently with my knuckles and was relieved to hear Maggie call out absently, "Come in—but be careful." I edged the door open and stopped at the sight before me.

A beautiful, light-hued calico cat was on the long counter, her tail in the air, her back arched. Maggie was at the other end, holding a non-decapitated, fully limbed Melvin the Mouse. She waved Melvin in the air, and the calico launched herself forward, paws outstretched. She clamped one around Melvin's neck and drew the little mouse to her; then she rolled over on her back and held the mouse in her front claws, her back ones wiggling in the air. Her head lolled to one side, and her pink tongue was partially out of her mouth, a sure sign that she loved the catnip.

Maggie glanced up and her intense expression relaxed somewhat when she saw me. "Hey, Syd, meet Olive." She gestured toward the calico. "The poor girl was trapped underneath Bert Park's porch. He called me yesterday afternoon, and I managed to coax her out. I brought her over to Donna's for a checkup. She's expecting." Maggie let out a small sigh and ran her hand over the cat's belly. "You know what that means."

I sure did. It meant more kittens for a future shelter event. Olive would be spayed as soon as possible after giving birth, and then she too would be available for adoption, but it wouldn't be in time for this event. I walked over and looked down at the cat. "She's beautiful," I said. "I've always loved calicos. I especially love the colors on this one. Pale peach and gray."

"She's what is called a dilute calico," said Maggie. "People love them. I'm sure once she's ready, we'll have no trouble finding her a forever home."

"I'm sure we won't. She certainly seems to enjoy Melvin there. Toby does too, only he seems to enjoy making mincemeat of Melvin's body parts more than anything else. I'd hate to tell you how many he's decapitated so far." I eased one hip against the table. "I just hope that this penchant for beheading mice isn't an indication of, ah, some other behavioral problem."

Maggie angled her head to one side. "I doubt it, Syd. Toby was originally an outdoor cat, and now he loves to stay inside and play with toys. It says a lot that you've gotten him domesticated. He likes his new environment."

"He seems to," I said slowly.

"He does." Maggie's tone was firm. "He wanted to be with you, Syd. Lots of people showed interest in him, but he never behaved himself until he met you. As for the mouse thing, well, hunting's in every cat's DNA, and maybe it's just more pronounced in Toby. Remember his nickname—the Wanderer? If I recall correctly, there were a few, ah, gifts, shall we say, left on the shelter stoop that were most likely from him. His hunting tendencies won't disappear overnight, but consider yourself lucky he takes it out on rubber toys." Her lips curved upward. "Look on the bright side, though—you and Kat will probably never have a rodent problem."

I burst out laughing. "I guess you're right. I'm probably worrying over nothing."

"Rest assured, you are. So, what brings you by this morning? I didn't see your name on the schedule."

"It's not." I paused and then said the first thing that came into my mind. "I wanted to work on some ad copy at home, but I left my notes here. I stopped by Dayna's for some coffee, and she insisted I try out some of her treats she's making for Saturday. I thought maybe you might like to try them too."

"How thoughtful of you. Yes, I would. I skipped dinner last night, and I didn't have much time to eat this morning." She inclined her head at me. "You never forget your notes, Syd, and I'm sure you didn't get up early just to bring me Dayna's pastry to try. So why don't you just come right out and tell me what's on your mind."

"Okay, I will." I shoved both hands into the pockets of my light jacket. "I came to talk to you about Saturday."

Maggie's brow furrowed, and she let out a deep sigh. "I thought so. Look, I'm sorry for the little tantrum yesterday. It's just when I heard her name . . ." Maggie bit down hard on her lower lip. "It stirred up emotions I thought were long buried, but it's got nothing to do with you or Kat, and I'm sorry I reacted like that. It's just the last thing I ever expected was to hear that Ulla Townsend was replacing Dudley Simmons at that book signing. It . . . it took me by surprise."

I looked Maggie straight in the eye. "You went to high school with Ulla, didn't you?" I asked. "Grace Topping mentioned it the other day."

"How on earth did Grace . . . ? Oh, right—her cousin was also in our class." Maggie let out a sigh. "Yes, Ulla and I went to school together. I actually tried to be nice to her, but . . ." She ran her hand through her hair. "That was a losing proposition."

"Ulla was in with a bad crowd?"

Maggie's lips twisted into a grimace. "Ulla *was* the bad crowd. A real hellion, all on her own. Suffice it to say she pulled some pretty dirty tricks on me, and on some of the other girls too. A lot went down back then, and it didn't exactly leave a good taste in too many people's mouths."

"A lot of that goes on in high school," I said. "And even if Ulla was a bad seed back then, she seems to have redeemed herself nicely."

"Hmpf," Maggie muttered with a deep scowl. "She might come across all sweetness and light on that cable show now, but I know the real deal. She wasn't a nice person then, and a leopard doesn't change its spots." She clasped her hands in front of her. "Look, I don't really like to talk about it," she said. "It brings back bad memories. I hope you understand."

"Of course," I said, although I didn't. My curiosity was burning now, but what else could I do but respect Maggie's wishes. "If you don't want to talk about it, well, then you don't have to. It's fine with me."

Maggie looked relieved. "Thanks for not pressing me on this, Syd. I know how much you're intrigued by a puzzle or a mystery, but trust me—this is something you're better off not knowing. Everyone is."

I tried not to let Maggie see just how much more curious her words had made me. "If you say so. It's just that Kat and I hate to see you upset, Maggie. You're very important to the shelter—and to us."

"Thanks for that," Maggie said, and I noted the catch

in her voice. "I appreciate your loyalty. Trust me, I wish the circumstances were different. You have no idea," she added softly. "I really couldn't stand to be within ten feet of Ulla Townsend—no, wait; make that ten inches. I'll be more than happy to make it up to you gals some other way, but as far as Saturday goes, count me out. I'm sorry—I really am—but I just can't."

"I understand, but if you should change your mind . . ."

"I won't," Maggie said firmly. She turned her back to me and her attention to the cat. I waited a few more minutes, and when Maggie didn't turn around again, I walked out of the playroom, got my things, and left. I pondered the situation on my short drive home. It was very clear that something had happened between Maggie and Ulla, and even clearer that Maggie, at least, held some sort of grudge. What could it be?

I sighed as I turned into my driveway. One thing was for sure: I wasn't going to find out from Maggie. If I wanted to solve this mystery, I was going to have to find some other source of information. Who knew? Maybe if luck were with me, I might even find out something from Ulla herself.

Chapter Four

"What have we gotten ourselves into?" Kat moaned.

Saturday, or "Caturday," had finally arrived, and Kat and I were both in the shelter van, staring out of its windshield at the line that had already formed outside Crowden's, and it was only ten AM! The signing wasn't scheduled to begin until noon, but already a slew of Ulla Townsend fans had started camping around the front of the bookstore. There had to be at least two hundred people there, maybe more.

"Well, per Tara, that's just the tip of the iceberg," I said as I started up the van and pulled away from the curb. "She told me that she's expecting five hundred people, maybe more, even. The news about Ulla's appearance hit several major newspapers, plus she was talking about it on all her cable shows. Tara thinks people might even come here from North Carolina and Georgia, maybe even farther away."

"Grand," my sister moaned again. "Maybe we should

have come here earlier. *Now* where are you going?" Kat asked as I made a sharp left down a narrow alley.

"I'm parking in the back lot. No way I'm carrying cats past all those people—unless you want to wait for Viola and Sissy?" Viola was our eldest volunteer and Sissy Arledge, a high school junior, our youngest. Neither would have a problem pushing through that crowd with our precious cargo.

"No, they weren't sure what time they'd be able to get here." She let out a sigh. "I do wish Maggie wasn't so stubborn. She's always good at things like this."

"I know, but she was very firm about not getting within ten feet of this place, so we're on our own." I exhaled a breath. "Let's do it."

There was a myriad of trucks in the back lot, most of them emblazoned with the cable channel's logo. I managed to squeeze into a space not too far from the back entrance, and then Kat and I each picked up a carrier and hot-footed it to the back entrance. Fortunately, the back door was open, so we walked in and went straight through to the main store area, where we stopped and gawked at the scene before us. The bookstore was hardly recognizable—there were wires and cameras everywhere, and people wearing microphones scuttling to and fro. A wide table had been set up to the left of the register, and it was loaded with copies of Ulla's book. I balanced the carrier carefully in one hand and reached for a volume with the other. A very flattering photo of Ulla in a pink suit and white blouse graced the cover, while the white block print above her photo screamed out: **SHOP TILL YOU DROP—MY STORY**.

I flipped to the first chapter, entitled "Bargain Barracudas," when a girl wearing a white CNC cable channel shirt and headphones whizzed past, paused, did a one-eighty, and snatched the book out of my hand. "We've got that set up just so," she informed me in an icy tone as she returned the book to the pile. "For the *paying* customers," she added. Bright blue eyes swept me up and down. "You are . . . ?" She stopped speaking as she noticed the carrier I held in one hand. "Good Lord. Is that a *cat*?"

Before I could answer, a loud voice called out, "Oh, Kat! Syd! I'm so glad you're here!" I turned my head and saw Tara emerge from the back room. Her face lit up in a smile that looked more relieved than anything else. If she hadn't spoken, I might not have recognized her. She'd traded in her usual uniform of jeans and a sweatshirt for a red and white floral dress. The platform wedges she had on easily added another three inches to her petite five foot two frame. Instead of her customary swipe of lip gloss and mascara, I noted that her face had been professionally made up. Her high cheekbones were highlighted by a soft rose blush, and the taupe shadow on her eyelids brought out the flecks of green in her hazel eyes—eyes that right now were wide and looked frightened. The girl in the white shirt beat a hasty retreat as Tara reached out to grasp Kat's wrist. "Sorry to sound so panic-stricken; it's just nice to see a friendly face."

I shifted the carrier in my arms. "That's okay, Tara. I would too. All this does seem to be a bit overwhelming."

"Overwhelming doesn't even begin to describe it," Tara murmured. Her normally soft voice was even lower-pitched right now, and she ran a hand nervously through her hair. "I have a section cordoned off next to our café especially for the kitties," she said. "And our storage room has been set up as a sort of catch-all for your supplies and Ulla's. It's right near the restroom and the back entrance. We usually keep the back door locked, but today we're leaving it wide open"—she gestured around—"because of all the activity."

"Understood." I gave her outfit a once-over. "You certainly look beautiful," I ventured. "That's a lovely dress."

Tara looked down at it, plucked at the hem with nervous fingers. "I guess. It's my cousin Wendy's. She said I needed to wear something bright so I'd stand out in the publicity photos. She's around here somewhere—oh, there she is."

A tall girl, hair cut stylishly short, wearing a black pencil skirt, plum-colored silk blouse and matching vest, came striding toward us. "Tara, there you are. The publicity department wants to get a shot of you, if you've got a minute." Her head swiveled and her dark gaze settled on Kat and me, one eyebrow raised in silent inquiry.

"These are the girls I told you about. The McCall sisters." Tara swept her arm toward us. "Katherine and her sister, Sydney. They run the Friendly Paws Shelter. This is my cousin, Wendy Sweeting. She produces Ulla's segments."

Wendy gave us both a curt nod. "Tara makes me sound

way more important than I am. I'm only one member of a highly skilled team." She glanced at the clipboard she held in her hand and then let out an exasperated sigh. "I have to find Freddie. We've got to be certain all the microphones are in good working order."

"*Shopping Your Way* is taping today's signing to use for on-air promotion," Tara explained. "Also for Ulla to celebrate her fifteenth year with the show, which is coming up soon."

"Wow," remarked Kat. She smiled at Wendy. "That's a lot of extra work for you, I imagine."

"Oh yes," Wendy said, a wry tone to her voice. "We were originally just going to send a photographer and get some still shots, but Ulla insisted on a full taping. It was her idea to use this event for her fifteenth anniversary celebration. Never let it be said Ulla Townsend missed out on any opportunity to bleed as much publicity as she could from anything." She paused and rubbed absently at her forehead. "Sorry. I don't mean to sound so cynical."

"No problem." I smiled at her. "I used to work in advertising, so I can imagine how stressful your job must be."

Wendy's pert nose wrinkled, and she reached up a hand to rub at the base of her neck. Her gaze dropped and for the first time she seemed to notice the carriers Kat and I held. "So, those are some of the cats you're going to try to get adopted today?"

"Yes." I held up my carrier. "This beauty is Princess Fuzzypants. She's a Maine Coon."

Wendy leaned forward for a closer look. "She's gorgeous,"

she remarked. "I'm sure you'll have no trouble finding her a home. And this one?" She waved her hand toward Kat's carrier.

"Annie Reilly. She's a Ragdoll."

Wendy leaned forward, and as she did so, the silver chain that was looped around her neck swung forward. Annie's paw shot out like a flash, twined in the thin chain.

"Yow!" Wendy reached out and disengaged the cat's claws from her necklace. "It looks like this little cutie likes jewelry."

"Annie does seem to have a penchant for shiny things," I admitted.

"A cat after my own heart. What self-respecting gal doesn't?" chuckled Wendy. "We're expecting a large crowd, but we wanted to keep the kitties away from Ulla's signing area, you know, to avoid distraction."

For the author or the cats? I wondered. I smiled at the woman. "Well, if you'll just show us where the cats are to be stationed, we'll start bringing everything in. We're expecting two other volunteers as well."

"Wendy, there you are!" came a harsh-sounding voice. "What I need right now is to take a pee. And I could use a smoke. Find Savannah—she's got my cigarettes. And is there any sparkling water around here? I'm simply parched after that wild ride to get here. All those people outside! I thought some of them were going to jump across the hood of the limo—hey, hold the phone. Are those some of the kitties?"

Even though she was clearly at least ten years older and just about as many pounds heavier than the photo on the book's cover, I recognized Ulla Townsend instantly. She swept toward us on a cloud of Chanel No. 5, her arms outstretched. She had on a pink suit that was a definite ringer for the one on the book's cover, but a high-necked white blouse instead of a V-necked one. Her ash-blonde hair was done up in a beehive style, and a thin chain from which dangled a bullet-shaped charm rested against her blouse. The red-lipped smile she shot us was wide, displaying a row of perfect, snow-white teeth that were, probably, caps. Her dark brown eyes darted first to Kat, then me, then back to Kat. She pointed a long red nail straight at us. "You must be the shelter folk. The McCall sisters, right?"

I saw Kat's jaw tighten at the term "shelter folk," but she plastered a wide smile across her face and said, "Yes. I'm Katherine McCall and this is my sister, Sydney. We're so grateful that you could step in for Dudley Simmons today."

"Of course you are, dear." Ulla fairly purred the words. "What better way to ensure the success of your event. And I know you want it to be a *big* success. After all, you're getting a percentage of *my* sales, right?"

The proprietary way she said *my sales* wasn't lost on me, nor on my sister. Kat drew herself up to her full five foot nine and looked the woman straight in the eye. "That is correct, *the shelter* is getting a percentage. A much-needed one, I might add," Kat corrected quietly. "It was very generous on your publisher's part . . . and yours too, of course."

Ulla looked startled, then barked out a laugh. "Touché, young lady. Well, *the shelter* will certainly be raking it in today. Have you seen that lineup of people? They're stretched around two blocks. Looks like the whole darn town of Deer Park turned out."

"That does seem appropriate, since you grew up here, right? Possibly some of your local fans might even remember you from back then."

Ulla tipped her head back and let out a deep laugh. "Lord, I hope not," she said. "I'm a much different person now than I was then." Her tone grew almost wistful. "It seems like two lifetimes ago. I doubt anyone still lives here who might remember me."

Ah, there was my opening. "Funny, you should say that; it seems one of our volunteers—"

I never got to finish the sentence, however, as a loud voice boomed out, "Ulla, there you are. I've been looking all over for you."

Ulla turned toward the speaker, a tall, handsome man wearing a gray, striped suit. His expertly cut dark hair was streaked with gray at the temples, and there were a few lines around the corners of his blue eyes. I placed his age at somewhere in the late forties, early fifties. Ulla's eyes narrowed slightly, and I saw her shoulders tense; the next moment she relaxed, and a bright smile crossed her face. "And now you've found me," she said. "Fancy that." With that flippant remark, she turned and flounced off toward the rear of the store. The man stared after her, his expression clearly one of annoyance; then his face cleared, and he turned to look at us.

"Forgive my client's rudeness," he said. "I'm her manager slash literary agent, Ken Colgate." He glanced at the cat carriers and added, "And you two ladies must be from the shelter, am I right?" Without waiting for an answer, he moved forward, grabbed Kat's free hand, and started to pump it up and down. "Allow me to apologize in advance for anything Ulla said or might say to you today. She doesn't mean to come across as condescending and belittling, but unfortunately . . . she does. Believe it or not, it's part of her charm."

"Oh, Ken . . . Mr. Colgate."

We all turned toward the speaker, a willowy redhead in a bright blue wrap dress. She minced over, on four-inch strappy sandals that looked like they cost a fortune, to where Colgate stood, and waved a sheaf of papers at him. "I have those contracts you wanted to see." She frowned as her gaze wandered to rest on Kat and me. "Maybe now isn't the right time?"

"No, no." Colgate extended his hand. "Now's perfect." He took the papers from her outstretched hand and riffled through them. "They're all in order," he said crisply, handing them back to her. "Make sure you put them away. Now, where did Ulla go? We should get started."

"I think she wanted to freshen her makeup," murmured the girl. "I'll go check." With another small smile, she sauntered off, papers tucked firmly under her arm. I noted that Colgate's eyes never left the redhead until she'd vanished around the corner.

Kat gave me a soft poke in the ribs. "We should get moving," she said. "Make sure everything's ready to go on our end." She inclined her head toward Colgate, who'd whipped out his iPhone and was busy tapping something into it. "Nice to have met you."

"Oh. Likewise," he murmured.

As Kat and I turned to go, Ulla barreled into the room, the redhead trailing in her wake. Ulla held an iPhone in one hand, and as she approached her manager, she waved it under his nose, almost hitting him in the face. "Just look at this," she rasped. "It's the cover story on this month's *Star* magazine. They're actually considering that harlot for Glow."

Colgate reached out and pulled the phone out of Ulla's hand. "Now, my dear, you shouldn't look at those gossip rags at all, and especially not before an appearance. You know how upset it makes you. We don't want you to have one of those nasty panic attacks." He started to slide his other arm around her shoulders, but Ulla raised her hand and swatted at it.

"I'm not having a panic attack," she snapped, "but I do believe there is something wrong with the people I employ to keep my best interests at heart." Her finger shot up, jabbed at the air under his nose. "You know more about all this than you're letting on. I can tell."

Colgate must have realized there were other people standing nearby, because he cleared his throat and said in an even tone, "Now, Ulla, this is not the time, but we do need to talk."

"Darn right, we do!" she growled. She turned and snapped her fingers at the redhead. "Savannah, find me some aspirin. I'm starting to get a raging headache."

"We can't have that," Ken murmured. He looked around and caught sight of Wendy just entering the room. He motioned to her and said imperiously, "Wendy. Water for Ulla, please. And two aspirin. We'll be in the back area."

For a split-second, Wendy seemed taken aback; then she quickly recovered. "Sure," she murmured. She watched Ken lead Ulla out, her lips screwed into a pained expression. Then, as if she'd just become aware of the fact that Kat and I were standing next to her, she summoned up a quick smile. "Ulla's water can wait. Do you need a hand with the animals?" she asked.

"We're short two volunteers, so that would be great, if you can spare someone," Kat said.

Wendy scanned the bookstore. "Looks like everyone's pretty busy," she said at last. She turned to us with a wan smile. "Tell you what. I'll lend you a hand. Where are the kitties?"

"Outside in the shelter van," Kat said. "Thank you so much."

"No problem. It's what I do."

With Wendy in the lead, we made our way toward the rear entrance. The door to the storage area was slightly ajar, and as we passed I caught a glimpse of Ulla inside. She was slumped in a chair, her head thrown back, hand pressed against her forehead. Ulla looked almost pathetic, and for a moment I felt a bit sorry for her. We reached the back door. Wendy flung it open, and we trooped down the short flight of stairs and over to the van. As I walked around to open the side door, Kat cleared her throat and inclined her head toward a white Lincoln parked a few spaces away. Seated in the front seat were Ken Colgate and Savannah. The two of them were locked in what appeared to be a passionate embrace. We quickly took out the carriers and hurried back up the steps. Once we were inside, Wendy turned to us.

"You didn't hear it from me, but that little scene you just saw? That's not unusual for those two."

I raised an eyebrow. "I thought they seemed a bit . . . intimate."

Wendy shrugged. "You could say that. But I doubt it's anything serious. Savannah's just out to further her career, and as for Mr. Colgate . . ."

"I noticed he seems to like the ladies," I remarked. "Good thing he's not married."

"Oh, but he is," Wendy said. "He doesn't wear a wedding

ring, but he and his wife just celebrated their fifteenth wedding anniversary."

I shook my head. Having just ended a relationship in which I'd been cheated on, I couldn't understand women who put up with it. But I imagined everyone was different. "Do they have children?"

"Nope. Mrs. Colgate had a Persian cat, Samantha, but she died a few months ago."

Wendy pushed open the back door again, and we went back to retrieve the rest of the cats. I noted that the Lincoln was empty now. As we made our way back up the steps, we heard a screech of brakes. A dark sedan was just pulling into a space under a large tree. Wendy glanced over at the car. "Speak of the devil. There's Mrs. Colgate now. I guess now that they're local, she doesn't want to miss an opportunity to check up on her hubby."

I looked at her. "They live locally?"

"Now they do. Mrs. Colgate is originally from Deer Park too. Her father passed a few months ago and left her the family home, along with a good stash of stocks, bonds, and investments." Wendy leaned in a bit closer to me. "Cathy Colgate's net worth now makes her husband's income look like chump change. He's got about two million reasons to be a good boy and not rock the boat."

I turned to watch as Mrs. Colgate exited the sedan. She was rather plain looking, her hair pulled back in a low ponytail, no makeup on her face save for a dusting of blush on her cheekbones. Her outfit was even a dull gray: pea coat over a matching skirt, leggings, and ankle boots. Something about her seemed familiar, though, and as she started toward us, I suddenly realized why.

Mrs. Colgate was the woman I'd seen in the shelter last Saturday morning, the one who'd left before completing the adoption application. Talk about a small world.

Chapter Five

Thanks to Wendy's help, Kat and I soon had the cat play area up and ready for business. In keeping with our previous cat café theme, Tara had placed the pop-up cat play area right next to the café, and within a half hour we had it set up with scratching posts, cat trees to climb, and assorted toys. Sissy and Viola arrived shortly afterward, accompanied by Dayna, her niece Louise, and, surprisingly, Donna Blondell. "Donna," Kat squealed when she saw her. "You're helping Dayna out today?"

"She sure is," Dayna said with a wide smile. "My cousin Clarice was going to, but she called this morning and said she was sick as a dog. Probably ate too much chili last night. Anyway, Donna was in the shop, having a latte, and she volunteered her services."

"I'm happy to help out," the pretty blonde vet said with a big smile. "We only have two checkups booked for today, and Amanda said she'd be fine on her own. Besides, this will be fun. I haven't been a waitress since college." She made a face as she opened a large box. "The only downside is wearing this." *Shopping Your Way* had provided frilly white aprons, each emblazoned with the name of Ulla's book in the corner. I couldn't hold back a sigh of relief. Thank God the show hadn't thought to get us similar smocks!

The signing was scheduled to run from noon until three PM. At a little past eleven, they let in a small contingent of reporters to interview Ulla, which Ken laughingly called the "meeting the press hour." I saw Leila in the crowd and waved to her. Jim Wantrobski was close at her side, his trusty Nikon slung around his neck. A few people who were interested only in the cats and not Ulla Townsend stopped by the pop-up area, and one couple applied for Rocco, a feisty, albeit large, tuxedo cat. Leila wandered into our section a few minutes before twelve. My bestie hurried up to me, her face flushed and her eyes bright.

"I owe your friend Tara," she said with a big smile. "She put in a good word for me with her cousin, and I was one of two reporters who got to ask Ulla more than just the usual canned questions." She held her phone aloft. "Got it all here, and you'll read about it in tomorrow's special edition. Jim got some good pictures of her too."

"Great," I said. "Maybe now your editor will realize you're more than just a pretty face and give you some meatier assignments."

Leila wrinkled her nose. Her editor, Bert Parker, gave new meaning to the term *male chauvinist*. He was a firm believer that a woman's place was in the home—and a female journalist's place was reporting on fashion shows and garden parties. "One can only hope." Leila leaned forward and lowered her voice. "By the way, our staff reviewer gave me an advanced reader's copy of Ulla's book. I only skimmed it, but *hot* doesn't even begin to describe it . . . especially when she gets into all the behind-the-scenes stuff with the other hosts and staff." Leila gave her hand a quick shake and blew on her fingers for emphasis. "It makes you wonder how she can look some of those people in the eye, especially Candy Carmichael."

"Candy Carmichael? Really?" Candy was an attractive woman and another popular host on the channel. She and Ulla sometimes hosted shows together, and on the few shows I'd seen, there seemed to be an easy camaraderie between them. I remembered reading that Candy had recently been in line for a syndicated TV series that had fallen through, and she'd taken on more hosting duties. I wondered if Ulla's book deal was an attempt to one-up the younger woman.

"Oh, yeah." Leila rolled her eyes. "There's no love lost between those two, I can tell you that. She has some pretty unflattering things to say about most of the other hosts, but Candy's the one who gets the brunt of her wrath."

"I wonder if Candy's read the book, and if so, what she thinks of it."

Leila chuckled. "From what I've read about Candy, she's probably loving every minute. She was once quoted as saying, 'There's no such thing as bad publicity.' And I haven't even started on the chapter about the staff yet. Of course, none are mentioned by name, but I bet it's easy for an insider to figure out."

"Sounds pretty juicy." I looked longingly at the table, where Lenny had just tossed down another stack of books. "I'll have to pick up a copy before the event's over. The sale will benefit the shelter after all."

"Jim's picking up a couple copies too. I don't believe he's getting them signed, though."

I gave her a look of mock horror. "What? You don't want Ulla's autograph?"

"Ulla Townsend? Not so much. Now if it were Ryan Gosling . . ." She wiggled her eyebrows, then made a motion of fanning herself. "Just make sure when you read it, there's a fire extinguisher nearby."

"That hot, huh?"

"And then some." She glanced at her watch. "Oops. I'd better make tracks. The festivities should be getting underway, and I want to get a few fan interviews before things get too crazy."

"Good luck."

Leila made tracks for the signing area, and I went back to the pop-up. Kat was seated at a table with an older woman who was busily filling out an application. She looked up, saw me, and motioned for me to come over. "Would you mind getting some more cat toys out of the back? It appears some of them have grown legs and walked away."

"As long as the cats themselves haven't walked away, I'd say we're in good shape."

I returned to the storage area, which had been set up as a sort of catchall area for the cable equipment, Ulla's things, and our shelter supplies. Ulla sat at a small table while a woman brushed powder onto her cheeks. Ken Colgate was talking to her in low tones, and I noticed his wife standing off to one side, watching them intently. Ulla mustn't have cared for whatever Ken said, because she stood up abruptly, causing powder to fly about. "Not on your life," I heard her hiss. She jabbed her finger in the air, scant inches from Ken's nose. "You go back and set up a meeting. No more excuses. Or else." Her eyes took on a wicked gleam, and her gaze swiveled toward Mrs. Colgate. "Perhaps you think that just because your dear wife's circumstances have improved, you're above reproach now. I wouldn't forget, dear Ken, what I can do to your reputation, both business and personal."

Ken glanced quickly around. "We'll discuss this later," he said, then rose and walked over to where his wife stood. The two of them conversed for a moment, and then Mrs. Colgate turned and walked toward the side door, Mr. Colgate at her heels. I walked over to the myriad of totes and boxes that were marked "Friendly Paws Shelter" and started to rummage through them, looking for the catnip sacks and balls we always took along. Suddenly I heard a loud gasp from the other end of the room. I glanced over and saw Ulla pushing the makeup artist's hand away. "Not that, you fool," she rasped. She reached for a large, flowered tote at her feet, rummaged through it, and then whipped out a small, glossy brown cylinder. She unscrewed the top, and I saw that it was a white, waxy-looking stick. "This," she said to the makeup artist, "is my lucky charm." She tapped at the case. "This is Glow's new revolutionary lip shine. Doesn't plump, just adds shine. It's a great product. I'm going to be their official spokesperson, you know."

She started to hand the lip gloss to the other woman, when Savannah burst into the room just then, waving a cell phone in the air. "Ulla? It's Dr. Gray."

"Dr. Gray!" Ulla set the lip gloss on the table and then snatched the phone from the girl's outstretched hand and walked a few paces away, talking earnestly. Savannah stood there uncertainly for a moment, then shrugged and vanished into the hallway. I finished gathering up some catnip sticks and balls and was just about to go out the door, when I felt a hand on my arm. I whirled around and saw Ulla looking at me. "Are those for the kitties?" she asked. "I think I'd like to see them before I go out."

I swallowed. "Certainly. Right this way."

Ulla followed me back into the pop-up area. She stood for a moment and her face lit up as she took in the cats milling about the enclosed section. "What beautiful animals," she murmured. "I love cats. They're so elegant." She snapped her fingers. "Where's that reporter and the photographer who was with her? I think I'd like my photo taken with one of the cats. I can use it for promo for my shows."

"Why . . . uh, sure." I set down the heap of toys I was carrying and walked over to one of the cages. Princess Fuzzypants looked up from her grooming ritual and gave a soft meow. "Here's a pretty cat," I said. "The Princess is a pedigree Maine Coon."

Ulla's eyes darted from cage to cage. "She's very nice, but I see one that appeals to me more." She walked right over to Annie Reilly's cage and dangled two fingers inside at the cat. "What a beautiful cat. Ragdoll, of course. She looks a great deal like my Pandora, who's passed on."

Annie Reilly meowed softly, then butted her head against the bars of the cage.

"What a precious girl," cooed Ulla. She reached her fingers through the bars to scratch Annie under her chin. Annie's pink tongue darted out and licked Ulla's fingers. "Simply adorable," she said again. Her gaze snapped back to me. "How much do you charge for adoptions?"

"Kittens and cats up to eighteen months are a hundred-dollar donation; older cats are seventy-five. I'd have to check the paperwork, but I think Annie's two years old, so she'd be seventy-five dollars," I answered.

"Annie?" Ulla's gaze narrowed. "Who names a pedigreed Ragdoll Annie? You name it something dignified, like Coco or Chantal or . . ." She paused and brushed a tear from her eye. "Pandora." She looked at the cat. "Pandora the Second—that's what I'd call you."

"Oh my Lord, Ulla. You're not thinking of adopting a cat, are you?"

Ulla and I both turned at the same time. I recognized the newcomer right away: Candy Carmichael. The shopping host wore a flame-red dress and a chunky black necklace with matching dangling earrings. Her full, rosebud-shaped lips were curved into what I could only describe as a wicked smile.

Ulla's expression hardened as her gaze fastened on the younger woman. She stepped forward and said in a haughty tone, "So, what if I am? What's it to you? And what in hell are you doing here, at *my* event?"

"Now, now, Ulls, don't get your panties in a twist," Candy said with a throaty chuckle. "Management thought it would be, ah, a hoot if I interviewed you and did some narration during the signing—you know, to use as promos on the air." She cleared her throat loudly. "You know, since I'm such an integral part of your book and all."

The two women exchanged dagger stares and then Ulla snapped, "Best publicity you've ever gotten. Is that the only reason you're here? To do promos on my book?"

Candy shrugged "What other reason would there be?"

Ulla stared at her, hands on hips. "Oh, I think you know."

"Hey, Ulla? Paranoid much?" Candy held up both hands. "Don't shoot the messenger. *I* just do what *I'm* told."

Ulla moved closer to the other woman. She lowered her voice and said in a low tone, "I know the real reason you're here, and you're wasting your time. You'll get that deal over my dead body."

Candy put her fingers to her lips and simulated a yawn. "Promises, promises," she said with a throaty chuckle. Her gaze traveled to me. "Will the cats cooperate, or will they be scared by the cameras?"

"We take videos of the cats and put them up on Pet Finder, so they're used to cameras. Not all of them like it, though." I glanced over at the cages. "Rocco's a ham, and so is Bubba. You could probably film them without a problem."

"Great," Candy flashed us a wide smile. "I'll tell our cameraman. Can they be out of the cage when he does it? The studio wants to get the full cat café effect."

"I should be in these shots too," Ulla said smoothly. "It is *my* book signing after all."

"It is." Candy looked pointedly at the large gold watch on her wrist. "But aren't you running a tad late?"

Ulla's smile was frosty. "Exactly. So, what's a few more minutes."

"Whatever." Candy gave a noncommittal shrug. "I'll go get Ralph." She tossed a quick look over at the cats, then vanished.

"I swear, that woman isn't happy unless she's shadowing me or torturing me. Oh well." Ulla pointed to Annie Reilly. "I'd like to be photographed with her, if you don't think the camera will frighten her."

"It's not the camera that would frighten her," Viola muttered under her breath, and I bit back a giggle.

Viola got Annie out of her cage, and I went with her back into the storage area. Candy stood in the center, accompanied by a young man carrying a handheld camera, and another whom I assumed was the soundperson. He affixed a microphone to Ulla's dress while the cameraman started jockeying around for a good position. The makeup artist moved in with a lipstick, but Ulla waved her off. She looked at the table and frowned. "My Glow lip-gloss. I'm sure I put it here before. Where is it?"

"Is this it?" Wendy, who'd bent to look underneath the table, straightened. She held a shiny brown cylinder in her hand. "It must have fallen on the floor."

"That's it, thank goodness." Ulla snatched it from Wendy's hand and walked over to the table. She unscrewed the cap, swiveled up the pale stick, and reached for a mirror. She gazed at her reflection for a minute, then set the mirror down. "I think I look okay for now," she murmured. She replaced the top on the gloss and slid it into the pocket of her dress. "Now that's settled, where is the kitty?"

Viola placed Annie Reilly on Ulla's lap, and immediately the cat started to squirm. Viola motioned to the necklace around Ulla's neck. "Take it off and dangle it off to the side," she suggested. "That shiny charm should keep Annie occupied enough that she'll sit still."

Ulla complied without a word. She dangled the necklace

back and forth, and sure enough, the cat sat still on her lap, staring at the charm as if hypnotized. Ulla looked over at Candy. "Okay, make it fast," she growled.

Ralph swung the camera in Candy's direction, and she was immediately all smiles. "Hey folks, you're in for a treat tonight. Ulla Townsend's in her old hometown of Deer Park, North Carolina, here at Crowden's Bookstore, signing copies of her book. But she's also a big animal lover, and her signing today benefits the homeless cats at the Friendly Paws Animal Shelter, felines who are looking for their forever homes."

Ralph swung the camera right at Ulla. She smiled and looked down at Annie Reilly with an almost beatific look. "This charmer's name is Annie," she said. "And she's not the only kitty looking for a forever home here in Deer Park." The camera swung toward Rocco and Bubba, who were now fighting over possession of a catnip banana.

"These adorable kitties and more like them are one reason why Ulla Townsend chose to have her kickoff signing here," said Candy. "If any of you watching live in the Deer Park area, you should check out the residents of Friendly Paws. We'll have more details at the end of the program."

"Great. That's a wrap," Wendy called out. She walked over to me. "Can you get me the particulars on your shelter and the names of the cats who were up for adoption today? I'll have Candy do a voice-over later."

Ken turned to Ulla. "Okay, Ulla, time to meet your public. Believe me, they are anxiously awaiting you."

"I'm sure they are." She frowned. "Let's get this over with, shall we? We've got a trip to L.A. to finalize right after this too."

Ken laid his hand on Ulla's arm. "You go on," he urged her. "I've some . . . matters to attend to first."

Ulla's gaze settled on Ken, then wandered to Candy, then back to Ken. "Oh, by all means attend to your *matters*," she said, in a tone that dripped with venom. "By the way, I meant what I told you last night." She made a slicing motion across her throat with her hand. "See that Glow deal is locked up, or you'll soon have plenty of time on your hands to take care of *matters*. Our contract is up for renewal in two weeks, remember?"

"How could I forget?" Ken managed a tired smile at Ulla, then turned and walked off. Ulla turned her back, so she was unaware of the venomous look Candy shot in her direction before following Ken. Ulla started to put the necklace back on, then gave a cry. "Oh darn. The clasp broke." She looked around and spied the tote bag. She walked over, opened the bag, and threw the necklace inside. Then she tossed it carelessly into the storage area near the spot where we'd stacked the pet carriers. "I'll have someone repair it later," she said. "Right now, it's showtime." With a smile that I thought was directed more at the cat than anyone else, Ulla swept from the room.

"You can't make this stuff up."

I glanced over my shoulder and saw Wendy. I'd forgotten she was still here. "Ulla argues and threatens Ken one day, and the next they're all smiles," Wendy continued. "She and Candy are like Bette Davis and Joan Crawford. Nice for the camera, but don't turn your back. And it won't be long before we get to do this all over again. Rumor has it, Ulla's got a second book in the works. And that she had to change some names and label it fiction to avoid potential lawsuits."

*　　*　　*

Wendy made her way into the main part of the bookstore, and I turned to make my way back to the pop-up area. As I stepped into the adjoining hallway, I noticed the back door was slightly ajar. I walked over to close it, and as I grasped the handle, I gave a quick glance at the parking lot in back. I saw two figures in the shadows. There was something intimate about their body language, and as they moved out of the shadows and into the light I recognized the taller figure instantly. Ken Colgate. I craned my neck, trying to discern the identity of the shorter figure—Savannah, no doubt. But as she moved into the light, I saw it was Ulla. Ulla reached up, touched Ken's cheek, then pulled him down for a hard kiss on the lips. *Well, well,* I thought. It looked as if they were kissing and making up—literally—after their earlier argument. They remained locked in the embrace another few seconds, and then the two of them turned and walked around the side of the building. I started to close the door, when I saw another shadow detach itself from a dark alcove and walk swiftly in the other direction. Even though the figure was several feet away, I recognized the drab gray skirt and pea coat.

Cathy Colgate. Ken's wife.

Chapter Six

By the time Ulla sat down to sign books at twelve-thirty, the crowd had grown to epic proportions. I was glad that Tara had taken my advice and contacted the police department for extra "muscle." Two plainclothes officers were stationed at the front door to monitor the influx. Ulla sat at the small table in front of the counter, Wendy at her side. There were two large piles of books on the table, and as the people approached, Wendy asked each of them how they would like their book signed, then wrote the information on a small card and passed it to Ulla. I caught sight of Ken Colgate, standing off to one side, arms folded across his chest. His wife stood next to him, close enough so that their shoulders touched. Not exactly an intimate gesture, but one I imagined was close enough for them. Savannah lingered near the door, her gaze alternating between Ulla and Ken Colgate. I didn't see any sign of Candy Carmichael, but I imagined she was around somewhere. No doubt Ken had advised her to steer clear of the signing area. After all, it was Ulla's event, and I doubted the woman would appreciate anyone being there who'd steal any of her limelight.

Once their book was signed, some of the people ambled either out of the store or else back to the café area for one of Dayna's complimentary treats. I waited on the sidelines, ready to escort anyone who showed an interest in the kitties over to our pop-up play area. Not too many people ventured my way, however, and at last Ulla rose from her seat and clapped her hands at the throng still clustered around her table.

"Listen, folks. Part of the reason for my signing here tonight was to help the Deer Park shelter find homes for these dear, sweet, homeless kitties. I do hope some of you will at least look at them. If you yourself aren't interested, perhaps you might know someone who is."

No sooner were the words out of her mouth than a half a dozen people started making their way toward me. For the next hour, we were all kept busy with a steady stream of people inquiring about our adoptees. Inez Morton, one of the library volunteers, put in an adoption form for Princess Fuzzypants, declaring she was the spitting image of a cat she'd had when she was ten. "I want to bring her to work with me. I saw three mice in the basement just this past week. I just don't know how Rita can stand to work down there all the time." Inez gave a small shudder. "Plus her red fur reminds me of my Aunt Eunice," she added as she handed me a deposit check. "Aunt Eunice had flaming red hair, like Lucille Ball. And it was *natural*!"

A half hour later, three of the cats had gold stars on their cages, indicating an application for adoption had been filled out. I finished taking an application from Cyndy Moseby, one of the waitresses at Rosie's diner. The girl left with a big smile on her face, and I went over and put a gold star on a grey and white striped tabby's cage.

"Yeah, Bubba!" Viola grinned at me. "So Cyndy took a shine to him, eh?"

"I had a feeling they'd be perfect for each other," I said. "They both crave affection."

"Wonderful," Viola said, and then she let out a sigh. "Too bad we can't say the same for our gal Annie." I had to agree. Annie, while not shy around shiny things, *was* shy around people. She found a deserted corner and made that her home. While it lessened our headaches, it wasn't a quality especially conducive to getting adopted. I had the feeling the shelter might be Annie's home for quite a while yet.

There was a light lull in the prospective adoptions around two o'clock so I decided to see how the line for the signing was progressing. There were still a good number of people waiting. I craned my neck, trying to see if I could spy anyone I knew in the crowd. Diane Ryan had mentioned she might stop by, but so far I hadn't seen any sign of her. As I started to turn away, Wendy stood up and said to the crowd, "Ulla's going to take a short break, and then she'll be back to sign your books. In the meantime, please help yourselves to coffee and pastries, and feel free to check out the residents of the Friendly Paws Shelter."

Ulla got up, stretched, and walked off toward the rear entrance, Wendy at her heels. I turned back toward the café section to see how the others were making out. One glance was all I needed to see that they were totally slammed. Dayna caught my eye and made a frantic "come here" gesture. I hurried over to the counter without hesitation. "What happened?" I asked.

"Louise was fighting a migraine all morning, and it took its toll on her," she said through gritted teeth. "She offered to stay, but I told her to go on home. We were doing okay, just Donna and me—and then the floodgates opened."

"Ulla's on a break," I said. "But I'd be glad to pitch in and help you get this line down."

"Would you?" Dayna flashed me a grateful look. "Darlin', if you can do that, I'll give you free lattes for a week."

I tossed her a wink. "You're on." I knotted Louise's discarded apron around my waist. "Shouldn't be too much of a problem. I used to help Dad out when he got slammed too. I'll bet we get this down to half the size in less than twenty minutes."

"Okay then, Speedy," chuckled Donna. "I'll take the coffee orders, you deliver them. Dayna's on pastry. Got it?"

I made a mock salute. "Yes ma'am."

We worked steadily for the next ten minutes, and the line did start to rapidly dwindle down as satisfied customers walked off with their coffee and pastry. When the line was down to about ten people, Donna passed me her pad. "I've got to hit the ladies' room," she whispered. "Can you handle it for a few minutes?"

I puffed out my chest. "Is the sky blue? Next," I called out, pad poised to take the order. Next turned out to be a handsome man in a light blue suit. His dark hair was cut in a becoming fashion, and behind his wire-rimmed glasses two blue eyes held a slight twinkle as he turned to me. "I'll have a mocha latte, hold the whipped cream," he said. He flashed me a wide smile, showing off perfect teeth and cute dimples bracketing his smile.

I smiled right back. "One mocha latte coming right up."

As I turned toward the cappuccino machine, I glanced over at the pop-up area. Everything seemed to be under control there. My gaze wandered briefly to the hall beyond, and I saw Ulla standing there. Her hands were on her hips, and she appeared to be talking earnestly to someone who stood just out of my range of vision. Whoever it was, though, must have upset her, because her face contorted into a snarl, and her hands curled into fists. I frowned and craned my neck, trying to see just who it was who'd produced this sort of reaction from the shopping channel host, but all I could see was just the teeniest flash of red in the darkened alcove.

"Hey," I heard Dayna say. "Are you getting that guy's latte or what?"

"Sorry," I murmured. I dragged my gaze away from the scene in the hallway and finished making the drink. I put a plastic top on the cup and quickly carried it back to the counter, where I noticed, much to my relief, that there was only one other person in line now besides my customer. I set the latte down on the counter, maybe a bit too forcefully. The top (which I confess, I'd not placed on too tightly) popped off, and hot liquid spilled out and across the counter. The man jerked his hand away in time to avoid a nasty burn, but not quick enough to save his suit. I gasped as he lifted his arm and I caught sight of a very dark mocha stain marring the pale blue of the sleeve.

"Oh my God," I cried. "I am so sorry!" I reached beneath the counter, grabbed a rag, and started sopping up the dark liquid.

The man, for his part, didn't seem all that upset. He'd grabbed some napkins from the dispenser on the counter and was wiping his sleeve. "Hey, things happen. It was an accident."

"An accident caused by my clumsiness," I said ruefully. "I am so sorry. Your suit—I hope it's not ruined."

He plucked at the sleeve of his jacket. "No worries," he said calmly. "This is an old jacket anyway."

I frowned. The jacket looked new to me. I had a feeling the man was just being polite. "Regardless, please allow me to pay to have it dry-cleaned for you."

He waved his hand. "Not necessary. Tell you what, though. I could use another latte."

"Of course." Feeling slightly embarrassed, I quickly whipped up the latte, this time making certain the lid was on nice and tight. Then I selected one of Dayna's blond brownies and shoved that in a paper bag. I went back to the counter and handed the cup and bag to the gentleman.

"Here you go," I said. "With an extra treat for good measure."

He took the bag and cup and smiled that killer smile again. "Totally not necessary . . . but thanks."

"Wait!" I shouted as he turned to go. I grabbed one of Dayna's cards from the counter, scribbled the shelter phone number and my first name on the back, and handed it to him. "Just in case you change your mind about having that jacket dry-cleaned," I said.

He looked at the card, then at me. "Syd? That's a girl's name?"

I chuckled. I was used to that reaction when someone learned my name. "My parents thought I'd be a boy, and my mother promised her brother she'd name me after him, so . . . it's Sydney. With a Y."

He touched two fingers to his forehead in a salute. "Okay, Sydney with a Y. Maybe I'll see you again."

With one last dazzling smile, he turned and vanished back into the main part of the store. Behind me I heard Dayna chuckle.

"That's not the way to meet men, Sydney. *They're* supposed to spill stuff on *you*, and then take you out to dinner to make up for it."

"Thanks for the tip." I chuckled as I took off my apron

and tossed it on the counter. "I guess now I know why I don't meet more men. I'm too clumsy."

Dayna grinned. "I don't think Mr. Blue Suit there minded you being clumsy at all. It wouldn't surprise me one bit if he looks you up and asks you out."

"Oh, Dayna, really," I said. "He was just being kind, is all."

"Humph. I saw the way he looked at you, girl, and you mark my words. If he doesn't make a move to get in touch with you or ask you out within the next forty-eight hours, I'll give you a free sweet and coffee for a week."

"You're on," I said. "Make sure you have plenty of that Southern Jumbo Java on hand. And a good supply of those Dabby Doughs, because this is one bet I'm sure to win."

"Humph," Dayna grumbled again. "We'll just see, won't we?"

* * *

Donna returned and I left the café area in their capable hands. As I walked into the cat play area, I stole a quick glance toward the hallway. Ulla and her mysterious stranger had been replaced by a glaring Savannah and a flustered-looking Tara.

"I don't understand why we couldn't have a locked area," Savannah said petulantly. "I've chased four fans out of here already who looked like they were going to make off with Ulla's tote bag."

"I explained that to Mr. Colgate. We didn't have enough room to have designated spaces for the shelter and Ms. Townsend. Unfortunately, everyone must share, and it made more sense for the area to be open, in case the shelter people needed to get something. Besides, even you have to admit there's a lot of activity back here from Ulla's camera crew."

"In bigger stores that's never a problem," Savannah said with a sniff. "I'd certainly advise Ulla against a return visit here."

The two women moved off, still arguing. I felt a bit sorry for Tara, but at the same time I felt confident she could hold her own against Savannah. I started for Kat's table, and as I approached, she looked over and mouthed "more applications" at me. I gave her a brisk wave and turned in the direction of the storage area. As I entered, I saw Ulla standing uncertainly off to one side. She looked a bit flustered, so I walked over to her and touched her gently on the shoulder. "Ms. Townsend? Are you all right?"

She whirled, and I saw a red flush creeping up one side of her neck. She saw me staring and raised one hand self-consciously to rub at the spot. "Oh. Yes. I just came here to put on some more lip gloss." I glanced down and saw that she held the tube in her other hand. As she stood there, still looking dazed, I walked over and touched her arm. "Ms. Townsend, are you all right?"

"Hmm? Oh, yes, yes. Fine, thank you." She walked over to where the flowered tote lay and snatched it up. She dropped the tube of gloss inside and then casually tossed the bag aside. It landed on its side right next to some of the Friendly Paws rubber bins. Ulla didn't bother to retrieve it, just turned and walked out without a backward glance in my direction. I shook my head, then walked over to the stack of boxes and opened the top one. Fortunately, that was the one the adoption applications were stuffed into. I grabbed a handful and made my way back to the pop-up. Kat eyed me as I entered.

"What took so long?" she asked.

"Nothing really. Ulla was in the storage area. She didn't appear to be feeling too well." I glanced at my watch. "Maybe it's a good thing there's only a half hour to go."

"I hope she's able to finish." Kat inclined her head toward the cat area. "We were pretty busy for a while, but it's seemed to slow down. Nearly all the cats we brought have applications for adoption, though, so that's a good thing."

I clapped my hands. "Yay! Maybe we'll have a hundred percent success rate."

Kat shook her head. "That won't happen, not unless Ulla decides to adopt Annie Reilly *and* Sylvie. They're the last two."

I glanced up. A man and a woman stood uncertainly in the doorway. "Well, who knows," I said. "Maybe they'll want two cats." I detached myself from Kat and walked toward the newcomers. "Welcome. Are you interested in adoption?"

"Yes, we are." The man held out his hand. "I'm Jay Johnston and this is my wife, Susan. We've just relocated here from Boston and our eighteen-year-old tabby passed away a few weeks ago."

"I wasn't sure if I wanted another one after her," said Susan Johnston, "but Jay here convinced me that we should have a pet. We read about this event in the paper so . . . here we are."

"Well, you've come to the right place," I said with a broad smile. "We have two kitties in need of a forever home here right now. If neither of them appeals to you, we have more at the shelter."

I left them looking at Annie Reilly and went over to Viola. "Do we have any of those flyers left, the ones that show the cats we didn't bring?"

"Yes, but I think Tara put them on one of the outside tables. Want me to get one?"

"No. You go chat up those prospective parents. You're so good at it. I'll get the flyer."

I went outside and found the flyers without any trouble. As I passed by the signing table, I noticed that Ulla was frowning and scratching her arm. She leaned over and whispered something to Wendy, who immediately got up and headed toward the back. Ulla smiled at the person standing in front of her and asked how he wanted the book inscribed. As she signed it, I noticed she seemed to be having trouble breathing. Suddenly she tossed the pen and book aside and jumped to her feet, almost knocking her chair over. I set the flyers down and hurried over to her. "Ms. Townsend, are you all right?"

She pressed two fingers to her sternum. "I—I'm not sure," she said in a strangled tone. "My chest feels so tight. . . . Maybe I need to splash some water on my face."

She turned toward me and I frowned. Her lower lip looked a bit puffy, and the flush on her neck had now morphed to a bright candy-apple red. "Do you want me to come with you to the restroom?"

She shook her head. "Just tell Wendy and Savannah where I am," she murmured. She raced down the hall to the bathroom, and I heard the door slam.

There was an excited buzz in the room. As I debated whether to say something, Wendy suddenly appeared at my elbow. "Where's Ulla? Why isn't she at the table?"

"She said she felt sick—her chest was tight. She went to the bathroom to splash some water on her face."

Wendy let out a strangled cry. "A panic attack. Just what we need in the last twenty minutes."

I frowned. "It didn't seem like if it was a panic attack."

"Oh trust me, it probably was. She does this all the time, although it's usually to get Ken's sympathy."

"I don't know about that," I said. "Her lip looked a bit puffy, and she really was having trouble breathing."

Wendy ran a hand through her short hair, glancing over at the people who were milling around the table, craning their necks, and whispering excitedly. "I guess I'd better do some damage control." She turned toward the crowd and said smoothly, "Not to worry, folks. Ulla will be back in a few minutes . . . I hope," she muttered under her breath to me, and then she hurried off in the direction of the bathroom.

Tara came over to me, concern etched on her face. "Is Ulla sick?"

I frowned. "I'm not sure. It seemed that way. I think I'll go check on her as well." I hurried down the hall, and I could hear Tara saying to the remaining people, "Don't worry, Ulla will be back shortly. In the meantime, there's plenty of goodies at our café." As I passed the side door, it suddenly swung open, and Savannah breezed in. Her gaze swept me up and down. "You look concerned. Is something wrong?"

"Ulla didn't feel well. She went to the bathroom to splash some cold water on her face. She doesn't have high blood pressure, does she?"

"One twenty over eighty since I've known her. Her pressure's fine. She just manages to raise other people's," Savannah said, and then she frowned. "How bad is she? I wonder if I should call Ken."

"He's not here?"

Savannah shook her head. "He and his wife left about fifteen minutes ago." Her lips twisted into a wry smile. "Neither one of them looked very happy. Man, would I love to be a fly on the ceiling of *that* Mercedes. Come to think of it, he might appreciate an interruption."

Savannah put the phone to her ear and moved off.

I shifted the tray in my arms and was just about to enter the playroom when the bathroom door banged open and Wendy emerged, pale and wide-eyed.

"Someone call nine-one-one!" she shouted. "Something's terribly wrong with Ulla. I—I don't think she's breathing."

Chapter Seven

I slid my hand into my pocket for my phone, but Savannah beat me to it. "I need an ambulance at Crowden's stat," she said in a clipped tone. "Ulla Townsend's had some sort of attack. She's barely breathing. Please hurry." She was silent a few moments, listening, and then said, "Yes, tell them the back entrance is open. And please, no siren. This has to be kept quiet, for now at least." She hurried into the bathroom, clutching her iPhone. I imagined her next call would be to Ken Colgate.

I turned to Wendy, who stood rigid, her hands at her side. "What happened?" I asked.

"I don't know," Wendy answered. "I knocked on the door a few times, calling out her name. When she didn't answer, I opened the door and went inside. I found her . . . just lying there . . ." Wendy paused and coughed lightly. "The sight of her lying there like that—well, it startled me. I'm used to her being hell on wheels, ya know? I called her name again, and she didn't respond, so I bent over her. She didn't look like she was breathing. That's when I figured I'd better get help." She pushed the heel of her hand through her hair. "God, what a mess! I hope those EMTs get here soon."

We didn't have long to wait. Less than five minutes elapsed before an ambulance, lights flashing, pulled up in front of the café entrance. A pair of paramedics burst through the café doors, pushing a gurney loaded with resuscitation equipment. I recognized one of them: Cherry Dunphy, a bright-eyed medical student who also volunteered at the shelter one or two nights a week. She tossed me a quick wave as she hoisted a defibrillator off the stretcher. Then she and the other paramedic, a middle-aged woman, hurried inside the bathroom.

I couldn't resist a peek inside, and what I saw caused my breath to catch in my throat. Ulla lay on her back in the middle of the bathroom floor, and both paramedics were kneeling next to her, their expressions grave. Ulla looked lifeless, her features slack, her limbs splayed out like a broken doll. I half-expected to hear one of the paramedics call out the time of death and pull a sheet over the woman's head. I clutched at my stomach; the sight had made me feel queasy.

Kat touched my arm. "We should give them some space to do their job," she whispered.

I knew my sister was right. There was nothing I could do to help Ulla. She was in good hands with the paramedics. I followed my sister back into the main portion of the store. I saw Wendy and Savannah conversing in low tones.

Something brushed against my arm, and I whirled around to face a pale-lipped Tara.

"Is it true?" she whispered. "Is she—is Ulla dead?"

"I don't think so," I replied. "She did have some sort of attack, though. The paramedics are with her now."

Tara swiped a hand across her forehead and gestured toward cluster of fans who were still awaiting their turn to meet their shopping channel host. "What do I tell them?"

"Nothing. I would imagine it would be up to Ulla's manager to make some sort of announcement," I said.

Tara frowned. "That doesn't seem right. I'm the store manager. I should say something."

Savannah detached herself from Wendy's side and hurried over to us. She looked straight at Tara. "Please refrain from saying anything about Ulla just yet," she said. "We're waiting for Ken to get here before any announcements are made."

Tara pursed her lips. "Fine, but I hope he arrives soon. The crowd is getting very restless."

Kat touched my arm. "There's nothing we can do. Let's get back to the pop-up." We hurried back, arriving just as the EMTs emerged from the restroom. Cherry was talking into a mic that was pinned to the front of her uniform. "ETA ten minutes." Ulla lay on the gurney, an oxygen mask strapped to her face. Her eyes were closed and her cheeks were a mottled shade of red. Cherry made a motion, and then she and the older paramedic wheeled the gurney out the back door and into the waiting ambulance.

I hesitated for only a fraction of a second, then walked swiftly after them. Cherry was standing by the ambulance, scribbling something on a sheet attached to a clipboard. I walked over to her and asked, "How bad is it?"

"Bad," she said grimly. "She's got no detectible pulse, and her airway seems blocked." She reached up to rub at her forehead. "Does she have any allergies?"

"Don't know." I frowned. "Why? You think she had some sort of an allergy attack?"

"She's got all the symptoms," Cherry replied. "It looks like a pretty severe one too." She leaned toward me and said in a low tone, "Just between us—I've seen people succumb to attacks not half as bad as this looks. If she has any next of kin, my advice would be to notify them." Her expression was grim.

Cherry's walkie-talkie beeped just then, and she hurried off toward the ambulance. I went back into the play area and found Kat waiting for me. "Cherry mentioned that Ulla's symptoms seemed to be those of a severe allergy attack."

Kat's eyes popped. "An allergy attack? Really? What might have brought that on?"

I remembered an incident back when I'd worked at Reid and Renshaw. A young associate had eaten a muffin that contained peanut oil, and had nearly died. "Did you see her eat anything?"

Kat frowned as she thought. "I remember Sissy offered her a pastry, and Ulla told her she didn't eat sweets."

Hmm, I thought. *Is Ulla diabetic?* It could be insulin shock. But I had no idea if insulin shock mimicked an allergic reaction. Someone, Wendy or Savannah or maybe even Ken, had to know something about the woman's medical history. "If she does have allergies, then she should have an EpiPen or some sort of allergy medication, right?"

"Right. Where's her assistant?" Kat craned her neck. "She'd probably know."

I glanced out the window at the curb, where a sleek silver Mercedes was just pulling up. "There's Ken Colgate," I said. "He might know. I'll ask him." I thrust the flyers I still held in my hand at Kat. "You take these back to the Johnstons. Who knows, maybe they're ready to adopt Annie Reilly by now."

"We could only hope," Kat said. She moved off just as Colgate barreled into the store. He saw me and hurried over, his expression grim. "Ms. McCall. What happened here?"

"Ulla didn't feel well and went to the bathroom," I said. "She didn't look well at all. Wendy went to check on her and found her on the floor. She wasn't sure if Ulla was even breathing. Savannah called nine-one-one, and the paramedics came. They took her to the hospital. As a matter of fact, you just missed them." I decided to omit the part about Ulla possibly being DOA at the hospital.

"Great." He flicked his gaze toward the café. "I take it Wendy and Savannah are still here? They didn't follow the ambulance to the hospital?"

"I think they wanted to wait for you to arrive. Wendy

said she wanted to get a diagnosis from the EMTs before making any announcements." I laid a hand on his arm. "Do you know if Ulla is diabetic or if she has any allergies?"

"What? No—I don't know." He shook his head, obviously confused. "I'm not sure. Why do you ask?"

"I overheard one of the EMTs mention anaphylactic shock. We thought perhaps if Ulla had allergies, she carried some sort of medication or an EpiPen with her?"

"Ulla is a very private person. She's never discussed her medical history with me, but she might have with Savannah. I can check." With that he strode into the main bookstore. I debated briefly going back to join Kat, but in the end curiosity won out. I followed Colgate in time to see Wendy and Savannah converge on him. They huddled together for a few minutes, talking in low tones. Then Wendy detached herself and started for the back area, while Ken walked up to the front by the now-vacant signing table and clapped his hands for attention. The crowd's buzzing ceased, and all eyes turned to him.

"Ladies and gentlemen, we thank you all for coming out today. Unfortunately, Ulla has suffered a slight attack and has been taken to the local hospital."

A collective cry of dismay went up. "Oh no!" someone called out. "Was it a heart attack?"

"We're not certain what it was," Ken said.

"But she'll be okay, right?" another person asked. That started more murmuring. Ken clapped his hands and said loudly, "We hope that Ulla will recover soon; however, we are unfortunately going to have to call a halt to today's signing." The murmuring grew more intense at that, and he clapped his hands again. "If you'll leave your names with Ms. Blade, we'll see that you get a copy of Ulla's book, free of charge."

As Savannah seated herself behind the table and the people surged forward to give their names, I caught sight of a familiar face in the crowd. I elbowed my way over to Diane Ryan and tapped her on the shoulder. She whirled and let out a gasp when she saw me. "Oh, Syd, what an afternoon!" she cried. She held up a copy of Ulla's book. "I was one of the lucky ones. I managed to get mine signed right before she jumped up and vanished. Lois wasn't so lucky, though."

"Lois?"

Diane looked around with a frown. "Heck, she was right next to me. Where'd she go . . . oh, there she is." She motioned to a short, thin woman with a pixie haircut in a dull gray jacket who'd emerged from the back area and now walked in our direction. "Here she is now. Lois, where have you been?"

The woman walked over and regarded me with a heavy-lidded blank stare. Her lips curved in a smile before she turned her attention to Diane. "I want to see if the restroom was free, but it's a nuthouse back there. They're chasing everyone away from the area."

"Yes, Ulla's manager just announced she had some sort of attack." Diane gave a little shudder. "It's such a shame."

"It certainly is." Lois turned and made a gesture in the

direction of the café. "I've heard she wasn't very well liked. Maybe someone should take charge of whatever food's left, and not touch it. You never know. The police might want it bagged."

Diane's eyes popped. "Bagged? You mean . . . you think someone might have poisoned Ulla's food?"

"I'm just saying that the police will probably consider every possibility. Then again, I do watch *CSI* reruns way too much." She thrust out her hand to me. "Sorry. I'm Lois Galveston. And you must be one of the McCall sisters, right? Diane told me all about your shelter and about how a percentage of sales today was going to be donated to it. It's such a shame the event had to end like this."

"I'm Sydney McCall and yes, it is a shame." I held out my hand and Lois's fingers closed over it. I had to fight to keep from wincing. The woman had a strong grip! "Are you new in town?"

"Sorta kinda. I grew up in Deer Park. I've been away for a while, and I recently got laid off from my job, so I decided I'd move back here."

"Lois interviewed for one of the open clerk positions at the station," Diane put in. "We hit it off right away."

Lois's lips twitched slightly. "Yeah, I always get nervous during interviews. Diane put me right at ease. The station seems like a great place to work, but I'm not getting my hopes up."

"Well, I don't see why not," Diane huffed. She looked over at me and added, "She has better qualifications than most of the others did. Plus, she did security work at her last job."

I eyed the woman. "Were you a security guard?"

Lois shook her head. "I was a member of the physical security team. We focused on keeping unauthorized personnel from getting into places that were off limits to them. It was a pretty interesting job. Sometimes it was as simple as locking a door; other times, more complex, like preventing the bypass of alarm systems or guard control."

Diane giggled. "Lois is too modest. Actually, she was kind of a female James Bond. She could get in and out of places like Houdini."

"Not that good, to be sure," Lois said with a small smile. "Unfortunately, that skill set hardly qualifies me to answer phones and take messages. If anything, the nice detective who interviewed me—Will something—said I was overqualified."

"Will Worthington. He's Syd's boyfriend," Diane put in. "Maybe Syd can put in a good word for you," she added hopefully.

I didn't answer right away. So, Will had added interviewing to his list of job duties. No wonder I hadn't seen too much of him! Captain Connolly was, no doubt, taking advantage of Will's good nature and his obvious desire to slide into Bennington's spot. I wondered if Charlie Callahan was also doubling as an interviewer. My hesitation caused Lois to cluck her tongue at Diane. "See? Now, you've put her on the spot," she chided.

"No, it's all right," I said quickly. "It's just I haven't seen much of Will lately—and now I guess I know why." I turned to Lois. "I'm not sure exactly what type of work you're looking for, but I do know Dayna Harper mentioned she needed to hire some more staff, if working in a sweet shop interests you."

"At this point anything that pays a steady salary interests me. Thanks for the tip. I'll be sure to check it out."

"You can mention my name when you do," I said. "Hopefully it might carry some weight."

Diane nudged her friend. "We should get going. I'll see you at the shelter when I come in for my shift Monday night, Syd."

Diane and Lois moved off. I started to retrace my steps back to the cat area, when Wendy suddenly popped up in front of me. "I can't find Tara," she said. "Could you tell her I'm going to the hospital with Ken?"

"Sure." I withdrew one of the shelter cards from my pocket and handed it to her. "My cell phone's on the back. Could you call when you find out anything?"

"Will do." She took my card, jammed it into her pocket, and then pushed out the front door and into a silver Mercedes that idled out front. I didn't see Leila or Jim anywhere, so I figured they'd probably followed the ambulance to the hospital. Worst-case scenario, I was certain Leila would be full of details when I saw her next.

I returned to the pop-up. The Johnstons were just handing a completed form to Kat, and I saw that a tag had been placed on Sylvie's cage. Susan Johnston looked up as we approached. "What happened? We heard the ambulance, and then I peeped into the hall and saw someone being taken out on a gurney."

"Ulla had some sort of, uh, attack," I said. "They took her to the hospital. We're waiting to hear how she is. It ended the signing rather abruptly."

"Oh, dear. Thank God I got my book signed before she took ill," said Susan. She clutched the volume to her chest as if it were made of gold. "I do hope she'll be all right. I just can't imagine shopping for my favorite sweater or shampoo without seeing Ulla."

"Now, now dear, I'm sure she'll be fine. The woman has the constitution of an elephant." Jay Johnston patted his wife's hand. I had the impression that he was fighting very hard to keep from rolling his eyes. He glanced up at me and said, "I'm a freelance motion graphics designer. I had gig a few months ago down at CNC where Ulla's show is filmed. That woman is an experience."

Susan turned to me. "He loves to exaggerate, especially if you get him talking about his job. He thinks every television personality is difficult."

"Well, a lot of them are," he said peevishly. "Ulla wasn't very well liked, I can tell you that. I remember one woman in particular—"

"Oh, Jay." His wife cut him off with a shrug and an eye roll. She sighed. "Ms. McCall isn't interested in any of that gossip. I swear, sometimes you're worse than an old woman."

I saw Jay's chin jut out, and I decided a change of subject was in order. I gestured toward Sylvie's cage. "I see you found a new kitty."

"Yes. She's very sweet. In many ways, she reminds me of my beloved Trixie," said Susan. "I liked the Ragdoll too, but—there was just something about the tabby that called out to me."

Jay Johnston pulled a face. "Besides, pedigrees always seem to need so much attention, you know." He pointed a finger at Annie Reilly, who lay quietly in the far corner. "That one seems like she'd be a handful."

I decided not to tell Mr. Johnston just how right he was. Instead, I smiled and said, "Well, I'm sure you made a good choice. Sylvie is a very sweet cat." I gestured toward Kat. "Our director will review your application and contact you to let you know when you can pick up Sylvie."

"Oh, thank you," said Susan. "Now that we've filled out the application, I can't wait to bring her home."

I walked out to the main part of the store with the Johnstons. I noticed as we walked through the store that all the recording equipment had been taken out and that the remaining books had been packed up and put in two large cartons by the side entrance. Susan Johnston asked a few questions as we walked, most of which dealt with basic cat care and were easy enough to answer. I assured her that Sylvie had been pronounced healthy, but I did recommend that they take her to Donna's clinic should they have any major concerns. As we approached their SUV, I spotted Lois Galveston and Diane Ryan standing across the street, sipping some sort of beverage from Styrofoam cups. Lois glanced up, saw us, and murmured something to Diane. The two of them quickly ditched their cups and went back inside the store. No sooner had the Johnstons pulled away from the curb than Sissy came flying out the front door. She saw me and hurried over. "There you are. Do you think Ulla's going to be okay?"

"I hope so," I answered. I decided not to say anything about Cherry's diagnosis until it was confirmed. "She didn't look good; I can tell you that."

"People are saying she's not gonna make it." Sissy dug into her pants pocket and whipped out her phone. "It's all over social media."

I stared at her. "Already?"

"Yep. My friend Carlene texted me about this." She opened up Facebook on her phone and showed me a photograph that someone must have taken as Ulla was being wheeled out. It showed her on the stretcher, her face covered by the oxygen mask. The caption below the photo read **"Shopping Queen Suffers Attack at Local Café Signing."**

"Swell," I muttered.

"And that's not all. It's on YouTube too," Sissy announced. "Someone else took a video with their phone and uploaded it. See?" She pulled up the video on her phone and handed it to me. Sure enough, someone had taken a clip as the stretcher was wheeled out of the café, onto the street, and into the ambulance. Suddenly, I let out a sharp gasp as the video ended.

"Play it again," I directed Sissy. "Is there any way to freeze it at a certain point?"

"Don't use YouTube much, do you, Syd?" chuckled Sissy. "Sure, I can halt it. Just tell me when."

The video rolled again. When it got to the point where the EMTs lifted the gurney up to put it in the ambulance, I yelled out, "Stop!" Sissy obligingly froze that frame. I took her phone and stared at the screen. The image was a bit grainy, but I could swear the woman huddled at the fringe of the crowd, looking very furtive, was none other than Maggie! She'd come down here after all—but why? She'd been so adamant about not wanting to see Ulla. . . . What had changed her mind?

My cell chirped just then, and I pulled my phone out. The number was one I didn't recognize, but I heard sirens in the background.

"Ms. McCall," said a wobbly voice. "It's Wendy Sweeting. Ulla didn't make it. I don't even think she had a pulse when she was admitted. The doctors pronounced her DOA."

Chapter Eight

E ven though Wendy's announcement wasn't entirely
unexpected on the heels of Cherry's prognosis, I still
felt a chill pass through me. I always found sudden death
to be disturbing, especially when its victim was relatively
young and healthy, as in Ulla's case. "I'm sorry to hear that,"
I murmured. "Did the doctors say what they thought might
have caused it?"

"It's too early to tell," Wendy responded. "I understand
the coroner is on his way here now." She made a little sound
that sounded somewhere between a gasp and a strangled sob.
"If you'll excuse me, I have to get a statement ready. Those
reporters at the event followed us here, and more are on the
way." She paused before saying, "I just thought you should
know what happened."

Wendy hung up and I just stood there for a minute, star-
ing at my phone. I glanced up and saw that Kat had joined
Sissy, and the two of them were looking at me expectantly.
I just shook my head, and both gasped. Sissy put her hand

to her mouth. We all stood in silence for a few moments, and then Kat asked, "Did Wendy know the official cause of death?"

"She said it was too early to tell. The coroner was supposed to be coming right down." I imagined that Angus McKay, the county coroner, was probably going to bask in this for a while. Celebrity deaths weren't exactly a commonplace occurrence in our neck of the woods.

Sissy looked at me curiously. "Official cause of death? I thought she had a heart attack."

"According to Wendy, they're not certain."

Sissy's eyes widened. "Do you think it could have been foul play?"

"Sissy! What a thing to say!" Kat admonished.

The teen didn't look at all repentant. "It's a natural assumption," she defended herself. "Ulla wasn't too well liked, and she had more enemies than friends. She talks about it in her book."

I looked at her, surprised. "You read her book?"

Sissy's grin was mischievous. "Some of it. Somebody left a copy on one of the café tables, and I skimmed through it. She made a lot of enemies back when she lived here. There's a whole chapter on it. Who knows? Maybe someone she wronged saw an opportunity for revenge."

Kat shook her head. "Sissy, you are so dramatic. That sounds a bit farfetched to me."

"Oh, I don't know," I said. "You don't watch enough crime shows, Kat. Actually, Sissy's theory sounds very 'fetched' to me." I pushed the grainy image of Maggie on that video clip out of my mind.

Sissy beamed at me. "Thank you, Syd."

"Well, all this is speculation until we have more details," Kat huffed. "And since Leila was probably one of the first reporters over there, I'm sure we'll get the scoop later. In the meantime, we should start getting the cats ready to go."

"Good idea, but first I want you to see something. Sissy, show Kat what you just showed me." I turned toward my sister as Sissy pulled out her phone. "Ulla's exit in the ambulance went viral. Someone put it on YouTube."

Kat wrinkled her nose. "Ew! And you think I'd be interested in seeing that?"

"Just look at the video carefully, particularly the last few seconds, and tell me if you recognize anyone in it." I motioned to Sissy. The teen stepped forward and replayed the video, with both Kat and me hanging over her shoulder. When Sissy got to the part where they showed the crowd, I asked her to slow the video down as she had before.

Both Sissy and Kat squinted at the screen. After what seemed like an eternity, Kat said reluctantly, "The image isn't all that clear, but . . . that woman kinda looks like Maggie."

"I think it *is* Maggie," said Sissy. "Or at least, it's Maggie's red jacket." She frowned. "I thought she said she wouldn't touch this place with a ten-foot pole."

"She did say that," Kat agreed. "So, either we're mistaken,

or . . . I don't know. Maybe curiosity won out in the end after all."

"I hope that's all it was," I muttered. Kat heard me and gave me a sharp look.

"It's an easy mystery to solve," she said. "We'll just ask her. Right now, though, we need to take care of the cats."

Sissy slid her phone back into her pocket, and the three of us went back to the pop-up area. Dayna and Donna were starting to box up what was left of the goodies. Suddenly Tara raced over to us, her face pale, her jaw set. "Ulla's dead," she said flatly.

"I know," I said. "Wendy called me from the hospital. It's a terrible thing."

"Yes, in more ways than one. The police just called. A detective is on the way over here now. Her death is being classified as suspicious."

That didn't surprise me. I knew police generally considered a death suspicious if it was unexpected and its circumstances or causes were either medically or legally inexplicable. That might mean Cherry's initial assessment about Ulla's having a severe allergic reaction was correct.

"They didn't come right out and say it, but I think they suspect foul play," Tara added.

Sissy let out a triumphant cry. "Told ya," she muttered.

Tara frowned at the teen, then turned back to us. "This type of publicity is *so not* what I need right now."

"Oh, Tara, don't worry." Donna Blondell stepped out

from behind the café counter to slip an arm around her friend's shoulders. "No one blames you for what happened."

Tara sighed. "Maybe so. Anyway, the detective who called asked that we detain as many people as we could. I guess they want to question everyone about what they might have seen or didn't see." She glanced over at the counter and its neat row of boxes. "I wouldn't box up the food just yet," she said. "The police said that we should leave everything as is and not touch a thing. They were especially emphatic about not touching any food."

My first reaction was that Lois Galveston's assessment had been correct. I had to admit it made sense. If Ulla had died from an allergic reaction, the first logical assumption would be that it probably came from something she'd ingested. I moved off to the side, took out my cell, and punched in Will's number. It went straight to voicemail. So much for finding out anything in advance, not that Will would tell me anyway. He's a stickler for doing things by the book.

Unbidden, the mental picture of Maggie lurking furtively on the edge of the crowd in that video popped into my head. As quickly as the thought came, I pushed it out of my mind. What possible motive would Maggie have for harming Ulla, unless . . . I gave my head a brisk shake. I could hear Grace Topping's voice in my mind: *The two of them hated each other.*" There had to be a reason for that, but what? Aloud I said, "Well, we can get the cats ready to go at least. Maybe the detective will take our statements first so we can get the cats back to the shelter."

"Good idea," said Donna. "If you need more help, let me know."

Kat, Sissy, and I headed back to the storage area, where we found a harried-looking Viola on her hands and knees, looking underneath a small table in the far corner. She glanced up as we entered. "Oh, so this time it's you. I heard someone at the door before, but when I called out, they scurried off."

"Probably one of the staff or another fan looking for an opportunity to go through Ulla's stuff—or a mouse." I grinned at Vi. "Lose something?"

"Yeah, one stubborn cat." Viola got to her feet and smoothed down her tunic top. "I had her in her carrier, but the lock is loose, and that little stinker is getting too good at unlatching the door." Her lips curved upward. "As a matter of fact, Annie reminds me a lot of Toby. She's enterprising and resourceful. Maybe the two of them should get together."

I chuckled. "I think one cat is about all we can handle right now. I'm lucky Leila agreed to let me adopt Toby." I glanced around the room. "Annie shouldn't be too difficult to find. There aren't that many places she can hide."

"Oh, don't kid yourself. Cats are masters at hiding, and Annie wrote the book. She didn't get that name for nothing, you know. I thought it was an odd name for a cat, so I looked it up on the Internet. Do you know—"

Vi stopped speaking abruptly as we heard a plaintive meow behind us. We all turned and saw the cat in question sitting in her carrier. "Merow," she said again, and then raised her paw and started to wash her face.

Sissy started to giggle. "See, Vi? Annie knows where her place is. She was probably just having a little fun with you."

"Fun my—never mind," Vi said with a sigh. "We're either going to have to get that carrier fixed or find her another one."

"I hate to do that. The cat is used to Irene's carrier," Kat said. "I'll just make a note to have Ed McGee look at it next time he's at the shelter." Ed McGee, the owner of McGee's Hardware, often fixed things around the shelter for free.

"Well, maybe someone will adopt Annie before it becomes an issue again," I said, and turned to Vi. "That reminds me, you didn't finish telling your story. You said you looked up Annie Reilly online?"

"I did." Viola cleared her throat and puffed out her chest, a mannerism she employed when she had what she felt was something of importance to impart to the rest of us, which was usually quite often. Don't get me wrong; I love Viola, but the woman does tend to be right a good deal of the time, and she knows it. "The real Annie Reilly was actually rather . . . notorious." Viola reached into her smock pocket, pulled out her smartphone, entered something in her browser, and then passed it over to me. "See for yourself."

I took the phone and, with Kat looking over my shoulder, read the brief article on the screen. When I'd finished, I shook my head and handed the phone back to Viola. "The cleverest woman in her line of work in America, huh?" I said.

"Yep," Viola said brightly, pocketing her phone. "Annie Reilly was one of the best thieves and con artists in America in the late eighteen hundreds. And this little stinker is the feline version. If you haven't noticed, she's a real pack-rat. She'll snag anything that's lying around, although her preference is for shiny things, and the shinier the better. You saw the way she went after Ulla's necklace." Vi pursed her lips. "Speaking of Ulla, any news?"

"She didn't make it," I said quietly.

Vi was silent for a long moment, and then she said, "She didn't seem to be a nice person, but still, it's such a tragic end to this event." She paused and then said, "Maggie would have been pleased at what a nice turnout we had today. I wonder why she didn't come in."

My ears perked up. "What do you mean? Maggie was here?"

"Yep. Or at least I thought she was here. I only caught a quick glimpse. She was standing over by the back entrance, and I'm certain that was her red coat, but—I could be wrong."

"You didn't see her face?"

Vi shook her head. "Nope. Like I said, I only had a quick glimpse." She waved her hand. "But I'm probably mistaken. After all, if it had been Maggie, she wouldn't have been lurking around; she'd have come inside to help."

"Absolutely," Kat agreed briskly. "Maggie's first priority would always be the animals."

The two of them moved off to help Sissy with the cat

toys. I hung back, unable to shake the vision of Ulla arguing with someone who stood in the shadows. Had it been Maggie? I pulled out my cell and hit the button for Maggie's number; once again, it went to voicemail. I left a message, short and sweet: "Maggie, it's Syd. I need to talk to you. Call me ASAP."

"You sound serious," said a familiar voice. I nearly dropped my phone as I whirled around and found myself staring right into Will Worthington's eyes.

Chapter Nine

At first glance, my boyfriend looks more like a movie star than a homicide detective. He has a high forehead, black curly hair that begs to have fingers run through it, sparkling blue eyes, and a wide, generous, very kissable mouth. Make no mistake, though—behind that handsome face is a mind like a steel trap, a mind that's well honed when it comes to things like murder and detection. I looked up at him with a sweet smile as I slid my phone casually back into my pocket.

"Why, Will Worthington," I purred, in my best Southern maiden impersonation, "we've just got to stop meeting like this. People will talk."

He gave my arm a quick squeeze. "I'm happy to see you, although I wish it were under different circumstances. Like my picking you up for a Friday night dinner."

"Me too." I gave a quick look around. "Are you working this alone?"

"I wish." His nose wrinkled, almost as if he'd smelled

something foul. "Charlie should be here somewhere. Connolly wants us to work this together."

"As in 'team'?"

He nodded. "I think he's going to use this case as a yardstick to determine which of us gets the senior position."

I resisted the urge to stamp my foot. "That's so unfair! You've been a homicide detective longer than Charlie!"

"We both put in the same amount of time on homicide; we just did it in different towns. And I hate to admit it, but Charlie might have a slight edge."

"You mean his connection to the mayor," I sniffed. "You know I'm going to hate this Charlie Callahan, right?"

"Your loyalty is appreciated. But you don't have to dislike him on my account, Syd." He shot me a lopsided grin. "Charlie can come across as quite personable."

"Personable, huh?" It had always been my experience that folks described thusly were often anything but. "Does that mean you think he should get the senior slot?"

"Oh, heck no. I'm better qualified." Will pulled out his notebook and pen and flipped to a clean page. "So let's get your statement down. What happened here today?"

I recounted the afternoon's events. "Ulla really didn't look well," I finished. "Cherry Dunphy was pretty certain she'd had some sort of allergic reaction. Her manager didn't seem to be aware Ulla had any allergies; then again, he also said he wasn't privy to her complete medical history. Which reminds me, he was going to have her assistant, Savannah Blade, check on it."

"Thanks. I'll be sure to follow up on that." He scribbled on his pad. "How about right before her attack? Notice anything unusual?"

Aside from her arguing with the mysterious shadow? As I debated whether to bring that up, someone standing near me cleared his throat. Loudly.

"Ah, Will. There you are."

I turned my head and saw a tall guy with curly hair standing there. My first impression from the man's muscular build was that he probably spent a great deal of time in the gym. The tan blazer and matching chinos he wore seemed molded to his angular frame. I'm bad at guessing ages, but I put his as a few years younger than Will and myself, somewhere around thirty, thirty-two. I had no doubt that when he was younger, he'd most likely been characterized as a pretty boy. His features seemed Ken-doll perfect, as were the white teeth he flashed in a quick smile. His ice-blue eyes widened for a moment as they rested on me, then narrowed as he switched his gaze to Will. "Harris and Robertson are taking names and statements, but it doesn't appear that any of the people who were here for the signing noticed anything significant."

"You never know," was Will's terse answer. "Sometimes the least significant thing turns out to be a real clue."

"Noted. I'm also having Ramirez bag everything from the café area. And the trash too. Any food wrappers, cups, or bottles with lipstick stains."

"I don't recall Ulla eating anything," I said, "but of course she wasn't within my range of vision for most of the event. I do know she was drinking some bottled water."

Charlie Callahan's gaze rocketed back to me. "And you are?"

"Sydney McCall. I'm one of the shelter directors."

"Ah, so you're the infamous Syd," he said with a wide grin. He held out his hand. "I've heard all about the part you played in tracking down Trowbridge Littleton's murderer."

I felt my cheeks start to sear as he pumped my hand up and down. "I think the press overplayed my role in that," I remarked.

He released my hand with a deep chuckle. "Modest *and* pretty." He pointed a finger at Will. "Don't let her go, Worthington." Abruptly he snapped his gaze back to me. "So, she ate nothing that you noticed? Not even a breath mint?"

"That's right, but as I said, I was in the cat pop-up area for most of the event. Her staff could probably tell you more. I know her assistant and producer were right out there at the table with her, and so was her manager."

Charlie Callahan raised a hand to scratch behind one ear. "Harris is talking to them. What about Ms. Townsend's things? Where are they?"

"In the storage area, along with our supplies. I'll show you."

I took both men over to the storage area and pointed out the section that had been assigned to Ulla. Both pulled out latex gloves, and just as they were snapping them on,

Wendy appeared in the doorway. She looked at them, then at me, and planted both hands on her hips. "What's going on here?"

Will started to step forward, but Callahan was a second quicker. He peeled his jacket back and flashed his badge. "Detective Charles Callahan, Deer Park PD." He picked up a tote bag from the floor and held it aloft. "Is this Ulla Townsend's purse?"

"No, it's mine. Ulla never carried purses. She didn't like them, claimed no one ever made one big enough to house all of her paraphernalia." Wendy glanced around and then pointed to a tote that was lying on the floor, yawning open, at the other end of the room where the shelter supplies were. "That looks like her bag, but what is it doing on that side of the room?"

"She tossed it over there," I piped up. As three pair of eyes swung toward me, I added, "I ran into her here shortly before her attack. I saw her toss the bag over toward our side of the room, but as far as I can recall, the bag was closed, not wide open like that."

"Fans have been sneaking in and out of this area all day," Wendy remarked, stamping her foot. "We told the store manager we should have been assigned a locked area, but—" She suddenly clamped her lips together and frowned. "Never mind."

I laid my hand on Will's arm. "This was the only spot that could accommodate everyone's needs," I said. "There were people milling around back here all day, so I imagine it's possible that a fan could have gotten in, maybe taken a keepsake."

He arched his brow. "So what you're saying is it's probably a waste of time to dust for prints."

"Well, you'll probably get more prints than you bargained for."

"We have to take everything that belongs to the CNC crew into evidence," Charlie Callahan barked out. "We'll take a complete inventory and notify you when you can pick everything up."

"And when might that be?" Wendy asked.

"A day, possibly two or three."

Wendy's eyes widened. "You mean . . . we have to stay here?"

"It's standard operating procedure in an investigation of this sort."

"'An investigation of this sort'?" Her eyes narrowed, and then she let out a gasp and took a step backward. "Good Lord! You think that Ulla was . . . that someone deliberately . . ."

"We're not making any assumptions now," Charlie said smoothly. "We don't have the exact cause of death yet after all." He whipped a small notebook out of his pocket and flipped a few pages. "According to a statement given by her manager at the hospital, Ms. Townsend had no known allergies."

"Yes, I heard him say it," Wendy said impatiently. "I was standing right next to him."

"Wonderful." Callahan snapped his notebook shut. "Then you understand that we're still not certain if her death was related to an allergic reaction, or if something else might have caused it. Until then, her death is labeled a 'suspicious death,' and yes, I—and my partner, here—are advising you and the others not to leave town until we sort this out."

I saw Will's cheeks flush slightly, and I could tell he was annoyed at the way Callahan had seemed to swoop in and take charge. I remembered the way Bennington had handled the investigation of Littleton's death. As much as I'd disliked Bennington, he hadn't been half as high-handed with Will as Callahan appeared to be. Then again, he wasn't fighting for a top investigative spot on the force.

Wendy looked perturbed. "So this is a murder investigation," she said slowly.

"Not at the moment. Right now, it's an 'unofficial' investigation into some strange circumstances," Charlie Callahan said smoothly. "It would definitely speed things up, though, if you could provide us with the name of Ulla's doctor."

Wendy let out a snort. "Ulla didn't have a doctor per se. She wasn't a big believer in the medical field. She felt people went to doctors too quickly with every little ache and pain, and the medicine they prescribed often made you worse. Cured one thing and broke down another. She preferred natural remedies for healing purposes. She went to a New Age physician."

Charlie Callahan looked completely confused. "New

Age? You mean a doctor who heals with crystals and potions? Stuff like that?"

Wendy's lips curved slightly upward. "Hardly. Most New Age doctors provide customized and individualized health care solutions focused mainly on nutrition and lifestyle modification. They shy away from traditional medicine in favor of age-old remedies."

Callahan let out a derisive snort. "Sounds pretty prehistoric to me."

"Don't knock it unless you've tried it, Detective. Ulla was rarely sick since I've known her. Savannah's known her longer, and she says the same thing." She pulled absently at her earlobe. "Maybe there is something to this natural healing stuff. I don't know; it seemed to work well for Ulla—until today anyway."

I noticed a flush similar to Will's start to creep up Callahan's neck. "I don't suppose you have the name of this New Age doctor?"

"Was it Dr. Gray?" I piped up. As the two detectives turned to stare at me, I added quickly, "I heard Savannah tell Ulla she had a call from a Dr. Gray. She seemed very anxious to take it."

Wendy frowned. "I don't know who Dr. Gray is, but Ulla's doctor's name is Raymond Lewandowski. I'm sure Savannah can give you more information." She paused, and her tongue darted out and swiped at her lower lip. "Ulla had another motive for being here in Deer Park, besides helping out the shelter," she said.

Both men had started to put their notebooks away, but now they pulled them out again. "Would you know what that other motive was?" Will asked.

"Only what I happened to overhear earlier. She was on her phone, and she was telling someone that it was imperative she find her, and the last she'd heard, she was in Deer Park."

Callahan glanced up from his scribbling. "She? A woman?"

Wendy inclined her head. "Yes. That's all I know. I'm sorry. I believe that Ulla was trying to trace someone, and she hoped to find her here in Deer Park. Whether she did or not, I have no idea." She paused. "And now we'll probably never know."

"Or maybe we will," Callahan murmured. He tucked his notebook back into his pocket and plucked at Will's sleeve. "I'm going to round up the rest of these cable people and escort 'em to the station, get their statements. Can you supervise the cleanup here?"

Only the muscle twitching in Will's lower jaw betrayed his annoyance, at least to me. "Sure," he said tightly. "I'll wrap things up here and meet you back at Headquarters."

"Good man," said Charlie, and then he motioned to Wendy to follow him. They walked off, and once they were out of earshot, I turned to Will.

"He's acting like he's already in charge."

"Yeah, well, having a political connection will do that every time," Will muttered. He brushed a hand across his eyes. "You and the others can take the cats back to the shelter," he said. "I'll come by either later or tomorrow and get all of your formal statements, okay? Like you said, you were back here with the cats, not out front." He gave me a brief nod and was gone. I stood rooted to the spot, thinking.

I knew Will, knew how to gauge his reactions. I also knew the circumstances surrounding Ulla's death bothered him. I could tell he wasn't pleased that this investigation had become a job contest between him and Charlie Callahan. Both men would be eager to solve the case, which meant they'd grab onto any lead they found like a starving dog clutching a juicy bone. Case in point: Wendy's revelation regarding the real reason Ulla had agreed to replace Dudley Simmons at the book signing event. Suppose Ulla had been trying to track down someone to settle an old score . . . how did Maggie fit in? Had the person Ulla had been trying to locate been Maggie? Had she found her, and had they had some sort of argument that escalated into . . .

I shook my head. No, I absolutely was not going there. No way.

I whipped my phone out and punched in Leila's number. She answered on the first ring. "Hey, I was just gonna call you. I'm on my way to the office to write up my story. It's not exactly the way I expected today's event to end."

"Me either," I said. "We're still at Crowden's. The police are here."

"I figured. Is Will in charge of the investigation?"

"Funny you should ask. It seems Ulla's demise has turned into a sort of job interview."

"Did you just say 'a job interview'? What the heck?"

I quickly explained about Charlie Callahan, ending with the little kernel of information Wendy had provided. "I'm afraid that when this investigation kicks into high gear, Maggie might pop up high on the suspect list."

"Maggie?" The surprise in Leila's voice was evident. "As in Kat's assistant Maggie Shayne? Why would you say that?"

"It's a long story, best told over a good meal," I said. "I could use some advice. I need to come up with some course of action."

"I know what that means. You're planning on investigating Ulla's death, aren't you? I thought after your last experience you said you'd leave all future investigations to the police."

"That was before it appeared as if Maggie might be suspect numero uno and before the investigation started taking on Keystone Cops aspects."

"I take it you're not too impressed with Callahan's detective skills?"

"He seems like a grandstander, one who'll latch onto someone and hone in on them without even looking at other options."

"In other words, you're afraid this Charlie Callahan will railroad Maggie, and Will won't be able to stop him."

I tried to keep the smile out of my voice. "I knew there

was a reason why I've always liked you. You're quick on the uptake. So, what do you say? Do you want to help me or not?"

My bestie sighed. "Sure, why not. Who knows, maybe I'll get another front-page story like last time. Only, please, please, promise me you won't confront the killer again. That shaved a few years off my life."

"You? Think what it did to *me*," I joked. "So, we brainstorm tonight? What shall I order? Chinese? Thai? Or the classic double-cheese pizza?"

"Mm . . . none of the above. I think we should go a little crazy," Leila said.

I frowned. The last time she'd suggested doing something crazy, I'd gotten a butterfly tattoo on my right hip. "What did you have in mind, exactly?"

"How about Antonio's at six thirty? Everyone raves about that place, and I'm dying to try it. This is a great excuse."

Antonio's was a new, upscale Italian eatery that had recently opened at the other end of town. I'd been hoping to experience it for the first time with Will, but it didn't seem as if that was going to happen anytime soon. "Okay. It's a date," I said, and hung up. Before I went to help get the cats ready for transport, I tried Maggie's number once again. Voicemail.

This time, I didn't leave a message.

Chapter Ten

We managed to pack up all the cats and supplies and made it back to the shelter a little after three. While Sissy and Viola got the cats settled back in, Kat took the stack of paperwork back to her office to start reviewing the applications. I locked myself in my little cubbyhole, fired up my laptop, and the first thing I did was Google "Ulla Townsend collapse." News of her collapse was all over the Internet—no big surprise there, considering her popularity. I clicked on one article that had been written by Joan Niven, a reporter for the *Charleston Chronicle* and read:

> A source at City Hospital reported that Ms. Townsend appeared to be suffering from anaphylactic shock. Anaphylaxis is a sudden, severe allergic reaction. Within minutes of being exposed to an allergy trigger, a chain reaction is started that can cause several things to happen, such as widening of the blood vessels, lowering of blood pressure, hives, and

swelling. Epinephrine was administered, but not fast enough to prevent the attack from being fatal.

The cause of the allergic reaction is not yet known, but local officials are investigating to determine what might have caused the reaction. A source at the hospital revealed that anaphylaxis attacks are most common after the victim consumes an item he or she might be allergic to, such as peanuts. It's unclear right now as to whether Ms. Townsend's reaction might have been the result of something she consumed at the event.

I sat back, drumming my fingers on the arms of my leather captain's chair. I was willing to bet that if Ulla had an allergy, it wasn't to food. What else could cause anaphylaxis attacks? I hit Google again, and a few seconds later I found my answer on a popular medical site. Anaphylaxis, a severe, sometimes life-threatening condition, could affect multiple organs, such as the heart or lungs. There were many things that could trigger a reaction, like eggs, peanuts, soy, insect bites, or stings from bees or hornets—and even some pain medications.

I leaned back in my chair and laced my hands behind my neck. It didn't seem as if any of the causes listed could have possibly contributed to Ulla's death. She hadn't eaten anything as far as I knew, and there hadn't seemed to be any insects around, at least none of the flying kind. She hadn't had a vaccine or a blood transfusion, and, according to Wendy, she didn't take prescription medicine. I scrolled back to the beginning of the article and found what I was looking for: symptoms typically occurred within 30 minutes of exposure and in most cases developed rapidly. It was considered rare for the onset of symptoms to be delayed for hours.

Rare, but not unheard of. I sighed. It would figure that Ulla Townsend could be one of the rare cases. Of course, this was all still speculation until the official cause of death was revealed. In the meantime, what was another possibility? That she might somehow have been poisoned? If she hadn't eaten or drunk anything, the "how" was certainly a brain-teaser.

I was just about to Google "poisons whose symptoms resemble anaphylaxis," when my phone rang. I scrambled for it, hoping that it might be Maggie at last, but the caller ID came up Deer Park Inn. Puzzled, I pressed the answer button. "Hello?"

"Ms. McCall? This is Savannah Blade." The admin's voice sounded a bit strained. I was willing to bet that Charlie Callahan had put her, as well as all the other CNC people, through the wringer. "I was just calling to find out if perhaps you might have found something of ours mixed in with your things."

"Oh?"

"Yes. It's Ulla's necklace—the one she was wearing. She took it off when she was being photographed with that cat, and the clasp broke."

"I remember," I said. "She tossed it into her tote bag."

"Yes, the police went through it, and it's not there. I thought perhaps, since the tote was over near your things, it might have fallen out and gotten mixed in with the shelter supplies." She paused and added, "The Glow people gave her that necklace. The charm is solid silver, and in the shape of a lip gloss tube. It's quite unique."

"Well, we unpacked everything when we got back here, and I didn't see the necklace. I can have Sissy go through everything again, though."

"Are you absolutely certain? I'm sorry. I don't mean to be rude, it's just . . . well, it's quite a valuable piece." She continued with a catch in her voice, "Ulla loved that necklace. She told me that if anything ever happened to her, I could have it. As a remembrance."

That remark surprised me. "I didn't realize you were that close to Ulla," I said.

"I know. It surprised me too. I never expected to like her but . . . I do—did," she amended. "Oh, she could be condescending, sure. But I learned a lot from just watching her. She was the Queen of Shopping, you know? She was tough as nails, but she had her Achilles' heel too. For example, she was super nervous about coming back to Deer Park."

"I know she grew up here. I'd heard her childhood here wasn't exactly idyllic."

Savannah let out a snort. "That's putting it mildly. I saw some of the notes that she had written down about her early years. Lots of that didn't make the book, but if it had . . . There was one girl in particular she had issues with back in high school—really big issues. And another girl who tried to be her friend, but that went down the drain when Ulla pulled a dirty trick on her. A real dirty trick."

Hmm, that tallies with what Wendy told us about Ulla's ulterior motive for coming here. "Lots of stuff like that goes down in high school," I said lightly. "I don't imagine Ulla named actual names in her book. Or did she?"

Savannah barked out a laugh. "Oh, goodness no. Legal would have had her head. No, the names were changed to protect the innocent—sort of."

" 'Sort of'?"

"Well . . . according to Ulla, if anyone she knew back then read her book, they'd recognize themselves right away, name change or not." She lowered her voice. "She was desperate to get hold of one person from her past . . . someone she referred to as Miggs."

"Miggs? That was this person's last name?"

"I have no idea. It was a woman, though, because she always referred to Miggs as a 'her.' She said that she simply had to speak with her before we went back to Charleston— no ifs, ands, or buts. And I know why."

I held my breath, and Savannah did not disappoint. "Just between us, Ulla was working with a therapist."

The lightbulb was shining now so brightly above my head, I could have reached out and touched it. "A therapist? It wouldn't be a Dr. Gray by any chance?"

"Yes, exactly! Have you heard of her?" Without waiting for an answer, Savannah rushed on. "Ulla wanted to put a lot of her trust and anger issues behind her. She enrolled in an anger management program with Dr. Gray. A large portion of this program involved making amends with people that she felt she'd wronged in some way in the past. That's why she was so frantic to get hold of this Miggs person."

"I see," I said slowly. "And you're certain that the name was Miggs? It couldn't have been . . . Maggie?"

Savannah paused. "Maybe," she said at last. "At any rate, I saw her talking with a woman in the back hallway. It seemed to be a very intense discussion. And shortly afterward is when Ulla collapsed!" She lowered her voice. "I don't know the details, but from what I could gather about that relationship, it seemed to me like this Miggs person had an excellent reason for hating Ulla. Maybe even a good enough reason to kill her!"

I was getting a sinking feeling in the pit of my stomach. "This woman you saw—do you remember what she looked like?"

"I didn't get a good look at her. She had a pink scarf with white dots wrapped around her head that hid most of her face. And she had on a really worn-looking red coat." She sighed. "Not much of a help, is it?"

Quite the contrary, I knew someone who owned a pink scarf and a worn red jacket just like Savannah had described.

Maggie Shayne.

After promising to look again for the necklace, I hung up and dialed Maggie's number once more. After the voice-mail kicked in, I said, "Maggie! This is serious! I need you to call me pronto." I tossed the phone down on the desk, and as I did so, Kat stuck her head in my office.

"Is something wrong?"

"You could say that." I gave Kat a quick rundown of my conversation with Savannah. When I finished, Kat let out a low whistle.

"It sounds bad on the surface, but I can't believe that Maggie would actually do something like that."

"Well, in that video she had on her red coat," I said, my jaw clenched. "I recognized it right off. And she has a pink scarf with white dots on it. She had it on the other day."

Kat gave her head a brisk shake. "Lots of people own red coats, and I've seen a few women with dotted pink scarves. They had a sale on 'em a few weeks ago in Kings. It's a coincidence, that's all."

"Maybe." I raked my fingers through my hair. "But what about her not answering her phone? That's not like Maggie at all. She always answers her cell—you know, in case it's about a rescue or an abandoned animal or something." I eyed my sister. "She hasn't called you or texted you again, has she?"

"Not yet, but I'm sure there's a perfectly good reason." Kat shook her head. "I think you're making mountains out of molehills, little Sis. I mean, Miggs might be a nickname for Maggie, but then again, maybe it's not. Maggie's probably just busy. She's always been a straight shooter—you know that. I doubt that she's avoiding you."

I sighed. "I hope you're right." But deep down I had my doubts.

*   *   *

Kat still had some paperwork to finish up, so I handed her the keys to my car and told her that I'd walk home. She started to protest, but stopped when I held firm, telling her that a nice leisurely walk would help clear the cobwebs out of my brain. She drove off, and after leaving a note for Sissy to check for the necklace when she came in for her shift in the morning, I set off at a quick pace up the block. As I passed Crowden's, I glanced over at the shop and saw Tara leaning in the window, straightening a pile of books. She looked up, saw me, and motioned for me to enter. I hesitated, then walked over, noting as I did so that the display she'd been fussing over was of Ulla's book. The door suddenly swung open, and Tara stood on the threshold, her eyes bright.

"You wouldn't believe the crowd that showed up after you guys left. Her book has been flying out of here."

I shook my head. "It's amazing how a tragedy can boost sales sometimes, isn't it?"

"You can say that again." She took my arm and pulled me inside the shop. "I've got about a dozen copies that Ulla signed for me in the back. I was going to put them out, but that girl who used to work for Ulla—Savannah, I think her name is—was in here earlier and told me to hang onto them and sell them on eBay. She said I could probably get a couple hundred each for them. Can you imagine that?"

Sadly, I could. "Sometimes celebrities become even more famous after they're dead. Look at Marilyn Monroe."

"You're right." Tara's head bobbed up and down. "I'm thinking of doing it, though, and giving all the proceeds to the shelter. What do you think?"

"Selfishly, I think it's a great idea," I said. "But maybe you should wait a few days."

"Yeah, that's what I thought too. If I do end up getting a lot for 'em, I guess I'll have to send Savannah a thank-you note."

"I guess the shelter will too," I agreed. I glanced at the pile of books in the window and plucked one from the pile. "You know, I think I'll buy a copy myself. Everyone who's read it has said it's pretty spicy."

"Yeah, Wendy said that too. Of course, with Ulla as the subject matter, how could it be anything but."

I took the book over to the counter, and Tara rang up the sale. As she was slipping it into a green and white Crowden's bag, I asked, "Why did Savannah come back?"

"She wanted to know if Ulla's silver necklace had turned up somewhere. She seemed quite concerned about it."

"Yes, she called me too. Ulla told her if anything ever happened to her, the necklace would be hers."

"That doesn't surprise me. Wendy always said that Savannah was an opportunist."

"Really? She seemed sincere to me. She went on about how she'd miss Ulla and how much she'd learned from her."

Tara let out a snort. "She might have learned a few tricks from her, but miss her? Doubtful. Wendy overheard her on the phone a few days ago, telling someone that her ship was about to come in and, boy, was she ever going to enjoy having the last laugh."

I frowned as I slid my credit card back into my wallet. "Last laugh? On who? Not Ulla?"

"Who else? Anyway, Wendy said Savannah's seemed very different the past few weeks. Very confident. Who knows, maybe she interviewed for another job somewhere. She has a degree in something . . . English, I think."

I tucked my purchase under my arm. "I take it you don't think she was sincere when she said she liked working for Ulla?"

Tara wrinkled her nose. "I hate speaking ill of the dead but . . . who would? After all, she didn't get the name "Dragon Lady" for nothing."

* * *

Back out on the street, I pondered what Tara had told me. Ulla had argued with Ken about getting the Glow Cosmetics deal, had even threatened to quit if it weren't awarded to her, yet they'd been all cozy and cuddly afterward. She'd been upset over Candy Carmichael's appearance, and about the former beauty queen's running for the Glow position as well. I wondered what had been so darned important to Ulla about getting that contract. Was it ego, or was it the fact that she just didn't want Candy Carmichael to have it? Then there was Savannah—what was up with that? Did she genuinely care about Ulla, or had it all been an act? She might have hated Ulla, but if hatred were a crime, a lot of people would be in jail. I was so lost in my thoughts that I hadn't realized I'd turned in the direction of Maggie's house until I saw the quaint ranch loom up in front of me. Maggie's beat-up Honda wasn't in the driveway, but the garage door was shut. I walked up the short flight of steps to the porch and rang the bell. No answer. I knocked twice on the door, as hard as I could. Still nothing. I sighed and started down the steps, when the next-door neighbor's door opened, and Jeannie MacGillicuddy thrust out her gray head.

"Hello, Syd," she called. "Are you looking for Maggie?" At my nod she went on, "I saw her leave earlier, around three I think. She had two big suitcases with her. Said she had some sort of family emergency and had to go out of town for a few days."

"A . . . a few *days*?" I cried.

"Yep. She wasn't certain just when she'd be back." Jeannie eyed me curiously. "You look upset, Syd. Is something wrong?"

"No, no. I'm just still a little flustered after what happened earlier today," I said quickly.

"Oh, yes, Ulla Townsend. Such a dreadful thing. Maggie was quite upset over it too."

My head snapped up. "She was?"

"Sure seemed to be. She turned pale when I told her." A soft "ding" sounded from within the house, and Jeannie shot me an apologetic smile. "Oh, that's the timer for my pie. See you, Syd."

Jeannie shut the door and I just stood for a moment, trying to assimilate what she'd just told me. Maggie was ignoring my calls. Maggie had seemed upset over Ulla's death. Last but not least, Maggie would be out of town for a few days.

I tried, unsuccessfully, to tamp down the phrase that kept running through my mind: flight is considered evidence of guilt.

"But she's not fleeing," I murmured to myself. "She's got a family emergency." Or so she'd said. I struggled to remember what Maggie had told me about her family. She had one sister who lived in San Francisco and another who lived in Detroit. Both were married, and each had two kids. Her parents were both deceased, and she had an aunt who lived in a nursing home in Weddington and a second cousin who lived on the other side of Deer Park.

And just as I was racking my brain, trying to remember if there was anyone else, my phone buzzed that I had a text. I snatched it up and looked at the message on the screen:

Sorry. I had to leave after what happened. I'll be in touch soon.

"Oh, Maggie," I murmured, feeling my heart sink right down to my toes. "What have you done?"

Chapter Eleven

I tried my best, but I couldn't shake off the feeling of trepidation that coursed through me after reading Maggie's text. On an impulse, I walked the three blocks over to Mulholland Street, where Maggie's second cousin Rhonda lived. I'd met her a few times at the shelter, and she was a pleasant, plump woman who'd moved to Deer Park after her divorce a few years ago. She did some telemarketing out of her home and was just finishing up a call when I rang her bell. She seemed happy to see me, and invited me in for a cup of tea. I informed her that I couldn't stay long, and then I explained about Maggie being out of town. "I really need to get in touch with her. You wouldn't have any idea where she might have gone, would you?"

Rhonda shook her head, letting a curl fall over one eye. "Sorry, no. I can't imagine what sort of family emergency it might be. Last I heard, Aunt Chloris was doing fine at the nursing home." She waved her hand in the air. "Maybe she just wanted to get away for a few days. It wouldn't surprise me. She was kind of upset at Ulla Townsend coming back to town. And even though that signing benefited the shelter, I know it ate away at her. She just never trusted Ulla, and I can't blame her—and now Ulla's dead. I'm sure Maggie didn't shed any tears, but knowing her, she probably feels bad. Like maybe her not wanting Ulla here might have caused it, which is ridiculous."

Is it? I thought. *I sincerely hope so.*

Rhonda got up and walked over to the large bookcase that took up one corner of her living room. She selected a thin blue book and walked back to me. "This is Maggie's high school yearbook," she said. "I was gathering pictures for our family reunion, and she let me borrow it. I need to return it to her." Rhonda flipped some pages and then held the book out to me. "Here's a photo of Maggie and Ulla in the Glee Club. They're right in front."

I took the book and peered at the black and white photograph. I recognized both Maggie and Ulla right away. From the happy expressions on their faces in that photo, one would never have suspected that they'd end up being enemies. I shut the book and handed it back to Rhonda. "I know something happened between them in high school a long time ago, and I get the feeling it was something pretty bad. Would you know anything about that?"

Rhonda looked a little uncomfortable. "I'm not privy to all the details," she said at last. "It's really better if you ask Maggie. It's her story to tell." She paused. "One thing I will say, though, is that yes, it was bad. Really bad for Maggie."

I tried to pry more out of her, but Rhonda held firm. We exchanged a few more pleasantries, and then I thanked Rhonda for her time and headed home. Toby greeted me at the door when I arrived, and I noticed a headless Melvin the Mouse lying a few feet behind him. I bent down to retrieve the mouse, then dangled him above Toby's head.

"You just can't leave poor Melvin alone, can you?" I chided the cat.

He looked up at me, eyes wide. "Merow?"

"Okay, I know. Better Melvin than Leila's couch." I walked over to the kitchen island, set down my tote bag, and fished out my copy of Ulla's book. I held it up for Toby to see. "See this poor woman, Toby? She was the main attraction for the shelter benefit. And now she's dead."

Toby stared at the book, then cocked his head. "Rrr."

"She died from an allergic reaction, but no one seems to think she had any allergies—hence Will's on the job. And a new guy, Charlie Callahan. They're both competing for Bennington's senior slot. Will seems to think that whoever solves this case will get the job."

Toby lay down, crossed his paws in front of him. "Mrrr?"

"Exactly. I know how badly Will wants that job. I think I should help him solve this mystery so he can get it. What do you think?"

The cat stared at me for a minute, then opened his mouth in a wide yawn.

"Sorry to bore you," I said with a chuckle. I took the book and settled in one of the kitchen chairs. Leaning back,

I started to flip idly through it. The book was divided into thirty chapters and three sections: Ulla's early years, her years struggling to find her niche, and her last fifteen years as a successful shopping channel host. The first section no doubt, was my best bet on finding a clue, if one were to be had, but curiosity over all the salacious parts of the book won out and I flipped to the third part.

It didn't take me long to find out that Ulla wasn't above revealing skeletons in the closets of her coworkers. She didn't name names, but the descriptions were so spot on, I imagined that people who were regular viewers would be able to read between the lines. She intimated that two hosts, both happily married, were embroiled in an affair, while another was a closet alcoholic. She ripped apart several staff members as well, and finally I found the section where she described her relationship with another female host as "dealing with a two-faced barracuda." From her description I was almost positive the host, whom she called "Ms. X," was Candy Carmichael.

I'm convinced Ms. X, whom everyone thinks of as Little Miss Goody Two Shoes, isn't so goody at all. She never talks about her past at all, which makes me wonder just what she has to hide. After all, everyone has secrets. She's all light and sweetness when the cameras are rolling, but when they're off? At times it seems as if she holds some sort of grudge against me. I chalk it all up to jealousy. Believe me, Ms. X isn't above using any means possible to get what she wants, and what she wants is my job. She's always around; it's like she's stalking me, just waiting for her chance to move in on my territory.

I flipped a few more pages and found a reference to a girl I was positive was Savannah:

Every good personality needs a good admin, and I'm not without exception. I've gone through many, as some people have hinted I'm difficult to work for (???), but one does stand head and shoulders above the rest. She always seems to be able to anticipate my every need, so much so, it's as if we've known each other in another life. She knows all my faults and, unlike many of my coworkers, understands them.

It sounded like high praise, coming from Ulla. I couldn't help but think of that old adage: Keep your friends close and your enemies closer. Was that what she was doing with Savannah?

I perused the remainder of the section. There were a few more veiled references to a man I was pretty certain was Ken Colgate and a brief reference to a "mealy-mouthed producer" that I had an idea was Wendy. When the juicy tidbits ended, I flipped back to the first chapter, entitled "Growing Up," and skimmed through it. Ulla mentioned her parents, her roots, growing up with her brother, typical sibling skirmishes. The second chapter and the third dealt with other, typical family issues, honing in on the fact that her parents, especially her mother, took every opportunity to put Ulla down while bolstering up her brother. Chapters Four and Five touched on her interpersonal relationships in grammar school, most of which were fraught with angst. She developed a tough skin, which she would need in the years ahead. I started Chapter Six, "Deer Park Darlings," with interest, as Ulla described attending high school and always feeling like an outcast. Her feelings of insecurity and jealousy grew to such epic proportions that when her senior year rolled around, she rebelled and decided to do something about it.

Chapter Seven, however, was where I hit pay dirt. Entitled "Little Town Blues," she went into even more detail. One paragraph was particularly insightful:

One thing I regret deeply was my inability to make long-lasting friendships during my school years. Unfortunately, most of the relationships I formed weren't exactly friendly. There was the girl whose Coke I put itching powder in, another whose sixteenth birthday party I sabotaged, and yet another girl who suffered a tragic breakdown I was blamed for instigating. If I had to do it all over again, I would probably have tried to let go of my anger. Hindsight is a wonderful thing. Now I have to pick up the pieces and move on.

I shut the book and drummed my fingers on the cover. It certainly sounded as if Ulla had indeed turned over a new leaf, felt sincere regret over the way she'd treated people in the past. Ulla had come here seeking forgiveness, but what if this person, this Miggs, hadn't been so inclined? I wondered if Miggs might be the person named here, the one who suffered the breakdown Ulla said she was blamed for. I frowned. I needed more details, but how to get them? I could only think of two sources: Ulla and Maggie. One was dead, the other . . . MIA.

I set the book aside and dug my laptop out of my tote. Firing it up, I typed in "Deer Park High, Deer Park, North Carolina" and the year of Ulla's graduating class. A list of alumni popped up, and I clicked on it. There were two hundred students, and I went through the list carefully.

Ulla's name wasn't there. There was a Jerry Townsend, but no Ulla in any way, shape, or form. I frowned and went to the white pages site. I punched in Rhonda's name, and a few minutes later I had her on my cell phone. "Hello, Syd," she said, and I could hear the surprise in her voice at my calling her so soon after my visit.

"Hello, Rhonda. I just had a quick question. That photo you showed me. Was it taken their senior year?"

"Why, I'm not sure. Hold on a sec." I heard the clunk as she set the phone down, and then rustling in the background. She came back on the line a few minutes later. "Yep. October of Senior year."

"Interesting. I just pulled up the alumni list from their graduation year, and Ulla Townsend's name isn't on it."

A soft chuckle. "That's because her name was Beckman back then."

Duh! I slapped my forehead with my palm. "That's right! Now I remember Grace mentioned that."

"Don't feel too bad. You wouldn't have found her there anyway. She didn't graduate Deer Park High. Her folks moved to Weddington halfway through the school year."

"Oh?" That was curious. "Did her father get transferred for his job, or something?"

"No, nothing like that." Rhonda sounded decidedly uncomfortable. "I was two years behind them, you know, so I'm not privy to all the details. You'll have to ask Maggie."

That was what I'd been afraid of. I thanked Rhonda and hung up, trying to ignore the queasy feeling in the pit of my stomach that was telling me Maggie might be more connected to what had happened to Ulla than anyone suspected. I eyed Toby, who was now sitting next to my chair, watching me hopefully.

"Yes, of course I'm going to feed you," I informed the cat. He wound himself in and around my ankles as I moved over to the cabinet to select a can of Fancy Feast Shredded Tuna. I spooned it into his bowl and then glanced at the clock. While he hunkered there slurping, I headed off to my room to shower and change for my dinner with Leila. When I emerged from the bathroom a half hour later, I found Toby sprawled across my comforter, washing his face.

"Have a nice meal?" I asked, shedding my robe. I pulled on underwear and then fussed in front of my closet, trying to decide what to wear. When I pulled out a pair of dressy boot-cut jeans and a checkered shirt, Toby sat up and let out a loud yowl.

"Hmm, maybe you're right. After all, this is an upscale place. That outfit's probably too casual."

My furry fashion advisor raised a paw in the air. "Merow."

I pulled out a navy and red–checked, mock turtleneck tunic with matching wide-legged navy pants. Toby gave his head a quick shake. "Ow-orr."

"Geez, Toby. Have you been reading *Glamour* when I'm not around? This outfit is nice, isn't it?"

Toby stretched full length out on the bed and covered his eyes with his paw.

I put back the tunic and slacks and rummaged around some more. When I pulled out a pair of black slim-leg pants and a black wrap top with a sweetheart neckline, Toby sat up on the bed and gave a loud yowl of approval. "About time!" I said, throwing up both hands in the air. I changed quickly, then slid into black strappy sandals with a modest two-inch heel. The dressing portion of the program complete, I sat in front of my vanity mirror and brushed my hair until it shone. I pulled it back into a sleek ponytail and added black hoop earrings and a gold locket. A final spritz of Chanel No. 5, and—voila!—I was done. Toby gave me another merow of approval as I gave myself a final once-over in my full-length mirror.

"Not bad, right? Maybe I should consult you on what to wear all the time."

"Ow-orr," he replied, then stretched out full-length on the bed and promptly closed his eyes. I figured being a kitty fashion consultant must be very tiring. My phone jangled, and I scrambled for it, hoping for Maggie's name to pop up, but it was Leila's name I saw onscreen.

"What's up?" I asked after pressing the talk button. "Don't tell me you're canceling?"

"Not at all. I'm just running a tad late, so let's make it six thirty instead of six." Her voice crackled with excitement. "I found out some interesting tidbits that may or may not help you," she said. "You'll have to decide that."

"Ooh, the suspense is killing me. See you soon." I hung up and then consulted my watch. "I could go and check out the bar," I said to Toby. "It's supposed to be very nice, and a 'hotspot' for singles—not that I'm looking. But it's very close to the Deer Park Inn, where Ulla's troupe is supposed to be staying. You never know who I might run into, right?"

"Merow," said Toby. Then he closed both eyes, curled his furry body into a ball, and started snoring.

Chapter Twelve

Antonio's was located at the far end of Deer Park, about a fifteen-minute ride from Leila's house. I pulled into the crowded parking lot at six-fifteen and was thankful to find one spot left, to the left of the large dumpster. I locked the car and pulled my light tan, cashmere jacket around my shoulders. It was a seasonable evening considering it was late summer, but there was a light breeze that brought a hint of a welcome chill in the air, a hopeful sign that fall—my favorite season—wasn't too far away. I stepped into the dimly lit vestibule and paused before the full-length mirror there for a final inspection. The wind had mussed my hair a bit; too bad I didn't have that can of hairspray that Vi kept stashed in the desk in the storage room back at the shelter. It would have come in handy now. I fiddled with my curls for a minute, then after deciding that was as good as it was going to get, took a moment to look around. There was a podium directly in front of me, behind which stood a tall brunette in a wine-colored, cold-shoulder blouse and long, wine and black printed skirt. Off to the right was the main dining room, and over on the left was the bar area. I could hear raised voices; it sounded like everyone was having a good time.

I checked in with the hostess at the podium, and since Leila hadn't arrived yet, I decided to check out the bar. I slid onto one of the leather-covered stools and leaned my forearms against the polished dark counter. I was debating between going out of my comfort zone and ordering a sweet Riesling or sticking with my usual Merlot, when I felt a light tap on my shoulder. I spun around and found myself staring into the eyes of the man whom I'd spilled coffee on at the bookstore. He wasn't wearing his glasses, and I couldn't help but notice how blue his eyes were.

"Well, hello," he said, "Sydney with a y. Fancy meeting you here." He gave me his movie star, megawatt smile, showing off his white, perfect teeth.

"Hello yourself." I smiled back, and held up both hands. "As you can see, I'm not armed. With coffee or anything else, for that matter. At least, not yet."

He chuckled. "I've just realized we were never formally introduced. I did stop by Dayna's café to rectify that matter, but you weren't there."

I stared at him, frankly surprised that he'd gone to the trouble to try to look me up. "That's because I don't work there. I was just helping out. I'm the publicity director for the animal shelter. Sydney—"

"McCall," he finished, his smile widening. "I should have known."

"You've heard of the shelter?"

"Yes—or rather, I've heard of you in particular. About your flair for detection." His hand shot out and closed over mine, and I noted his grip was very firm. "I'm Douglas Harriman. All my friends call me Doug."

I smiled back. "Nice to meet you too, Doug. And I'm sure reports of my skill as a detective have been greatly exaggerated."

"Somehow I doubt that." His eyes twinkled as he went on, "And now that's out of the way, tell me: Are you meeting someone?"

"Yes, I'm meeting a friend for dinner, but I'm a bit early."

He motioned toward the bar. "Might I buy you a drink while you're waiting?"

I paused, wondering if this qualified as being asked out and if I should tell Dayna she'd won the bet. "Sure—that is, if you trust me not to spill wine all over that nice suit you're wearing."

He flashed that killer smile again. "No problem. I'll order you white wine. That way if you spill it on me, it won't be so noticeable."

We adjourned to the very crowded bar area. There was a vacant chair all the way over on the left side. He propelled me over and held out the stool for me. I slid onto it, and he stood just behind me, his hand resting lightly on the stool's back. The bartender looked over, and Doug signaled him. "I'll have a Bulleit neat. And the lady . . ." He paused and looked at me questioningly.

"A Riesling. Sweet, please." There was a bowl of peanuts on the bar. I pulled it in front of me, grabbed a fistful, and popped one into my mouth. "So, how about you? Are you meeting someone here too?"

"Guilty. Mine is business, though, not pleasure." He reached into the bowl for a fistful of nuts, popped one in his mouth and chewed it before he added, "So, tell me. Is the friend you're meeting for dinner your boyfriend?"

I almost choked on my nut. Doug certainly didn't pull any punches! I coughed lightly to cover my confusion. Fortunately, the bartender set our drinks down just then. I grabbed my glass and took a swallow. "Unfortunately, no. I haven't seen too much of him lately. He's been putting in a lot of overtime."

The corners of Doug's lips drooped downward. I wondered if he was disappointed over the fact that my boyfriend put in so much overtime, or just, in general, that I had a boyfriend. "Ah, so I take it he's a hard-working corporate type?" he asked.

"Hard-working, yes; corporate, no. Will is a detective."

He threw back his head and laughed. "Why am I not surprised? I imagine you're a big help to him. It's a demanding job."

"It is that, but Will prefers I stick to publicity and keep my detecting to a minimum."

He chuckled. "He's probably trying to keep you safe. I heard you had a rather close call."

I took another sip of my Riesling. For a newbie in town, Doug certainly seemed to be very familiar with local gossip. "One might say that."

Doug's gaze bored into mine. "Still . . . you'd think he'd appreciate the help, especially when it comes from one so charming. I do hope he appreciates you. Demanding job or not, he still should manage to take some time off. You know that old saying about too much work."

"I've heard it," I said dryly. "I'm not sure Will has."

Doug laughed. "Has he heard this one? The early bird catches the worm? Or, perhaps in this case, the girl?"

I felt heat sear my cheeks and I coughed lightly. "So, what brought you to Deer Park, Doug? A job? A woman?"

He laughed. "Not a woman," he said with finality. I felt an odd fluttering in my chest at those words. "Actually, I'm surprised you hadn't heard. I—" He paused as his jacket pocket started to vibrate. He took out his iPhone, glanced at the screen, and held up a finger. "Excuse me, Sydney. I have to take this." He motioned to the bartender as he moved away. "Put the lady's drink on my tab."

Doug moved off and I sipped at my Riesling, letting my eyes rove over the bar. It was indeed crowded, mostly with girls dressed in sexy-looking dresses and guys in suits and ties. Had I been in the market for a boyfriend, this was definitely an upscale meeting place. I waited a few minutes more, and when Doug didn't return, I downed the rest of the Riesling and slid off the stool. I started to move toward the vestibule, when I happened to glance over at the bank of small tables near the rear of the bar. A couple sitting at the corner table near the back entrance, partially shrouded in shadow, caught my attention. There was something familiar about them, so I moved closer. The back door opened, letting in two giggling girls dressed to the nines, and light spilled over the table, briefly affording me a better look. I recognized the man at once. Ken Colgate. The woman's face was still in shadow. I was betting it was Savannah, so I let out an involuntary gasp as she leaned forward and I recognized Candy Carmichael. Their heads were bent close together and they looked like they were having a very earnest conversation. I couldn't resist a chuckle. Colgate certainly got around! No wonder his wife felt the need to keep tabs on him.

The couple seated at the table just off to Ken and Candy's left scraped back their chairs and started to thread their way out of the bar area. Without a moment's hesitation, I wended my way over to the newly vacated table, elbowing two girls right out of my path. As I slid onto the chair, I stole a quick glance over my shoulder. Ken and Candy were completely absorbed in their conversation. I greatly doubted they'd noticed me. I shrugged out of my jacket, draped it across the back of my chair, and picked up the drink menu.

A waitress sidled up to me, pad in hand, and after only a second's hesitation I ordered another Riesling. "Would you tell the bartender this goes on Mr. Harriman's tab?" I added sweetly. She moved off and I leaned back in my chair. I was less than two feet away from Ken and Savannah. Maybe, with a little luck, I could hear a bit of what they were discussing. I leaned back as far as I dared without toppling the chair—and me—over. I couldn't hear whole sentences, but they were talking loud enough that I did manage to catch a word or a phrase here and there.

"She knew some . . . not everything," I heard Ken say.

Candy let out a snort. "Don't kid . . . knew plenty. Enough . . . lives miserable."

Out of the corner of my eye, I saw Ken reach for Candy's hand. "Don't worry," I heard him say. "Your secret is safe with me."

Their voices lowered, and it was darn near impossible to make out another word. They hadn't mentioned any names; it was possible they were talking about Ulla. Then again, maybe not. Perhaps they were speaking about Ken's wife. And what secret was Ken talking about? Something connected with Ulla? Or did it have to do with Candy herself? I glanced at my watch and noted it was almost six-thirty. I was just about to grab my jacket and head for the vestibule, when the waitress appeared with my Riesling. Never one to waste good alcohol, I lifted it to my lips and took a sip, but I almost dropped the glass as Ken's voice rose slightly.

"You do realize that if the police should find out you took it upon yourself to come here today—"

"It might not look good. Of course, I know that," Candy

snapped. "Anyway, no one will find out the network didn't send me unless you tell them. Besides, you're the only one who knows."

Colgate leaned in closer to her and said something in a low tone. I was afraid my chair would topple over, I was leaning over so far, straining to hear more. Candy's appearance today hadn't been network dictated. Why had she come here then? Could it have had something to do with that cosmetics deal that Ulla had wanted so desperately? I tightened my grip on the stem of my glass as another thought occurred to me. Had Candy come to the signing with the intention of getting her rival out of the way permanently? And had Ken Colgate somehow been a party to it?

Ken scraped back his chair abruptly, and Candy did the same. I turned my back and concentrated on my half-finished drink until I saw the two of them disappear out the door. Then, glass still in hand, I slid off my chair and hurried into the vestibule after them. I wasn't quick enough, though. The two of them were nowhere to be seen, so I returned to the bar area. As I passed the table where Ken and Candy had been sitting, I glanced down and saw a scrap of paper peeping out from beneath the table. I bent down and picked it up. It read:

Terry Finley 213-555-1958

The name and number weren't familiar. I tucked it into my purse, intending to share with Leila later. I shrugged back into my jacket and sauntered back into the vestibule. I was just about to peek in the dining area to see if perhaps Ken and Candy had stayed for dinner, when I heard someone yell my name. I whirled around and saw Leila coming through the front door. I had to admit, for a split second there I almost didn't recognize her. Dressed in a short red dress with matching red satin stilettos and chunky gold hoops, her auburn hair cascading like a waterfall down her back, my friend looked like a Victoria's Secret runway fashion model. I walked right over to her, touched her arm, and said, "Wow! You did all this for me? I'm impressed, but I have to tell you, I feel underdressed."

She waved her hand impatiently. "Oh, don't be silly. I just threw this old thing on. I had it in my locker at work."

"Old thing? Really?" I looked her up and down again. "I'm afraid to ask what you keep this at work for."

"You never know when you'll draw an assignment at a classy place like this one. And it never hurts to look your best." She squeezed my arm. "You look nice too."

Nice. Yeah. That was what I'd been aiming for. I gave her a little push toward the hostess podium. "Come on— let's get our table."

As my friend turned toward the podium, I happened to glance out the large picture window at the front of the restaurant. Douglas Harriman stood at the corner, helping someone out of a sleek, black Lincoln Continental. I recognized the woman instantly.

None other than Petra Littleton, the shelter's biggest benefactor.

I frowned. Doug had mentioned his dinner was of a business nature. What business could he have with Petra?

Or maybe the better question was, why did I care?

Chapter Thirteen

A few minutes later, the hostess led us to a table tucked in a far corner. She deposited a velvet-covered menu in front of each of us and then withdrew. A busboy appeared a few seconds later and filled our water glasses to the brim. I was dying to tell Leila what I'd just learned, but as I started to speak, my friend held up her hand. "Let's table all discussions till after the appetizer at least," she said. "I brainstorm much better on a full stomach."

I was anxious to get started, but just then my stomach gave a loud rumble. "Agreed," I said, albeit a trifle reluctantly.

A smiling, black-jacketed waiter appeared and we ordered drinks: another Riesling for me, the house Merlot for Leila. We both ordered eggplant rollatini appetizers, followed by the house salad. For the main course I ordered one of my favorite dishes, vegetable lasagna, while Leila ordered the rigatoni. The waiter deposited a basket of Italian bread along with some rolls and a dish of sweet butter, and for the next several minutes the only sound heard at our table was contented chewing. Our waiter returned a few minutes later with our wines and rollatinis, and once he'd gone, Leila raised her glass high.

"Here's to crime. The successful solving of it, that is," she added.

"Hear, hear," I replied, and we clinked glasses.

We sipped the wine and the next few minutes were spent devouring the simply delicious eggplant dish. I sopped up the last of the excellent sauce with a slice of crusty Italian bread and pushed my plate to one side. "Okay," I said. "I can't wait any longer. Who wants to go first? Me? Great!"

Without mincing words, I related what I'd overheard in the bar between Ken and Candy. "So if her appearance here wasn't ordered by the network," I finished, "then why was she here? I can think of two possibilities. It's connected to the Glow deal, somehow, or . . . she came with a sinister purpose in mind."

"You mean doing away with her rival?" Leila wiggled her eyebrows and reached for her wine. "It's an interesting possibility, but I'm not sure Candy Carmichael would have the smarts to plot a murder. And I do believe this was premeditated, not a spur-of-the-moment crime of passion."

"I'm not sure I totally agree," I said. "I think Candy is dumb like a fox. But I also think that if she did it, she didn't do it alone. She had help."

Leila paused, wineglass halfway to her lips. "Colgate?

Hmm. Interesting. Why would he want Ulla out of the way, though? He made big bucks as her manager."

"I heard her tell him earlier that their contract was up in two weeks. Maybe he wasn't going to be her manager any longer."

"And he would have lost all that income. But if he killed her, he would have lost it too, so . . ." She spread her hands. "It seems like a lose–lose to me."

"True," I sighed. "Unless he had a specific reason for wanting her out of the way."

"Like what?"

I dropped my chin into my palm. "I don't know. Yet."

"Well, let me tell you what I found out." Leila reached for her tote, dipped her hand inside, and pulled out a small notebook. She flipped a few pages until she came to the one she wanted. "According to one of my very reliable sources, Cathy Colgate consulted with Michael Fox a few days ago."

"Mike Fox!" I knew the name. He was a highly respected lawyer whose specialty was high-profile divorce cases. "Sounds like Mrs. Colgate might be interested in shedding her cheating hubby."

"Well, inheriting two million-plus dollars certainly does wonders for a woman's independence," Leila said, and chuckled. She picked up her wineglass and swirled the contents around. "She probably has had enough of hubby's endless string of affairs, if she knows, and I believe every wife knows at some point."

I remembered the dagger looks Cathy Colgate had thrown in Ulla's direction. "Do you think Cathy Colgate might have killed Ulla? For revenge?"

"I doubt she cared that much," Leila said bluntly. "Although . . . there's always the 'kill two birds with one stone' approach."

"Which is?"

"Get rid of Ulla and make sure Ken gets blamed for it. My source hinted there was some sort of connection between Cathy Colgate and Ulla, but he wasn't sure just what, only that the two of them seemed very familiar with each other whenever they'd cross paths." She put both elbows on the table and leaned forward. "The most interesting tidbit, though, concerns Ulla's assistant."

"Savannah Blade?"

Leila nodded. "That new novel Ulla was working on? She's not the author. Savannah is."

My fork clattered to the floor. "No! Are you sure?"

"Yes. My source is ninety-nine percent sure. Ulla somehow caught wind that Savannah was writing a book and that the main character was based on her. She managed to get a peek at it and hit the roof. Threatened to sue Savannah unless she signed all rights to the manuscript over to her. If you ask me, that's an excellent motive for murder. Now that Ulla's dead, Savannah can reclaim ownership and make a mint, with no one to stand in her way."

I thought about my conversation with Savannah and couldn't stifle a chuckle. "I think Savannah missed her calling. She should have been an actress." I related the gist of my conversation with her to Leila.

"There are a few good possibilities here," Leila said when I'd finished. "But we can't lose sight of one very important thing—if Ulla's death was indeed caused by an allergic reaction, then the killer has to be someone who would have been privy to that particular bit of information." She tapped the spoon on the table. "I was there at the hospital when the doctor told Colgate and company. They all appeared shocked—then again, they could have been acting, but are they really that good?"

"Savannah definitely could be," I said bluntly. "And as Ulla's personal assistant, Savannah would have had access to her medical appointments and even her medical history. If what you told me about that book is true, she jumps to the top of my list for sure."

The waiter set two good-sized plates in front of us, and for a few minutes we busied ourselves eating the delicious mixture of Romaine lettuce, cucumber, and tomato in a light honey mustard dressing. When we finished, Leila leaned forward. "There's something else to consider. She was venomous toward the staff and hosts in that book of hers, but the small section on hometown feuds is what got to me. You know, it might not have been one of those CNC people at all. There were a gazillion people at Crowden's, and that back door was wide open. Who's to say that someone she wronged in the past didn't sneak in there and somehow do her in?"

"I could see the wheels spinning around in both Will's and Charlie Callahan's minds when Wendy Sweeting mentioned something similar," I admitted. "That's why I want to get this resolved."

Leila's eyes narrowed. "Does this have something to do with your concern about Maggie?"

"Yep." I related the story of Maggie's high school connection to Ulla and then pulled out my iPhone and called up the video Sissy had played for me earlier. Leila let out a low whistle when it finished.

"The image is grainy as hell, but it sure looked like Maggie to me," she admitted. "This thing's right out in the open on YouTube. Once the police start digging . . ."

"It's only a matter of time before they hone in on Maggie. Couple the video and her history with the fact that she's flown the coop—"

Now Leila's fork clattered to the floor. "What!"

I showed Leila the text I'd gotten earlier from Maggie. Leila's brows drew together in a deep frown. "I agree, it doesn't look good," she said at last. "But it's all circumstantial right now."

"Plenty of people sitting on death row are there because they couldn't beat circumstantial evidence," I said tartly.

"Well, what does Kat think? She's known Maggie quite a while."

"She thinks I should give her the benefit of the doubt." I thought about the person I'd seen arguing with Ulla in the hallway. I'd only caught a flash of red, and Maggie had been wearing her red coat in the video, but it didn't mean that it had been Maggie. Lots of people had red coats. But how many had a history with the victim?

"What about this Miggs person Savannah mentioned?" Leila asked. "Any chance it could have been her?"

"It's possible," I said, the corners of my lips drooping down. "I'm just hoping Miggs wasn't Ulla's nickname for Maggie."

"Me too. Then again . . . maybe it's not this Miggs at all, whoever she is. Maybe it's someone else entirely." She flipped a few more pages in her notebook. "My source had something interesting to say about Ulla's producer, Wendy Sweeting. Last year she was going to file a lawsuit against Ulla, but the network brass talked her out of it. But I heard that she was thinking of starting it up again. And if she'd gone through with it, there's a good chance the station might have had to let Ulla go."

"That's juicy, but a motive for murder?" I shook my head. "More like one for Ulla murdering Wendy than the other way around."

"Not if Ulla had some dirt on Wendy that she was using to keep her in line," suggested Leila. "Wendy might have just gotten sick of it and seen a chance to get rid of the albatross around her neck."

Conversation came to a halt as the waiter brought our entrees and, thankfully, two more forks. My food smelled delicious, but my appetite had waned considerably from when I'd first sat down. Leila speared a rigatoni with her fork. "How certain are we that Ulla didn't eat anything at the signing?"

"Not one hundred percent certain. Why?"

"I did some research. Scombrotoxin poisoning has symptoms that mimic an anaphylactic reaction. Only problem with that is, you get it from eating poorly processed oily fish, and it usually takes a short time to develop. So, unless Ulla ate a tuna or a mackerel sandwich shortly before she collapsed . . . COD is a real puzzle." Leila popped the rigatoni in her mouth.

"I do remember Ulla taking some aspirin," I said, pushing my lasagna around on my plate. "I guess someone could have switched out the aspirin or maybe put something in her water. She did freshen her lip gloss right before her attack, so maybe she did eat or drink something. Bottom line—we need to ascertain the exact cause of death. Once we know that, maybe then all the puzzle pieces will fall into place."

"Good idea, but just how do you propose to do that? You know how Will feels about you investigating in general, plus he'd never share information on an ongoing investigation. And it's a sure bet Charlie Callahan's not going to let you anywhere near the coroner's report."

"That's for sure." I shrugged. "There are other ways to find out that information."

She paused, rigatoni midway to her lips, and raised a brow. "Yeah? Like what?"

I speared a hunk of lasagna. "Well . . . how about your friend Krystle? She was very helpful last time." Leila's friend worked in the County Lab, and had access to all the medical and coroner reports. She'd come through with flying colors the last time I'd needed info.

Leila made a guttural sound in her throat. "Oh, no. She almost got in big trouble the last time she did me a favor. I would only ask her as a last resort, and even then, I'd have to get on bended knee."

"No Krystle, huh? Bummer. Well, there's always Diane."

"True—if she gets a look at it. Will and Charlie are probably under orders to keep that report under lock and key. Ulla Townsend's death is big news, you know. Every reporter in a twenty-mile radius would like to get the scoop on what really happened. Myself included." She forked more rigatoni, chewed, and swallowed before adding, "We're forgetting another prime motive—money. Who stood to gain monetarily from her death? Savannah with her reinstated book deal, for one. But Ulla was, from all accounts, worth a small fortune. Who inherits that, I wonder?"

I frowned. "That's a good question. She wasn't married, had no children . . . wait!" I snapped my fingers. "I remember Grace mentioned something about a brother. Bart. Bart Beckman."

Leila whipped out her iPhone and her fingers went flying. A few minutes later she announced, "Yep. The obits listed already. 'Ulla Townsend is survived by a brother, Bart Beckman of Charleston, South Carolina.' No other relatives are mentioned. So, unless she left the whole shebang to a charity, maybe brother Bart gets it all."

"We need to consider his financial state," I said. "If he's deeply in debt, and he knew he was her sole beneficiary . . ." My fingers beat a swift tattoo against the white damask tablecloth. "It's a pretty safe bet that he'd have known what, if anything, his sister had an allergy to, wouldn't you think? And at the very least, if he didn't have something to do with her sudden demise, maybe he's got some insights on who might have wanted her dead."

"Really? And just who might this insightful person be?"

My head snapped around, and my heart sank as I recognized the man standing beside our table.

Charlie Callahan—and he wasn't smiling.

Chapter Fourteen

When I'd met Callahan earlier, he'd been pleasant, even affable. There was no semblance of that now as he stared down at me. His brows were drawn together, and the corners of his lips dragged down. I forced a smile to my own lips and said brightly, "Detective Callahan. What a surprise, running into you here." I glanced around. "Is Will with you?"

"Will's still at the station," he said briefly.

I couldn't resist a dig. "Stuck him with the paperwork, huh?"

"Actually, he volunteered." His gaze bored into mine. "So, I'm curious. Who's this insightful person you mentioned?"

I waved my hand in a careless gesture. "Oh, no one you'd be interested in."

"Oh, I doubt that. I'm sure I'd be greatly interested, particularly if it had anything to do with my case. Does it?"

I caught the proprietary way he said *my case*, and

I frowned. "I'm sorry, did you say *your* case? I thought you and Will were working this together?"

His face reddened slightly, and he took a step back. "Of course we are. That was just a figure of speech."

Hah, more like a Freudian slip. I gave him a tight nod and picked up my fork. He said nothing, just stood with his feet planted slightly apart and his hands on his hips. I felt his stare boring into the side of my neck as I pushed some lasagna around on my plate, and it was pretty apparent he didn't intend to leave anytime soon. After a few moments elapsed, I glanced up and said, "The circumstances of Ulla's death are odd; you've got to admit that. Plenty of people are speculating on it, and that's exactly what we were doing. Sitting here, having a nice meal, speculating on who might have wanted to see Ulla dead and why. There's no law against that, now, is there?"

"None, if that's all you were doing. You weren't planning to go off on your own and interrogate a witness, were you?"

I widened my eyes just a tad and let out a short gasp. "Goodness, is that what you thought?"

He looked at me for a long moment, then said, "That's exactly what I thought—do think. Look, you were helpful the last time—no one's denying that. Civilian interference in a criminal investigation, though, is a strict no-no. Will might not have minded it, might have bended a few rules to close the case, but I'm not like that."

"Oh, Will wasn't happy about it," I cut in. "Not at all.

He told me all the time not to get involved, and he never discussed details of the investigation with me. I butted in strictly on my own."

"And Will and Captain Connolly and everyone else was darn glad she did," Leila chimed in. My friend shot Charlie Callahan one of her extra-special dagger looks that she usually reserved for those she felt were especially annoying. "They gave her a citation."

"So I've heard," he said tightly. "One would think you'd have learned from your last experience, Syd. Confronting a killer is no laughing matter. You were darn lucky the last time." He leaned over, his arm resting lightly on the back of my chair. "You and your friend here can speculate on what might have happened and who might have done it till the cows come home, just as long as you don't act on it. Leave the detecting to the trained professionals. Trust me, we've got everything under control."

"Well, that's good to hear," Leila piped up. As Callahan's gaze swung toward her, she smiled sweetly at him and said, "Leila Addams. I'm a reporter for the *Deer Park Herald*. Considering your remarks, is it safe to assume that Ulla's demise has been upgraded from 'suspicious death' to an official homicide investigation?"

A red flush started to creep up the side of Charlie's neck. "You are to assume nothing. We aren't making an official ruling until the coroner's report comes in, which should be very shortly. Just understand this, ladies." He bent over and said in an almost menacing tone, "If I catch either one of you interfering in a police investigation, whether it's interrogating a witness or anything else, unlike Will, I won't hesitate to arrest you." He straightened, and his annoyed expression morphed into a frozen smile. "Enjoy the rest of your dinner."

"Enjoy it?" I muttered as he strode away. "I'll be lucky if I don't throw it up." I watched as Callahan made his way to a table at the other end of the room, where three other men were seated. I recognized the distinguished, white-haired man in the center immediately—Mayor Bascomb, Charlie's uncle. The other men were probably town council members. "Nothing like using your connections to get ahead," I grumbled.

Leila rapped her knuckles sharply on the table. "Want my first impression? I don't like him. He's conceited and arrogant, and he's chauvinistic. You can just tell."

"I agree," I said. "He's a big phony. This afternoon he was all smiles and praise for me. Tonight, he's telling me to stay out of his investigation 'cause, essentially, lightning doesn't strike twice." I let out a soft snort. "And Will thinks he's likeable—hah!" I stole another glance toward the table. "For all we know, he could be putting Will down to his uncle right now!"

"I wouldn't put it past him. As for Will's attitude toward him, well, they do have to work together. Plus, he's probably just trying to get the right mindset in case this joker does get the lead slot," Leila remarked. She tapped her finger against the side of her face. "If you want my opinion, I think all that bluster was to cover up the fact he's scared that maybe if you do get involved, you'll end up solving Ulla's murder and make him look bad."

"You could be right. The best defense is a good offense, right? Well, no doubt he thinks he put the fear of God into us, but all he succeeded in doing was making me more determined than ever to solve this case." I gave a small shudder. "No way do I want that guy within ten feet of Maggie, let alone getting that lead detective slot."

Leila raised her glass in a toast. "Atta girl."

I clinked my glass to hers, thinking I surely had my work cut out for me if I was going to stay one step ahead of Charlie Callahan.

*　*　*

We finished our dinner and, after some debate, decided to skip dessert and coffee. Charlie Callahan was still enjoying dinner with his friends and uncle when we left, and out of the corner of my eye I noticed that he angled his head just enough to watch us leave, as if he were wondering what our next move was. As we sauntered into the lobby, I saw Lois Galveston emerge from the bar. She was looking at something on her cell phone and didn't notice us approach until we were practically on top of her. "Hello Lois," I said. She jumped, startled, then barked out a tinny laugh.

"Why, hello—Syd, right?" She slid her phone back into her jacket pocket. "Sorry. I was a bit preoccupied and didn't see you. I was looking up some employment possibilities."

"No luck so far, huh?" I gestured to Leila at my side. "This is my friend, Leila Addams. Leila's a reporter for the *Herald*. She hears about job openings all the time."

"That's true," Leila said with a warm smile. "What field are you interested in?"

Lois's lips curved in a wan smile. "Right now, just about anything."

"Diane mentioned you used to work in security, right?" I asked.

"Hmm, yeah, but to be honest that's not cut in stone. Truth be told, I wouldn't mind a career change." She glanced at her watch. "Sorry, I've got to get going."

"I'll keep my eyes open for you," Leila said. Lois gave us a wave and departed. Leila decided to hang around the bar for a while; I had an idea that Jim Wantrobski might be joining her later. It would certainly explain the killer red dress and heels. I got in my car and debated stopping at DuBarry's for a brewski, thinking maybe Will might show up, but in the end I drove straight home. A sleepy-looking Toby met me at the door and wound around my ankles.

"Miss me?" I asked the cat, bending down to give him a scratch behind his ear.

He looked up at me and then over at his empty food bowl. "Merow."

"At least you're the type of guy a gal can depend on. Charlie Callahan is an ass. An arrogant, conceited ass. If he thinks he's intimidated me into giving up, he's dead wrong.

It's going to give me a great deal of pleasure to help Will beat him out for the head detective slot."

Toby sat up and waved his paw in the air. "Merow." I couldn't tell whether he was agreeing with me or just egging me on to get his food. I chose to believe the former.

I shrugged out of my jacket, tossed it across the counter, and got the sack of dry food out of the bottom cabinet. I filled his bowl up with crunchies, and as he slurped away, I sat back down at the table and pulled out my smartphone. I tapped in "anaphylaxis causes" and hit Enter. A few minutes later, I glanced up to find Toby sitting on his haunches beside my chair, staring hopefully up at me.

"Oh, no," I said. "I think you've had enough crunchies for tonight." I held up my phone and tapped at the screen. "Did you know that food is considered the most common cause of anaphylaxis, Tobes?" I read aloud from the website I had found: "The most common food triggers include nuts, shellfish, dairy products, egg whites, and sesame seeds. Wasp or bee stings are also common causes. It could also be caused by certain types of medications, or even by exercise, if the activity occurs after eating allergy-provoking food."

Toby blinked twice. "Merow?"

"I know. There's not much leeway here. The cause of Ulla's death is the real mystery, if you ask me. How I'd love to get a gander at that coroner's report. There's got to be a way, though, for me to find out that info. I just have to put on my thinking cap."

With another sympathetic meow, Toby flopped over on his side and closed his eyes. I put my phone away and went to change out of my slacks and top into sweats. I emerged from my bedroom twenty minutes later with a large white object tucked under one arm. Toby sat up and regarded me curiously as I set the whiteboard up on the kitchen island.

"Remember this, Toby?" I asked, as I whipped a Magic Marker out from one of the drawers. The whiteboard I'd purloined from my sister had come in handy during the last murder I'd investigated. I drew an oblong box and printed Ulla Townsend's name inside it, the word "VICTIM" right underneath.

I drew another box off to the left with an arrow linking it to Ulla's box and printed "Savannah Blade" inside it. Underneath that I wrote: *Actual author of Ulla's new book. Ulla blackmailed her into turning manuscript over to her. Ulla's death makes path clear for her to claim ownership. Motive?*

I drew another box next to that one and added Ken Colgate's name. Beneath that I wrote: *Ulla's manager. Had CLOSE relationship with her at one time. Now seemed strained. Ulla mentioned their contract was up—did she find out he intended to betray her in some way, either with Savannah or Candy?*

I studied what I'd written, tapping the marker against my chin, and added: *Wife consulting divorce lawyer. Motive for offing Ulla?*

After a slight hesitation, I drew another box underneath Ken's and printed Cathy Colgate's name inside. I wrote:

Rumored to have had some sort of relationship with Ulla. What? Consulted divorce lawyer—did she plot Ulla's demise with the thought of having Ken blamed for it?

I drew another box and printed Wendy Sweeting's name inside. *Worked with Ulla at CNC. Filed lawsuit, then retracted it. Why?* Right next to that box, I drew another and put Candy Carmichael's name inside. *Rival for Glow cosmetics deal—came to event on her own. Why? Ulla believed she wasn't above plotting against her—did she team up with someone else to off Ulla?*

I stood back and surveyed my handiwork, tapping the Magic Marker against my chin. I knew there was another box I had to add. I drew it and inside printed: *Miggs. Person Ulla was desperate to reach. What was that relationship, and could it have been volatile enough to drive Miggs to murder?* I hesitated and then added: *Is Miggs a nickname for Maggie Shayne? Is Maggie the person from Ulla's past? What happened between them?*

I added one more: *Mystery person from past or possibly brother? Who stood to gain the most from her death?*

I stepped back from the board and looked at Toby, who'd hopped up on the kitchen counter and was regarding the board with wide eyes. "I know," I said, scratching at my head, "The motives appear pretty thin, on the surface, but maybe when I start digging deeper, something will hit me. I've got to determine who had the best reason for wanting Ulla out of the way. Right now, Savannah's in the lead, but that could change."

Toby opened his mouth in a wide, unlovely cat yawn.

"I agree. It's late. I can figure out where to start tomorrow." I paused and then wrote across the bottom of the board: *What killed Ulla? If an allergy, who would have known what she was allergic to?* I knew with a chilling certainty that finding out that piece of information could be the key to unlocking the whole mystery.

I set the marker down and looked around for Toby. I found him in the corner, playing with a scrap of paper. I bent down to retrieve it and saw that it was the scrap of paper I'd rescued from the bar earlier, the one either Candy or Ken must have dropped. It must have fallen out of my jacket pocket, and anything on the floor was fair game for my cat. Toby dug his claw in as if he didn't want to give it up, but I snatched up a mangled Melvin and dangled it above his head. He released the paper instantly and made a dive for his favorite toy. I fished my cell phone out of my bag and sat back down at the table. First thing I did was check the area code on the scrap of paper; it didn't look familiar and turned out to be an LA area code. Then I typed in "Terry Finley, Los Angeles, California," into the search engine. A few minutes later I had my answer. Terry Finley was listed as an entertainment lawyer. I glanced at the clock. California was three hours behind us—it would only be a little after eight out there. I picked up my iPhone and punched in the number. I was fully prepared to leave a message, so it came as a surprise when a real, live male voice answered.

"Terry Finley."

"Mr. Finley," I said. I had to think fast. I wasn't as good as Leila at making up tall tales, but I confess hanging with my bestie the past few months has taught me a thing or two, not to mention all the tips I've gotten over the years from watching *Murder, She Wrote* and *CSI*. "I'm so glad you're working late tonight. I'm calling on behalf of Candy Carmichael."

"Who?"

Oops, try again. "Sorry, I meant to say Ken Colgate."

"Ken—oh, yes. Savannah's manager." I could detect a note of disapproval in his voice. "What did you say your name was again?"

"Ah, Jess. Jess Fletcher," I murmured, hoping that Terry Finlay wasn't a big Angela Lansbury fan. "I—ah—I've been working with Savannah and Ken Colgate on . . . that matter."

"Oh, yes, the book." Finlay's voice became more animated. "I'm glad you called. I wondered why I hadn't heard from them yet. I texted them both that I've got a pretty firm offer from Columbia Studios for the movie rights. I just need to know what publishing house the book's going to land with."

Pay dirt! "That's up in the air right now," I said.

"Oh? I was under the impression the auction had ended Friday? Sorry, I'm a bit out of touch. I had several contracts to finish, so I've been holed up here all day. I haven't even eaten."

Auction? They auctioned unpublished books off? "It was extended over the weekend." I said the first thing that came into my head. "Because of his commitment to Ulla Townsend. The charity book signing."

"Ah, yes. I remember him mentioning he had something going on this weekend, but I didn't know it was for Ulla. I thought he'd given her his notice."

So, he had been planning to leave! Notice wasn't necessary now, but it was apparent Finley hadn't heard the news. "Ah, not yet."

"He will this week I'm sure. He'll need to devote all his energies to Savannah and this book. Trust me, it's got all the earmarks of a big bestseller. It could be bigger than *Fifty Shades*."

Wow, what was in that book? "Yes, they're very excited."

"As well they should be." He coughed lightly. "Have they settled on a title? Last I heard it was between *Dealing with a Diva* and *Diva Behind the Scenes*. Personally, I like the former, and Columbia does too. You might mention that to Colgate."

"I sure will." I was still trying to wrap my head around the "bigger than *Fifty Shades*" remark. No wonder Ulla had wanted the manuscript. And now her death made it smooth sailing for both Ken and Savannah to reap the benefits. "You wouldn't happen to have the exact amount of this movie deal handy, would you? I'm sure Savannah and Ken would be interested."

"I discussed it with Ken just last week," Finley responded, clearly puzzled.

"Really? Well, he's been in rather a tizzy lately. Can't seem to locate any of his notes, so if you don't mind telling me, I can pass the info along."

"Well, okay." I heard paper riffling, and then Finley said, "Savannah's initial advance will be one and a half million dollars."

Whoa! "And Ken gets fifteen percent of that, correct?" Almost a quarter million for him. Nice. And that was just the movie rights. Who knew how much the actual book deal would command?

"I believe his percentage is higher for the movie deal. Twenty-five, if I'm not mistaken." His tone suddenly turned sharper. "What did you say your name was again?"

"Oops, that's my other phone. Gotta go." I rang off. Dammit, I didn't have a burner cell like Leila, so if he wanted to, Finlay could probably trace that call back to me. I was hoping that maybe that might not occur to him—at least not until he heard about Ulla's demise. Oh well, maybe my number had come up on his screen like so many did on mine, as "Out of Area." One could only hope. I started for my bedroom to get some shut-eye, when it hit me like a lightning bolt.

Finley had thought the book auction was Friday. He'd been working on this movie deal for a while, he'd said. He'd also mentioned Savannah as Ken's client, the author of the book. All of which could only mean one thing: Colgate had to have pitched it to Finley well before today, when Ulla died.

I leaned against the wall. Why would he have done that, particularly if Ulla had intended to claim ownership of the book? Had he and Savannah planned to work out some sort of deal with Ulla? Or did they figure they didn't need to, because by the time the deal came to fruition, Ulla would already be dead. Suddenly Ken Colgate's motive for wanting Ulla out of the way didn't seem so thin after all. Ken and Savannah were now at the top of my list.

I felt something furry wind around my ankles. I reached down and hefted Toby into my arms. "Well, well, despite Charlie Callahan's warning, it looks like I'll be doing some investigating tomorrow. What do you say?"

Toby burrowed into my chest and tucked his head underneath my chin. "Merow."

"I'm glad you agree. Because when push comes to shove, I'd rather Ken or Savannah—or anyone else, really—be guilty of Ulla's murder than Maggie."

I started for my bedroom, remembered my jacket that I'd left on the counter, and turned back. As I picked it up, another scrap of paper fluttered out of one of the pockets. Toby reached up and snagged it between his claws.

"Merow."

I frowned and held out my hand. "Let me see that, Toby." I said. I didn't remember having anything in my pocket other than the paper with Finlay's number on it.

Toby backed up, his prize still between his claws, but I found a Melvin underneath the counter and held it up. Distracted at the sight of his favorite toy, Toby let go of the paper and snagged Melvin instead. I picked up the paper and unfolded it, then gasped at what I saw printed crudely there:

U should stay out of what doesn't concern U . . . or else.

Chapter Fifteen

I spent a restless night, my dreams littered with thoughts of Ulla standing in front of a large book, laughing at Savannah, Candy, Wendy, and Ken, who all stood in front of her. She smiled haughtily at each of them, but when she turned, it was to point an accusing finger at a person who stood behind her, clothed in the shadows. A person wearing a well-worn red jacket. Then a faceless person in a long black robe started chasing me, waving the printed note aloft.

I woke to find Toby sprawled on the pillow on top of me, chewing my hair. At first I swatted him away, but that only made him more determined and he came closer, this time reaching out to swipe at my forehead with his tongue. It felt like sandpaper, and I pushed him away again. He returned, more determined than ever to groom me. He stuck out a paw and swatted gently at my cheek. I turned my head and caught a glimpse of the clock on my bedside table. Seven AM! I threw back the covers, startling Toby, and swung my feet off the bed and into my mule slippers. Toby glared at me balefully from where he'd burrowed back into my comforter. I reached out and gave him a quick pat on the head.

"Sorry, Tobes. Today's my early day."

Toby wriggled around on the comforter, into a sitting position. He raised his paw and pointed toward the piece of paper on my dresser. "Merow?"

"I have no idea how that got into my pocket, Tobes. It had to be someone in that bar, watching me, because I only left that jacket there for a few minutes. It could have been anyone, including Ken or Candy."

Toby widened his big green eyes. "Ow-orrr?"

I reached out to ruffle his hair. "Of course, I'll be extra careful. And yes, I plan on telling Will about it, even though I'll probably get a lecture."

Toby settled back into a supine position. "Merow," he said, and then began to purr softly.

I pulled on my bathrobe and padded into the bathroom, where I took what was no doubt the quickest shower in history. I emerged ten minutes later, nice and clean and ready to face the world. I threw on jeans and a Friendly Paws T-shirt, swiped on some lip gloss, and made my way to the kitchen, Toby padding along beside me. I gave him his morning bowl of crunchies, but when I walked over to the cupboard where we kept the coffee, I saw that we were out. Drat. There wasn't enough time to stop at Dayna's either. I'd just have to make myself a cup when I got to the shelter. I picked up my cell and punched in Will's number. Voicemail, of course. I left him a message, stuck my phone in my purse, and hurried out the door.

I pulled into the parking lot at one minute to eight, and I noticed Sissy's beat-up VW almost immediately. The teen was already feeding the cats when I stepped inside. She tossed me a puzzled glance when she saw me. "Did you forget we switched?" she asked. "You said you'd take the late shift today, because—"

"You wanted to go to the high school basketball tryouts today." I slapped my forehead with my palm and groaned. "Now I remember. I could have stayed in bed."

Sissy spooned some wet food into Annie Reilly's bowl. "Sorry."

"Don't be. Maybe it's better I get an early start today anyway. I'll come back tonight." I turned toward the doorway, then paused. "You didn't happen to find a silver necklace while you were unpacking the supplies yesterday, did you?"

Sissy finished filling the cat's bowl, put it inside her cage, and then looked at me. "Nope. If I did I would have given it to you or Kat. Why?"

I explained about the missing necklace and Savannah's call. "I do remember that necklace," Sissy said. "When I'm done with the cats and walking the dogs, I'll take another look. I'll text you one way or the other."

I said goodbye to Sissy and made my way to my car, pondering my next move. I knew darn well there was no way in hell Leila would be up yet. I'd heard her stumble in around two in the morning when I'd gotten up to go to the bathroom. I decided to make a stop at the Redi-Mart for some coffee and other sundries, but first I needed java desperately. I drove to Dayna's shop and found a parking spot two doors down. The minute I walked in the door, I spotted Lois Galveston. She was seated at the counter, a steaming mug near her elbow, head bent over a sheet of paper in front of her. I started toward her, but Dayna suddenly appeared in front of me, a mug of delicious-smelling coffee in hand.

"I saw you from the window," she said. She took my arm and steered me over to the opposite end of the counter from Lois. Once I'd slid onto the stool, she pressed the mug into my hand. "You look like a woman in dire need of caffeine."

"Thanks. I am." I put the mug to my lips and took a long sip. "Man, that's good!"

"Jamaican Jumpin' Java. Dark roast with a hint of coconut and hazelnut blended together." She cocked her head toward the glass case next to the counter. "How about a fresh apple raisin muffin with sweet butter to go with?"

"Sounds like heaven."

Dayna got a fresh muffin out of the case, split it in half, and slathered it with sweet butter. The muffin was still hot, so the butter was oozing and melting down the sides of the muffin and pooling on the plate. I took a large bite and sat back, rolling my eyes. "Oh . . . so . . . good." I inclined my head toward Lois. "New applicant?"

Dayna nodded. "She said you recommended my place for employment."

I drained my mug and set it off to the side. "She's a recent transplant. Seems to be having a bit of a problem getting a job."

"Well, times are tough these days. Maybe it's those eyes of hers. She's got that heavy-lidded way of staring at you, like she's looking through you."

"I noticed that too, but I don't think that's the reason. Her stare didn't seem to faze them down at the police station. She applied for one of the admin slots."

Dayna quirked a brow. "She did? Well, that will pay a lot more than I can offer."

"Not if she doesn't get it. She said Will told her she seemed overqualified."

Dayna let out a soft snort. "Well, if she's overqualified for that job, she's probably really overqualified for one here." She noticed my empty mug, grabbed it, and was back in a second with a refill. She set it in front of me and leaned both her elbows on the counter. "Any more news about Ulla's death?" she asked.

I shook my head. "It's definitely a puzzler. They expect the autopsy results in soon, though, so maybe that will shed some light on how she died."

"All I can say is, it's a good thing she didn't eat any of my pastry. Could you imagine the headlines? *'Shopping Channel Queen Felled by Local Baker's Brownie.'*" Dayna threw up her hands. "It didn't take much to see she wasn't a nice person. Most people were blinded by her peppy TV persona, though."

"Someone wasn't," said a voice at my elbow. I glanced up and saw Lois now standing next to me. She had a paper in her hand, which she passed across to Dayna. "Sorry, I couldn't help but overhear. I take it there's no suspects yet? Or no clue as to the actual cause of death?"

"Not so far as I've heard," I said.

"Her death—or should I say the circumstances of her death—is attracting a lot of media attention. People want details, which have been sparse, and they're starting to speculate. I'm sure the police want to resolve it as quickly as possible." Lois regarded me thoughtfully. "Any ideas? Diane told me you're a pretty good sleuth."

"Someone else apparently thinks so too. I had a warning note slipped to me last night."

"No!" both Dayna and Lois chorused. I repeated the note's contents, ending with, "My nosing around has struck a chord with someone."

"Maybe you should stop investigating," suggested Lois. "This person might mean business."

Dayna let out a loud guffaw. "If you ask me, whoever did it must be a real coward. They also don't know our Syd! When it comes to puzzles, she's like a dog with a bone."

"That's true," I admitted. "I imagine this was meant as an attempt to get me to back off, but it's having the opposite effect. If anything, I'm more determined than ever." *Not to mention the fact Maggie's welfare is at stake,* I added silently.

"You're pretty tenacious," Lois said. "I sympathize—I'm that way myself. Just be careful."

"I intend to be."

* * *

The front door opened and in came Tara Pitsenberger, her cousin Wendy Sweeting right on her heels. Tara had on a white skirt and a red and white flower-patterned blouse, her feet encased in red wedges. Wendy was dressed more casually, in gray Dockers with a white blouse underneath a cream and gray chiffon vest. Wendy slid into one of the small tables near the picture window, and Tara headed straight for the counter. She nodded her head in greeting and turned to peruse the delicious treats in the display case.

Dayna held up the application Lois had given her. "I'll review this and be in touch," she said. "Like I said, though, it's only a part-time position, no more than twenty hours a week."

"Anything's a help at this point, thanks," Lois murmured.

The door opened again and Jay Johnston strolled in. His eyes lit up in recognition as he saw me, and he headed straight for me. Lois mumbled something and returned to her seat as he approached. "Ms. McCall, good morning. I was going to give the shelter a call. My wife is most anxious to pick up Sylvie. We're going over to the Pet Palace later to pick out supplies. We threw out everything of Trixie's when she passed because she didn't want another cat, but . . ." He spread his hands and smiled.

"I'd say tomorrow is a good bet. My sister was reviewing the applications yesterday. I'm sure she'll be giving you a call."

"Excellent." He glanced over at Dayna. "I'll take two extra-strong coffees to go. You wouldn't happen to sell the paper in here, would you?"

"There's a magazine rack over by the door," Dayna sang out. Jay flashed her a quick smile and turned in that direction, bumping full tilt into Lois Galveston, who was making a beeline for the front door. Jay's hand shot out to steady her. "I'm so sorry," he said.

"My fault," mumbled Lois. She ducked her head and pushed through the door like her pants were on fire.

"Well, someone's in a big hurry," Dayna commented. She looked over at Jay. "Don't take all the blame; it was partially her fault too. She had her head down." Dayna rolled her eyes and then offered Tara a smile. "You decide, honey?"

"Yes, one of those muffins—is that one blueberry?" At Dayna's nod she went on, "A blueberry muffin and a raspberry scone. And do you have Hawaiian Kona coffee?"

"Not ready, but it will only take me a few minutes to brew some. Why don't you take the pastries over to your table, and I'll bring the coffee over when it's ready?"

"That would be great, thanks." She turned toward me and smiled. "How are you this morning, Syd?"

"Still recovering from yesterday's events, I think. And you?"

"The same." She wrinkled her pert nose. "I called my district manager yesterday. I figured it was best he hear it from me, before the news hit the national papers. He was distressed, of course, but he said I handled it just fine."

"That's good to hear." I glanced over toward the table at Wendy, who sat slumped in the chair, her chin in her hand, staring morosely out the picture window. "How's your cousin doing?"

Tara sighed. "Wendy's getting very antsy, as are the others. They need to get back to Charleston, and"—she lowered her voice and whispered to me—"I hate to say this, but I can't wait till she's gone. All she did yesterday evening was follow me around the bookstore and mope and complain."

"Maybe you should cut her some slack. She worked closely with Ulla. Her sudden death had to be upsetting."

"Oh, I know. It's just . . . there are times when I think she's relieved the woman is gone." Tara gave her head a shake. "She's more worried about her job than anything, I think."

"Really? I thought she produced other segments as well."

"She does, but she'd done the bulk of Ulla's for the past few months and now that she's gone . . . well, I guess she's wondering just how much she'll be needed around the set." Tara lowered her voice again and said softly, "Believe it or not, she doesn't think she's very well liked. I think that's what's got her worried."

Tara picked up the tray and I pondered her words as I sipped my own coffee. While my interaction with the CNC had been brief, I hadn't detected any animosity toward Wendy from any of them; rather, any ill will seemed to be directed toward Ulla. I remembered what Leila had said about Wendy instigating a lawsuit against Ulla. Ulla hadn't been well liked either, but I knew from experience that the mere mention of lawsuits could throw people into a tizzy. Maybe word had gotten out she was thinking of starting it up again. Could that be why she felt like an outcast?

Jay Johnston came over, brandishing the morning *Herald*. "Looks like Ulla's death is the top story," he said. He held the paper out and I glanced at the headline: "Celebrity Dies at Charity Event." Jay tapped the paper. "It's a thorough account. It blends information about the signing with the tragedy. The reporter did an excellent job."

"Thanks. She's my best friend and my roomie. I'll be sure to relay your praise."

Dayna set two large Styrofoam cups in a to-go tray in front of Johnston. He whipped out his wallet and extracted a five-dollar bill, which he handed to Dayna. "Keep the change," he told her. He reached up and tugged on his earlobe. "Funny thing, that woman I ran into—literally—at the magazine rack? Something about her just seemed so familiar to me."

"Perhaps she reminds you of someone you know," I suggested. "That sometimes happens to me. Or you could be remembering her from Ulla's signing. She was there."

He shrugged. "It's not important. My wife tells me I get too fixated on things like that." He picked up his tray and smiled at me. "I'll tell Susan to expect a call from the shelter soon?"

"You bet."

Jay sailed out the front door just as Dayna approached, balancing a tray on which rested two mugs, a small bowl of creamers and another of sugar. I held out my hands. "I'll take it over," I said. "I want to talk to Wendy anyway."

Dayna put the tray into my outstretched hands. "Here you go. Are you sure you don't want a part-time job here?" She winked and started to turn toward the stove, then suddenly did an about-face. "How about our bet? Has that nice young man tracked you down?"

Since Doug had said he'd come to the café asking about me, I figured there was no point in hiding anything. "I happened to run into him last night," I admitted. "I was waiting for Leila at the bar in Antonio's."

Both of Dayna's perfectly penciled eyebrows rose when I mentioned the upscale restaurant. She let out a low whistle. "And?" she prodded.

"He bought me a drink."

The eyebrows arched higher. "That's it?"

"He did inquire about my status. If I was in a relationship."

"You told him yes?"

"Yes, but it didn't appear to discourage him. So, truthfully, I'm not certain who won the bet," I admitted.

"We'll call it a draw . . . for now. He's a gentleman. He knows you have a boyfriend, but . . ." She picked up my left hand and stroked my ring finger. "So long as there's no diamond on here, chère, you're fair game."

"Oh, you." I pulled my hand away and thrust it behind my back. "I think he might already be involved with someone anyway," I said. "I saw him with Petra Littleton outside the restaurant."

"You think he's involved with Petra Littleton?"

"Well, he's an attractive guy—"

"He's a great-looking guy," Dayna cut in.

"Right, a great-looking guy, and Petra is, well, Petra." I looked down at my jeans and T-shirt. "No way can I compete with her."

"Maybe you don't have to," Dayna said. She refilled my mug, set it on the tray with the other two, and gave it a little push toward me. "You never know what Fate might have in store for you, down the road." She paused. "And most of the time we're better off not knowing. But I'll tell you this. If that guy's romantically involved with Petra Littleton, I'll give you free coffee for a year."

I narrowed my eyes. While Dayna loved to give away free stuff, she wasn't that generous. "What do you know?" I demanded.

But she'd already turned away to wait on an elderly couple who'd come up to the register. With a sigh, I picked up the tray and headed toward Wendy and Tara's table. They looked up, surprised, as I approached. "Dayna's shorthanded, so I thought I'd help out," I said. I set the two mugs down in front of them along with the creamers and sugar before picking up my own mug and settling into the chair opposite Wendy. "I hope you don't mind if I join you?"

"Not at all." Wendy poured two creamers into her coffee, stirred it, then took a long sip. "That's heaven," she murmured, setting the mug down. "Much better coffee than I got from room service at that inn this morning."

"The Deer Park Inn recently changed hands," I said. "A neighbor of one of our shelter volunteers bought it. They're doing a good bit of remodeling, trying to compete with the Mountainside Inn." The Mountainside Inn was a good bit larger and more upscale, located on the opposite end of town. They catered to more of a business clientele, while the Deer Park Inn was more of a homey, bed-and-breakfast type of establishment.

Tara nodded her head in agreement. "That's true," she said. "They're in the process of hiring new chefs along with other key personnel, but right now they're a bit in flux."

"I guess that's why the others all decided to jump ship and move over there. Especially Ken. He loves his morning coffee." Wendy let out a throaty chuckle. "Oh well, lousy coffee is a small price to pay in exchange for the suite they gave me. I definitely wouldn't have gotten that at the other hotel."

"Probably not." I took another sip of my own coffee and wrapped my hands around the mug. "So Ken is staying at the Mountainside? I rather thought he'd be with his wife. I heard she inherited some property in Deer Park."

"Hmm, well, kind of tough to move in with your wife when you get served divorce papers," Wendy said. Her tone seemed almost gleeful. "He got served yesterday afternoon, right at the police station. Talk about embarrassing. But he deserves it. Cathy should have done it ages ago."

"Some women get used to a certain lifestyle," Tara said. "They want to keep it no matter what."

"Cathy was a bit of a wimp, but no more," Wendy remarked. "I always thought she was too good for Ken anyway. He was little more than a blackmailer in a suit. He used things to keep people in line, mainly for Ulla. Take me, for instance." She pointed at herself. "Way back when I first started at CNC, I was a contingent worker. They put me on Ulla's show, and I was assigned to handle her publicity. She fought me at every turn, spoke down to me, made me do demeaning things. I couldn't take it anymore. I threatened to sue her for harassment and she laughed at me, so I got a lawyer and filed the suit. A week later I got called to the VP's office. Ken was there. They offered me a choice. I could go ahead with the lawsuit, which would end up being held up for years, or I could accept a permanent position as one of Ulla's producers. Bottom line, though: I could never reinstate the suit."

"So you chose the perm job," Tara said.

"Yep. Only in recent weeks . . . let's just say I was considering other options a lawyer friend of mine advised. Ken somehow got wind of it and told Ulla. She called me in and, with a big smile on her face, told me that if I pursued it, I'd never work in television again. And I've no doubt she could have done serious damage to me." Her head came up and she looked me straight in the eye. "I know what you're thinking. A good motive for murder, right? Except that Ken jumped the gun. I was only considering it because I'd had a bad day. I have had a pretty cushy job with Ulla. Her death puts me in a worse position. Anyway, Ulla and I reached an understanding. I made her see that Ken had misinterpreted the facts." She laced her hands in front of her. "That detective grilled me on this, and somehow I don't think he believed me."

My eyebrow quirked. "Will?"

"No, his name wasn't Will. It was Charles, I think. Yes, that's right. Charles Callahan. *Detective* Charles Callahan."

I could just imagine how Charlie Callahan must have put Wendy through the wringer. It sounded to me, though, that if her story checked out, she could be crossed off the list, which made me feel better. I hadn't liked the idea of Tara's cousin possibly being a murderer.

Wendy rolled her napkin into a ball and tossed it off to one side. "Getting back to Mrs. Colgate, at least she doesn't have to worry any more. She inherited a bundle from her dear old dad, and now Ken's out on his behind. It seems as if all the women in Ken's life were finally wising up. Ulla was getting fed up with him, too."

I leaned in and said in a low tone, "I'd heard that he had something going on with Candy Carmichael."

"Yes, but oddly enough it wasn't of a romantic nature. He was secretly working to get her the spokesperson gig for Glow lip gloss instead of Ulla. The advertising execs at the cosmetics company were split. Some thought Ulla was perfect; others thought she was too old, and they wanted someone younger. Ken was supposed to have a meeting with them tomorrow in Charleston to discuss, but I believe it's been postponed. Indefinitely, since we're stuck here, at least until the coroner's report comes in." She leaned forward and said to me, "Just between us, I'm positive that's why Candy hauled herself down here to this event. She wanted to discuss some last-minute strategy about Glow with Ken." She leaned back with a deep chuckle. "Bet she's sorry now."

I took another sip of coffee. "What about Ken and Savannah?"

Wendy blinked. "What about them?"

"Anything going on between the two of them? I happened to see them in a pretty tight clinch in the parking lot yesterday."

"Oh, that." Wendy waved her hand carelessly. "Like I said, Kenny always had a roving eye, and Savannah just likes men in general." She paused. "Funny you should say that, though. Ulla asked me the same thing only yesterday."

"She did?"

"Yep. It was during her first break. I was walking past the storage room, and suddenly she popped out, pulled me over to the side, and asked me if I knew anything about Ken representing Savannah in some sort of movie deal."

I tried to keep the excitement out of my voice. "Really? A movie deal? Was Savannah thinking of becoming an actress?"

Wendy shrugged. "I have no idea. She didn't go into detail. I knew she was mad—Ulla's face always got like a stone statue when she was furious—but I told her I hadn't heard, and she just said thanks and then walked off. Truthfully, after what he put me through, I was tempted to lie and make up something, but . . . I don't play that way." Wendy paused. "It was odd, though. While she was talking to me, I saw someone else slip out of the storage area behind us."

"Did you recognize the person?"

"Oh, yeah. It was Cathy Colgate. I figured that it must have been her who tattled on Ken and Savannah." She paused. "Talk about weird, right? I mean, Cathy used to go out of her way to avoid Ulla, and here she was, spilling info to her. Odd, if you ask me."

Tara and Wendy finished their coffees and headed out. I sat at the table for a few minutes after they'd left, thinking. Cathy Colgate had found out about her husband and Savannah partnering to market the book that had been Savannah's in the first place, and Cathy had blown the whistle on them. Why? Was there more to it than met the eye? Had Cathy done it to lull Ulla into a false sense of security, make her think she was her friend, and then . . .

On an impulse, I got my iPhone out and used the white pages app to find a phone number for Bart Beckman. Fortunately, it wasn't an unlisted number. I dialed it, and after five rings, an answering machine picked up. I left a brief message: my name, the fact that I'd been at the event when Ulla passed, and I had a few questions regarding his sister, if he wouldn't mind speaking to me. I left my number and hung up. I hadn't mentioned any connection to the police and hoped he might not ask when—or if—he returned my call. I'd cross that bridge when I had to. I chuckled, thinking that both Will and Charlie Callahan would probably not approve of my tactics, but oh well. Will would forgive me, especially if I could give information that would solve the case. Charlie Callahan—well, I couldn't care less about his opinion.

I started to put my phone back into my pocket, when it began to vibrate. I snatched at it, wondering if it might be Bart calling back so soon, but then I saw Leila's number. I hit the answer button. "Hey, sleepyhead."

"Hey yourself. You went out early this morning." Leila sounded chipper, but I detected the remnants of a faint yawn.

"I thought it was my morning for early duty at the shelter. I forgot that I switched with Sissy, so I don't have to go back till tonight. What's up?"

Another stifled yawn and then: "Have you had breakfast yet?"

"Just a muffin and coffee. Why?"

"Well, drag that famous appetite of yours out of retirement. My editor left a message. The Mountainside Inn is debuting what they advertise as an 'out-of-this-world brunch, the likes of which Deer Park has never seen,' so he wants me to go down there and get the scoop. It's on the paper, so of course I thought of you."

The Mountainside Inn, where Ken, Savannah, and Candy were all staying. That could be very interesting. "Aww, I'm touched. Are you sure you wouldn't rather take Jim?"

"He's actually covering another event in Browertown, but he might meet us there later for some pictures."

"Well, then, count me in."

"That's what I figured," Leila said, not even trying to keep the smugness from her tone. "Especially once I heard your pals Colgate, Savannah, and Candy Carmichael are staying there. If we're lucky, maybe we'll even sit near them at brunch, and you can interrogate them."

"You're no fun at all," I complained. "I only just found that out. How did you know?"

"I'm a reporter. It's my job to know such things. Plus, Jim and I ran into the new chef at the bar at Antonio's last night, and he told us all about the new guests. So, I'll see you at home in a few?"

"You got it."

I started to slide my phone back into my pocket, then on impulse decided to try Maggie one more time. Naturally, it went to voicemail.

"One of these days you'll pick up, Maggie," I murmured. "But what will you tell me when you do?"

Chapter Sixteen

"Okay, Sherlock, what's the plan?" Leila grinned at me from the passenger seat of my convertible and rubbed her hands together. "Or maybe I should be calling you Jess Fletcher?"

"Very funny. As for a plan, well, I don't have a formal one. It seems as if each one of them had a good reason to want Ulla out of the way, except for maybe Wendy Sweeting, provided her story about the lawsuit checks out."

Leila leaned her cheek against the headrest. "I'm actually liking Cathy Colgate for the deed. It all depends on how much she hated her husband and just what her connection to Ulla was. Are you going to share anything we find out with Will?"

"Of course. I want him to have all the credit for solving this," I said. "Either he's busy, or his phone battery died, because I left two messages and he hasn't called back yet." I sighed.

"You are going to tell him about that note, right?" Leila

asked. As I nodded she went on, "That's really creepy, you know. Do you think it was Ken or Candy who did it?"

"They had the opportunity. It had to have been put in my jacket when I left it in the bar. I was only gone a few minutes."

"You know what Will is gonna say."

I sighed. "Oh yes. But I'm not planning on listening. Right now all I'm interested in is having a meaningful conversation with one or all of our potential suspects. Who knows, maybe one of them will crack and say something useful."

"Yeah, well, if you're hoping for a confession à la Perry Mason, somehow I doubt it."

I pulled into the spacious parking lot of the Mountainside Inn and parked under a spreading elm. We exited the car and strolled leisurely toward the building, pausing for a moment to admire the beautifully manicured garden with its colorful foliage of magnolias, pansies, and English daisies. A large wrought-iron sign read: "Mountainside Inn. Visitors Welcome". The quaint cobblestone walk led up to a charming white building with two stone pillars on the outside, reminiscent of old-style Southern plantations. Inside was a spacious lobby with cypress paneling and a twelve-foot-high molded ceiling from which hung a cut-crystal chandelier. Straight in the center of the lobby was the large, oak-paneled reception desk, and over to the right was the large dining area where a sign outside the entrance read: "Sunday Brunch, 10–2." The sound of clattering silverware and lively conversation reached our ears, and we headed in that direction. Leila displayed her press pass, and a young girl wearing a royal blue maxi dress led us to a table in the corner, across from the sumptuous buffet table. I hadn't been particularly hungry, but the spectacular display of fruit and food made my mouth water.

We'd barely taken our seats, when a young busboy hurried over to our table and poured water into two goblets. Leila took a sip of water and looked around the room. "This table is excellent. It gives us a good view of the hall outside as well as the elevator doors. We can see our quarry as they enter, or if we spot one of 'em walking through the lobby, we can run outside and grab him or her." She paused. "Not literally."

"I know what you meant. We'll need some sort of pretext to talk to them, since I'm not officially on this case. I leave that up to your creative mind. You are the writer after all."

"Gee thanks. Now I need food. I don't lie very well on an empty stomach."

"If it's any consolation, you don't have to think up anything elaborate. Besides, it's not an interrogation. It's just a . . . friendly conversation. We might learn something of interest, and then again, we might not."

A tall, red-headed boy wearing a black jacket and a nametag that said "Desmond" sauntered over to our table. "Ladies," he said with a smile. "My name is Desmond, and

I will be your waiter this fine morning. Would you care to look at our breakfast menu, or will you be having the brunch buffet?"

"Brunch," we chorused.

Desmond smiled. "Excellent. There is a fine selection of juices on the buffet table, if you wish. Would you like coffee or tea?"

We both ordered coffee, and as soon as Desmond departed, we made our way over to the buffet table. There was indeed a wide selection of food: bacon, sausage, hash browns, grits, rolls and pastries, plus platters heaped with fresh fruit. A large chafing dish held heaping servings of eggs Benedict, my personal favorite. Two white-hatted chefs stood behind the white-sheeted table, one manning an omelet station, the other serving up pancakes and waffles. A bit farther down the line, I saw two large, silver, covered platters with placards in front. One said "Roast Beef" and the other said "Turkey."

"They start carving them at noon."

I whirled around and found myself staring straight at Doug Harriman. Today he had his glasses on. His eyes were still a brilliant blue, though, and they twinkled behind the tortoise shell–framed glasses. I noted he held a plate on which was piled an assortment of fruit, some granola bars, and a plain scone. He saw me looking and patted his stomach. "I'm saving myself for the main course," he grinned. "Although I confess I've always been a healthy eater."

That, unfortunately, was a claim I couldn't make. "How nice to see you again. You wouldn't be following me, now, would you?"

"Quite the contrary. I was about to ask if you were following me. I saw you and your friend walk in." He gestured toward the other end of the table. Leila stood in front of the omelet station, balancing one very full plate and extending an empty one toward the chef. "Is that who you were meeting last night?"

"Yes, Leila Addams. She's a reporter for the *Deer Park Herald*." I paused. "She's also my roommate."

"Really? Lucky her."

I wondered if my cheeks could possibly look as warm as they felt. "So," I said lightly, "how did your business meeting go? I assume that's why you left."

"Yes, and I'm really sorry about that. But with a new job and all, when the boss calls . . ." He lifted his shoulders in a shrug. "Anyway, I went back to the bar afterward, but you were gone. I should have checked the dining room, but I figured maybe you and your friend were discussing serious matters and wouldn't welcome a third wheel."

I barked out a laugh. "Serious matters?"

He leaned in close and said, "I've heard about your detective abilities. Considering Ulla Townsend practically died in front of you, I figured you'd have an interest in figuring out what happened to her." He paused. "They haven't yet released the official cause of death yet, right?"

I shook my head. "Not as far as I know."

"But I bet you're working on finding it out, aren't you?"

I stared at him. "Why do you ask?"

"Well," he said, eyes twinkling, "my motives are purely selfish, I'm afraid. I bet my employer that you would figure out what really happened to Ulla before the police did."

My eyes popped. "That's a pretty bold bet, don't you think?"

He chuckled. "Not really. I had a tough time getting my employer to agree to it. She has a very high regard for your deductive abilities. We reached a compromise on a timeline bet. I said you'd solve it well before Saturday. She said within two weeks."

"She?" Suddenly it was starting to make a strange kind of sense. "Don't tell me your employer is—"

"Sydney! How nice to see you here?"

I glanced up and, sure enough, saw none other than Petra Littleton striding toward me. Trowbridge Littleton's widow had not only been a former Miss North Carolina, she'd been a runner up for Miss USA in her heyday, and truth be told she didn't look much different twenty years later. Her dark hair, which she usually wore in a chignon or a French twist, today was loose and flowed like a waterfall around her slim shoulders. Her makeup, as usual, was flawlessly applied: she looked like an airbrushed canvas. The lime-colored sheath she had on looked very simple, but I figured it probably cost more than I'd made in a month at my last job. Her feet were elegantly shod in matching lime-green wedges that added at least three inches to her already impressive height of five foot eight. Both Kat and I had gotten in the woman's good graces when we'd introduced her to her little pup, Jonesy, and I especially had earned her approval when I'd exposed her husband's real murderers, taking her off the suspect list. I had a definite idea now who'd been singing the praises of my deductive ability to Doug.

I couldn't resist smiling back at Petra. While most people thought her stuck up and snobbish, I'd always rather liked her. "Hey, Petra. We haven't seen you in a while. You weren't at the last shelter board meeting." As Littleton's widow, Petra had inherited all his real estate holdings, one of which was the shelter. Petra had recently taken a slot on our Board of Directors, the result of a very large donation she'd made in her late husband's name. Although, if you asked me, it was more of a thank-you for us hooking her up with the little Bichon Frise pup.

She waved one heavily bejeweled hand in the air. "No, sorry. I've been so busy. I never realized managing all of Bridge's properties was so much work." Her hand came down to rest on Doug's arm. "Thank goodness I found a capable properties manager at last."

I looked from one of them to the other. "So, you are Doug's boss?"

She wrinkled her pert nose. " 'Boss' is such a crass term. I much prefer 'employer.' " She grabbed his arm again. "He signed the contract last night. He's such a dear too. I was running late and forgot to call him until I was outside.

Then I got my coat stuck in the car door, and he had to help me with it." Her hand came up, lightly caressed the side of his cheek. "I think he's going to work out splendidly, though, don't you?"

So, he hadn't lied—his meeting with Petra had been business, although I got the distinct impression Petra wouldn't mind mixing business with pleasure where the handsome man was concerned. Then again, Petra felt that way about most men. I felt an odd sense of relief as I smiled and remarked, "Oh, yes. Just splendid."

"I'm glad you feel that way, because you'll be seeing him a lot. Who knows, I may eventually give him my spot on the shelter board. We'll have to see." She turned to Doug. "Our table is ready," she said, pointing to the other end of the large room. "We still have a few more contracts to go over." She turned back to me. "Do say hello to Kat for me. I'll see you at next month's meeting." With that, she sashayed away. I noticed that several men turned to watch her as she wiggled past.

My eyes twinkled as I looked at Doug again. "So this is a working breakfast?"

He grinned. "Yes. Don't tell my new employer, but she can be a bit of a tyrant."

"Oh, you don't have to tell me." I smiled back. "Good luck in your new position."

"Thanks. Don't worry—we'll be seeing a lot of each other." He balanced his plate in one hand, leaned over, and hissed, "Remember, solve it before this coming Saturday and there's a nice dinner in your future. You and your detective boyfriend, of course," he added quickly. "We can make it a double date." With a broad wink, he turned and moved off in the direction Petra had gone.

"Well, with an incentive like that, I guess I'd better get busy," I murmured. Although I couldn't help but wonder . . . who would Doug be bringing to this double date? Petra? Or had he met someone else already?

I added a small fruit cup and a large blueberry muffin to the pile of bacon and sausage on my plate and wended my way back to my table. Leila was already there, digging into a scrumptious-looking helping of eggs Benedict. "Ew ahs unk ah aw oo it."

"Chew, swallow, repeat," I advised.

Leila obediently chewed and swallowed, then said, "Who was the hunk I saw you with?"

I unfolded my napkin and spread it across my lap. "That is our new properties manager. Petra hired him yesterday. He's also the guy I spilled coffee on at the event."

"What?!"

I repeated the story of my faux pas from yesterday. When I'd finished, Leila picked up her water glass, took a long sip, then regarded me over its rim. "Have you got the hots for him?" she asked bluntly.

"What? Who? Doug? No!" I sputtered.

She shot me a mischievous grin. "But you think he's cute."

"One would have to be blind not to think he's cute. I'm with Will, remember?"

"I remember. Does Will?"

I popped a slice of bacon in my mouth, chewed, and swallowed. "Your point?"

"You and Will haven't seen that much of each other lately."

"Because his partner up and left, and he's been working overtime. Things will get back to normal."

"Plus—and don't deny this—he hasn't kissed you yet. I mean *really* kissed you."

I bit down hard on my lower lip. "Okay, the time just hasn't been right yet. So?"

"Stop making excuses. I love Will, but he has always been a bit on the slow side when it comes to girls." She leaned across the table so her nose was almost level with mine. "The point is, it never hurts to let your current boyfriend think he might have competition."

I stared at her. "You want Will to think I'm interested in Doug?"

"It's not that much of a stretch. I think you could be interested in Doug. Heck, I could be—but I'm not," she added hastily. "The point I'm trying to make is, you were taken for granted once. Don't let it happen again."

"Will would never do that."

"Sweetie, he's a man. That's what they do best." Leila paused, fork halfway to her lips, eyes riveted on the doorway.

205

"Not to change the subject, but one of our quarries has just entered the dining room."

I turned my head slightly and glanced quickly over my shoulder. Sure enough, Ken Colgate stood in the entryway. I popped the last bite of muffin into my mouth and dabbed at my lips with my napkin. "Okay, it's showtime. Got your speech ready?"

Leila was already sliding out of the booth. "Watch and learn, my friend."

The hostess showed Ken to a table off in the far corner. I wondered if he'd requested that one on purpose. It was set back, out of the line of fire, so to speak, perfect for someone who didn't want to be seen. I wondered briefly if anyone would be joining him. I got my answer as the hostess handed Ken a green, velvet-covered menu and placed one on the seat next to him. She moved off, and a busboy appeared on her heels, filled Ken's glass with water, then withdrew. Leila, who was about ten paces ahead of me, marched right up to the table as soon as he departed.

"Mr. Colgate," she said, flashing a wide smile, "fancy meeting you here."

Ken Colgate lowered the menu he'd been studying, and his eyes narrowed a bit as he saw Leila. "I'm afraid I don't recall . . ." he began hesitantly.

Leila, never one to waste time, slid into the seat opposite him. "Leila Addams, from the *Deer Park Herald*. I covered the signing event yesterday at Crowden's." She rushed on before Colgate could answer. "Such a tragedy! I can still hardly believe it happened."

"Nor can I. I will never forget the doctor's face when he told us the news." He stopped, dabbed at his eyes. "It was a distinct shock to all of us. Ulla was a rare talent, one that can never be replaced."

I fought the urge to roll my eyes. *Oh, please.*

"Yes, she was truly one of a kind. I consider myself fortunate to have had that one-on-one interview with her, however brief." She glanced over her shoulder, saw me, and motioned me to come forward. "You remember my friend, Sydney McCall? Syd is the director of publicity for the Friendly Paws Animal Shelter."

Ken gave me a perfunctory nod. "Yes, of course." He fidgeted uncomfortably in his chair. "I know why you're here."

Leila and I exchanged a glance. "You do?" I asked.

"Yes. You're concerned about the money. Well, let me assure you, Ms. McCall, that you do not have to worry. I'll personally see to it that either Ulla's publisher or her estate makes good on the revenue the shelter would have gotten had the event been completed."

"That's so kind of you," I said, "but are you in a position to make such a guarantee? I mean, we do need the funds, but I wouldn't want to put you on the spot."

"Not at all, not at all. As the executor of Ulla's estate, it will be my pleasure."

I nearly fell out of my chair. "I'm sorry? Did you say you were the executor of her estate?"

"Ulla put that in her will a few years ago. Her attorney and I are co-executors. It's a rather large estate."

"I can imagine." And what was the rule? That executors usually got five percent of the total value of the estate? Ulla's had to be worth millions, surely. Add that to the twenty-five million he was going to get for Savannah's movie deal, plus fifteen percent for the book deal . . . and you had a few million motives for murder.

Chapter Seventeen

Ken Colgate cleared his throat and shot me a smile I imagined was supposed to be disarming. "As I said, the estate is rather a large one, and complicated. Ulla had many varied assets and investments, but I promise to be in touch with you and your sister shortly regarding the details," he said. "So, ladies, if that's all . . ."

"Um, actually, I have some questions," Leila piped up. She whipped a notebook and a pen out of her bag and set them on the table in front of her.

Ken held up his hand. "I'm really not authorized to give any interviews," he said.

"Oh, but this isn't a formal interview," Leila said quickly. "I just thought I might write a human-interest piece as a follow-up, about Ulla and how the public loved her. And since you and she were so close . . . you did work with her for a long time, correct?"

"Since the beginning of her career with CNC," he said

with a faint smile. "We started out colleagues and became"—here he paused to swipe at one eye—"very dear friends."

"Then you must have some wonderful stories about Ulla that you'd like to share." Leila gave him a wide, guileless smile that I knew meant she didn't believe one word of his tearful admission. Ken took another sip of water and glanced at his watch.

"Perhaps I could spare a few minutes," he said at last. "What is it you wanted to know?"

For the next few minutes, Leila peppered him with questions about how he and Ulla met, her ambitions, her rise on the cable channel from a virtual nobody to one of their most popular hosts. As I expected, Ken pretty much took credit for mentoring Ulla's rise to fame.

"And her book, what about that?" Leila asked. "What will happen now?"

He shot her a surprised look. "Why, the book will continue to sell, of course. The presale figures were through the roof, and I've no doubt they'll continue to grow. All the money will be funneled into her estate."

Leila widened her eyes. "I'm sorry I should have been more specific. I meant the second book."

"Second book?" His gaze traveled to a point just past my shoulder. I turned my head slightly and realized he was looking at the entrance, probably wishing that whoever was supposed to be joining him would hurry up. "I'm not certain what you mean," he said at last. "Ulla wasn't working on another book."

"Are you certain of that? I was informed she was. A fiction piece this time. Also, that a major movie studio had already expressed interest in it."

I watched Ken's face carefully as Leila spoke. Aside from a muscle twitching in his lower jaw, his face was a blank slate, his expression bland. From looking at him one would never guess that he'd been in the process of double-crossing his "dear client, colleague and friend."

"I don't know who told you that, but your source is incorrect," he said at last. His tone was flat, with an air of finality. "Ulla was advising someone who was writing a book—mentoring, if you will. But she wasn't the author."

Leila's eyebrows rose. "No? Then who was? Will you be representing this person?"

He shifted in his chair. "I've been approached," he said shortly. "I'm sorry, that's all I can say now."

"Of course," Leila murmured. She made a show of closing her notebook and capping her pen, and just as she was about to slide them back into her bag, she paused and looked straight at Ken. "What about the cosmetics deal that Ulla was talking about at the event? Have you any idea what will happen to that now?"

Again, I saw him glance toward the entrance, and this time I saw something more furtive in his glance. "I really couldn't say."

"Couldn't you?" Leila leaned forward, and jabbed at the air under Ken's nose. "Isn't it true that the Glow people turned Ulla down in favor of Candy Carmichael?"

His eyes flickered in surprise, but his expression remained impassive. "If I were you, Ms. Addams, I'd get another source," he said. "Candy was being considered right along with Ulla, but no deal for either was finalized. I will say this, though. Candy's got the looks and the personality to make Glow a stunning success."

"And Ulla's death puts her right at the top of the heap, doesn't it?" Leila persisted. "As a matter of fact, it might even cinch the deal."

His eyes narrowed down to slits, and he barked out a nervous laugh. "What are you implying? That Candy Carmichael came to the event with malice aforethought?"

Leila leaned back in her chair and shrugged. "I'm not implying anything. But the police might, once they find out that the studio didn't send Candy down here to do promos, that she came entirely on her own." She paused. "They might even wonder if she had help—possibly from someone else who might also benefit."

His fingers, which had been drumming on the tabletop, paused in mid-air. "That is a ridiculous assumption," he sputtered. "And if I were you, I'd refrain from mentioning it to anyone else."

I reached out and laid my hand on his arm. "I'm curious about something, Mr. Colgate. How did your wife take the news of Ulla's death? I'd heard a rumor they were pretty close."

He turned toward me, the affable smile back on his face. "I'm afraid that's a question you'll have to ask Cathy yourself. Unfortunately, I was served with divorce papers yesterday, so we're not on speaking terms now."

"Oh, I'm so sorry to hear that," I said, trying to inject a note of sympathy into my tone.

"Yes, well, it is difficult. We were married for fifteen wonderful years—or so I thought. Anyway . . ." He glanced again at the doorway, and this time his eyes widened a bit, and he inclined his head to one side. I glanced toward the entrance as well, but there was no one there. Ken raised his wrist and made a show of looking at his watch. "I just remembered another appointment I must get to. If you need more information for your article, Ms. Addams, you may contact me." He pulled a business card out of his pocket and threw it down on the table.

"One last question," I blurted as he rose. "Did you tell Savannah Blade she could have Ulla's necklace?"

He stared at me. "What?"

"Ulla's silver necklace, the one the Glow people gave her. Savannah called me yesterday. It wasn't in Ulla's tote, and she thought it might have gotten mixed in with the shelter supplies. She said that Ulla mentioned she could have it as a keepsake if anything ever happened to her."

Ken pressed his lips together, and he rubbed absently at the back of his neck with one hand. "That necklace wasn't Ulla's to give away. It was on loan for her to use in her publicity photos."

"Have you any idea why she might have promised it to her assistant?"

"None," he said shortly. "Ulla and Savannah . . . clashed a bit at times, and Savannah is rather a materialistic person. No doubt Ulla noted her interest in the necklace and was needling her. I'll be sure to set her straight." He paused and then added, "That necklace is worth a good deal of money. The bullet-shaped charm is solid silver. If you do find it, Ms. McCall, I'd appreciate it if you'd give it directly to me. It must be given back to the Glow people."

And passed onto Candy Carmichael, no doubt, I thought but didn't voice. Instead I just murmured, "Of course" in as sympathetic a tone as I could muster.

Ken turned and strode away, head held high. I watched him disappear out the doorway, then looked at my friend. "He flat out lied about that book. Makes you wonder what else he's not being forthcoming about."

"He did seem to be a tad on the nervous side," Leila said. She scooted over into the seat Ken had vacated. "He especially didn't like my insinuating Candy might have murdered Ulla with his help. That tidbit about the necklace was enlightening too. Sounds like Savannah was trying to pull a fast one. She probably knew Ulla was pulling her leg about the necklace and when she saw a chance, she just took it."

"She did seem to want it pretty badly. Or else she knew all along the necklace went to the Glow spokesperson, and since Ken seems to be involved with both her and Candy, maybe she just didn't want Candy to have it." I tapped the edge of my phone against my chin. "Or maybe Ulla's killer took the necklace."

"Why? As a trophy, you mean? Or—" Leila abruptly stopped mid-sentence, dug her nails into my forearm, and ducked her head down. "Don't look now, but Charlie Callahan's here."

"Oh, swell." I cast a furtive glance toward the front of the dining room. Callahan stood in the doorway, hands on hips, his gaze roving slowly over the room. I shrank down lower in my seat, wishing with all my heart that I could be wearing Harry Potter's invisibility cloak right now.

Another figure appeared in the doorway beside Callahan, and I relaxed slightly as I recognized Will. The two conversed in low tones for a few moments, then turned and left. I lightly disengaged Leila's death grip from my arm. "Wow, that was a close one. I wouldn't mind talking to Will, but I absolutely do not want to run into Charlie Callahan, and especially not here."

"He'd think we were horning in on the investigation for certain," Leila agreed. Then she chuckled. "Which we are. So—what do we do now?"

"Let's go to the shelter," I said. "I've got an idea."

We went back to our original table and found the check sitting there in a leather holder, square in the middle of the table. I put enough money in to cover the tab plus a twenty percent tip, even though the waiter had done little more than bring us water. Then we walked out of the dining room and right into Will, who'd been standing just outside the entryway. He raised two fingers to his forehead in a casual salute. "Ladies."

"Why, Will," I cried. "What a nice surprise. Did you come here for brunch?"

"Did you?" he countered. "Or did you have another purpose in mind, like interrogating Ken Colgate, perhaps? Don't bother to deny it. I saw you sitting with him earlier."

"Okay, I won't," I said. "I'm surprised that your—er—partner, Charlie, didn't march right over and arrest us for interfering in his investigation."

"He might, if he'd seen you. Fortunately, I managed to distract him. He's upstairs with Colgate now."

"Is Ken an official suspect or still just a person of interest?" At his look, I threw up both hands. "Okay, fine. I know. You don't have to share any details of an ongoing investigation with a civilian. This time, however, it might be to your benefit."

He arched a brow. "Really? How so?"

I glanced around the lobby. People were starting to come in and converge around the entrance to the dining room. I motioned to a secluded alcove. "Let's talk there."

"You two go," Leila said. She brandished her phone. "I just got a call from my editor that I have to take."

I spent the next ten minutes giving Will the Cliffs Notes version of what I'd learned so far regarding Ken, Savannah, and Candy. "You have to admit they've all got pretty good motives," I finished. "They could each have done it alone, or they could have worked together. And let's not leave out Ken's wife, Cathy. She's supposed to have some sort of history with Ulla, and she just served her cheating husband with divorce papers. But maybe that wasn't enough revenge for her. Maybe she wanted to kill Ulla and make sure her ex was blamed for it."

Will pulled on his earlobe. "A little melodramatic, don't you think? We interviewed Cathy Colgate, and she didn't seem the murderous type."

I crossed my arms over my chest. "Yeah, well, Ted Bundy didn't either."

The corners of Will's lips twitched upward. "I'd hardly compare the soon-to-be-ex Mrs. Colgate with a serial killer. Look." He put his thumb under my chin and tilted my head up so he could look into my eyes. "I know you're trying to help, and I do appreciate it, but right now, it might do more harm than good, especially if Charlie should get wind of it. He wouldn't hesitate, Syd, to arrest you for interfering in a police investigation, and there wouldn't be much I could do to stop him."

"Even if the interfering helps catch a killer?"

Now he let out a low chuckle. "Especially in that case."

"Yeah, that's what I thought. I had him pegged as the sore-loser type." I wrinkled my nose. "Will, you've got to let me help you. The thought of Callahan getting Bennington's job gets under my skin."

"Think how I feel," he said with a wry grin. "I have to say, though, his giant ego aside, the guy is a good investigator. He's already turned up a few leads—and no, I can't share that with you," he said before I could speak. He patted my arm. "I appreciate your support, but right now the biggest help you could give me is getting out of here before he comes back, okay?"

"Fine." I started to move away, then turned. "Can you at least tell me if the coroner's report came in?"

He hesitated and then said, "Yep. We got it early this morning."

"Did Ulla die from an allergic reaction? Or can't you share that detail with a civilian?"

"As a matter of fact, I can, since certain details will be made public later. COD was definitely an allergic reaction."

"Dare I press my luck and ask to what?" I said as he lapsed into silence.

"I can't share the details, but I will tell you this—it wasn't to anything she drank or ate. Frankly, it's puzzling."

I frowned. "What's puzzling? Her allergy?"

"No, just how she might have been exposed to it."

My frown deepened, and he wagged his finger in my face. "I probably shouldn't even have told you that much. . . . You and Leila had better scoot." He leaned over and gave me a quick peck on the cheek. "We do have a good lead, though, so hopefully we can get this wrapped up very soon—maybe even in time for us to go out this Friday."

"That would be nice." I hesitated and then said, "There was something else I wanted to talk to you about. Someone slipped this into my jacket pocket last night. I reached into my purse, pulled out the note, and handed it to him. Will unfolded it, read it, and then raised his gaze to meet mine.

"Looks like a warning to me," he said. "One I'm pretty sure you're not going to pay attention to, right?"

"Well, of course I'm going to exercise extra caution. But back off entirely? Heck no." I jabbed my finger at the note. "Think you could get any prints off it?"

"Doubtful, but I'll give it a shot." He folded the note and tucked it into his pocket. "You've heard me say this before, but here it is again: Be careful, Syd. Please do not take any unnecessary risks. Promise me."

"Of course." He kept staring at me, so I added, "I promise."

He sighed. "Why don't I believe you? Look, I've got to get going. Remember what I said." He gave me a quick kiss on the cheek and hurried off. I motioned to Leila, and the two of us left the hotel and went back to my car. Once we were inside with the motor running, Leila pulled out her iPhone.

"Listen to this," she said. "Captain Connolly confirmed Ulla Townsend died from an allergic reaction."

"I know. Will just told me."

"Did he also tell you that they're widening their suspect pool?"

I gripped the steering wheel hard. Widening the suspect pool was *not* good news, because they could mean they were looking at other people, most likely ones from Ulla's past who might have been at the event. And if that were the case, I had a pretty good idea who they'd be focusing on first.

"You said before Will waylaid you that you had an idea." Leila's voice broke into my thoughts. "Parker wants me to cover a ceremony at the Town Hall in Weddington, but I don't have to leave until two, so till then I'm all yours."

"Will said the police already interviewed Cathy Colgate but I'd like to pay her a visit myself. See if I can get her to tell me what her connection to Ulla is. She visited the shelter last week and started to fill out an adoption application, so I'm hoping that it's still on file."

As it turned out, it was but it took us until almost two o'clock to find it because Cathy had filled it out under her maiden name, MacGregor. I dropped Leila off at home so she could change before Jim picked her up, then swung by my sister's apartment. Her car wasn't in the driveway, and I remembered she'd mentioned visiting some friends today, so I decided to make the trek to the other end of Deer Park solo. First, however, I called Cathy MacGregor on the pretext of discussing her adoption application with her. She sounded very cordial and excited at the prospect of giving one of the Friendly Paws residents a "furever home," so I was very optimistic as I turned my convertible toward the north end of town, where the MacGregor home was located.

Once I arrived at the large, wrought-iron gate that bore the initial M emblazoned on it, I had to press a button on the black box next to it and state my name and business before the gate opened and I could pass through. I drove for nearly five minutes down a winding, graveled road that opened into a wide clearing. Off to the left was an enormous white building that did, indeed, resemble the plantation Tara in *Gone with the Wind*, right down to the large columns on the front porch. I half expected to see Scarlett or Rhett at the front door as I rang the bell. Instead, a tiny woman in a gray and white maid's uniform greeted me with a brisk "Afternoon" before leading me through an entryway that glowed from Victorian lamps reflecting off the dark wood paneling of the walls, past a wide, curving staircase and into a beautifully furnished parlor. A fireplace, complete with burning fire, was at the far end, a chintz-covered loveseat positioned directly opposite. I walked over and was admiring the landscape portrait above it when I heard someone clear her throat.

"Ms. McCall?"

I whirled and did an immediate double take. Cathy Colgate certainly looked a lot different from the last time I'd seen her. Her hair wasn't hanging in strings today; now it was softly curled and framed her tiny face like a halo. She had on a becoming shade of blush and lipstick, and she wore a formfitting, cranberry-colored sheath that hugged the slender curves of her body. I smiled and held out my hand.

"Yes. It's nice to formally meet you, Mrs. Colgate—or should I call you Ms. MacGregor?"

"Cathy will do just fine. Shall we sit?"

She motioned me to the loveseat, and I dutifully sat down. The same maid who'd answered the door appeared, bearing a silver tray on which rested an ornate silver tea service. She set the tray on the coffee table and withdrew. Cathy looked at me. "Tea?"

"Yes, please."

As Cathy poured tea for both of us, I reached inside my tote bag and pulled out the application. "Vi, one of our volunteers, said that you were interested in adopting a cat. However, you never completed the application."

"Yes, I'm sorry about that. I suddenly remembered I had to meet my attorney, and I was running late." Her lips twisted into a wry grin. "I had to sign the final papers for filing. I meant to come back, but . . ." She spread her hands. "Time just got away from me. I thought I'd be able to finish it at the event, but Ken irritated me, so I left early." She fiddled with the edge of her napkin. "He thought I was kidding about the divorce. Probably my fault. I'd threatened many times before but never followed through. Circumstances, however, changed." She reached for the application. "It was sweet of you to remember me."

"I'm always glad to find one of our Friendly Paws residents a home," I replied. I picked up the teacup and took a small sip. "Did you get a chance to look over the cats when you visited the shelter?"

"Oh, yes. There was one I liked. Honey Bunny. Is she still there? I didn't recall seeing her at the event."

I remembered the cat, a beautiful, long-haired one with big blue eyes. "I'm pretty sure she is. She's an older cat, and we didn't take her to the event because she can be skittish at times."

"I can't blame the poor thing. With all those people, I was a bit skittish myself," Cathy remarked. "Have you got a pen?"

I pulled one out of my bag, and we sat in silence for a few moments while Cathy finished the application. After she signed it with a flourish and handed me back the paper and pen, I said casually, "I imagine you saw Ulla at the event. You and she were close, weren't you?"

"Who told you that? Ken?" Cathy's tone dripped with scorn. "He was probably trying to divert attention away from himself. He was a lot closer with her than I ever was. I only knew her briefly from high school."

I had to grip the stem of the cup tightly to keep from dropping it. "You went to the same high school?" A mental picture rose in my mind, and I let out a sharp gasp. "You were in the Glee Club with Ulla, weren't you? I happened to see a photo of the club in a friend's old yearbook recently," I added quickly.

Cathy took a sip of tea before answering. "I know the photo you're referring to. That picture is deceptive. We weren't always as happy a group as we appeared to be. I was one of the few juniors in that club, and I was always getting picked on. Ulla was by far the worst."

I took another sip of tea. It tasted good and bracing, and I'm not a big tea fan. "What do you mean? Ulla was a bully?"

Cathy bobbed her head up and down. "Oh, yes. One of the worst. I think it was because she'd been bullied and ridiculed so much herself. As I said, I was only a junior, but I heard the stories." The corners of her lips tugged downward. "These days Ulla would have never gotten away with half the stuff she pulled back then."

"She touched on the subject a bit in her book," I ventured.

"So I heard." Cathy leaned in a bit closer to me and said, "You know the girl in the book, the one who got itching powder put in her Coke?" She tapped at her chest. "That was me."

I kept my expression neutral. "You must have been furious with her at the time."

"Back then it didn't pay to get furious with Ulla. She'd only pay you back double. She pulled lots of other pranks on me, but they were mild compared to some of the things she did to others." She leaned in a bit closer to me and said, "I heard she snuck into a party once and slipped liquor into the punch. That ended up a real mess, or so I heard. Thank God, my father pulled me out of Deer Park High and stuck me in that ritzy private school right afterward. Private school girls can be snotty and mean, but none of them could hold a candle to Ulla."

Now that Cathy had started talking, she didn't seem to want to stop. She leaned toward me and said in a confidential tone, "Ulla wasn't just in Deer Park for that signing. Ken called it her "rehabilitation tour." They were keeping it hush-hush, but she was seeing a therapist—wanted to work through her 'anger issues.'" She drew air quotes around the last two words before letting out a sharp laugh. "More like insanity issues, if you ask me. Of course, the real reason behind this sudden surge of humanity was Glow. She'd heard the top brass thought she was too confrontational. Anyway, the therapist convinced her that to maintain her mental well-being, she had to attempt to reconcile the bad feelings. Face those she wronged and make amends."

I looked her square in the eye. "Did she face you?"

Cathy's lips thinned. "She tried to. She called me several times, but I hung up on her. Then she tried to approach me at the signing. Said that there were some things I should know about Ken that would make up for all the pain she'd caused me in the past. I told her she couldn't possibly tell me anything about my cheating husband that I didn't already know, including the fact she'd slept with him. She was more than welcome to him—as are all his other lovers." Cathy's tone grew wistful. "I put up with all of his cheating for years because I didn't have much choice. My father wanted nothing to do with me after I married Ken, but he always knew I'd come to my senses someday. That's why he left me his fortune."

She set her cup down, and I noticed her hand was trembling. "I hated her," she murmured. "I hated her, but I certainly would never have wished her harm. I guess the fact that she died quickly was a blessing for her." She shook her head. "Have they determined what caused her attack yet?"

I twisted in my seat so I could look right in her eyes. "It was due to an allergic reaction."

"She had allergies? That seems so . . . trite somehow. I guess I just never realized allergies could be fatal."

She bowed her head, and I sat there, studying her. Was her reaction sincere, or could she be acting? The woman impressed me as a straight shooter. If she'd been aware of Ulla's allergies, she would have said so.

I set down my cup and rose. "Well, thank you for the tea and the conversation," I said. I slid the finished application into my bag. "I'll see this is processed quickly so that you can pick up Honey Bunny."

We walked down the hallway to the front door. "It will be so nice to have a feline companion," she said. "Someone who will love me unconditionally, someone I can count on." She sounded so sad that I found myself feeling a bit sorry for her. She opened the front door, but I paused just before I crossed the threshold.

"One more question, if you don't mind. When you were in high school, did you ever hear of anyone called Miggs?"

She pursed her lips. "Miggs? That's an unusual name."

"I thought perhaps it might have been Ulla's nickname for someone?"

"Now that's a possibility. Ulla had nicknames for everyone." Cathy's nose wrinkled as she thought. "There's only one person I could think of that it might fit. She and Ulla hated each other. Her name was Maggie. Maggie Shayne."

That was what I'd feared she'd say. I forced a smile to

my lips and said my goodbyes, then got in my car and drove off, my stomach roiling. My visit with Cathy MacGregor had only served to intensify my worry over Maggie being involved in some way with Ulla's passing. I drove past Maggie's house again, but all the blinds were still drawn, and there was no car in the driveway, no sign of life. I called Rhonda and asked if she'd heard from Maggie. Of course, the answer was no. I had the feeling that even if Rhonda had heard from Maggie, she wouldn't share that information.

I drove by Kat's place and spotted her car in the driveway, so I parked behind it, got out and rang the front doorbell. A few minutes later Kat opened the door. "Wow, you've got good radar. I only got home a few minutes ago." She peered at me. "You look upset. There's nothing wrong at the shelter, is there?"

"No, everything's fine there. But I've had a rather eventful day."

"You look like you lost your last friend." She slipped her arm around my shoulders. "Come in and tell big sis all about it."

I allowed her to lead me into her homey kitchen, where she immediately brought out a platter of chocolate-chip cookies—my favorite—and a pitcher of sweet tea. In between bites and sips, I brought her up to date on the day's happenings, ending with my visit to Cathy Colgate and what she'd said about Maggie. Kat listened impassively and, when I'd finished, leaned back in her chair, just staring off into space for several minutes. At length, she looked over at me and said, "I agree, on the surface it sounds bad. But I've known Maggie a long time, Syd. She's not capable of killing someone."

"Per Will, everyone is capable of murder, given the right circumstances."

"Of course Will would say something like that. He's a detective; they're supposed to be cynical. I'm telling you, no matter how much Maggie might have disliked Ulla, she'd never have killed her."

I took another sip of my sweet tea, set the glass down, then laced my fingers behind my head. "I sure hope you're right. You didn't hear how Maggie sounded that day, though. I could almost hear the venom in her tone when Maggie talked about Ulla. Whatever it was that went down between them had to have been bad—really bad."

"Putting itching powder in Coke isn't exactly a walk in the park," Kat said, wrinkling her nose. "How do you know this Cathy Colgate didn't have something to do with Ulla's death? Just because she says she didn't?"

"I don't," I admitted. "But when you add it all up— Maggie making an appearance at an event she said she wouldn't go near with a twenty-foot pole, then pulling a disappearing act . . ."

"It's not like she just vanished," Kat protested. "She texted you and me that she needed some time off."

"You don't think it's odd that she texted instead of calling?"

"Not really. She always texts, and she's always sparse on details. She's a very private person."

"Yeah, well, this time being private could cost her—a lot."

"You're not even certain that Maggie and Miggs are the same person. It could be someone else entirely."

"True. But how can I find that out? One person who could tell me is dead and the other is missing. I think Maggie's cousin Rhonda might know, but it's obvious she doesn't want to get involved."

Kat reached out and gave my arm a pat. "You'll think of something, Sherlock. You always do."

"Thanks for the vote of confidence." I held out my empty glass. "Could I have some more sweet tea? And maybe some more cookies?"

Kat eyed me as she reached for my glass. "I thought you said you and Leila went to that fancy brunch?"

"We did, and Leila ate like a pig. Me, not so much."

Kat glanced toward the stove. "I could whip you up a frittata," she offered.

My sister isn't what I'd call a master chef, and the last time she'd made a frittata, there had been bits of shell in it. I started to refuse, when my stomach let out a low growl. Kat laughed. "One frittata coming right up," she chuckled as she pulled a frying pan out of the cabinet.

"Fine. But no shells this time."

Kat pulled a carton of eggs out of the fridge. I slumped in the chair and closed my eyes.

"There's got to be someone else who can help me," I muttered. "Someone else who knew both Ulla and Maggie and . . ."

My eye suddenly fell on the little table by the back door, on which sat the floppy straw hat that Kat usually wore when she puttered in her garden. And just like that, it came to me.

I knew who I could talk to that might hold the key to this whole mystery. And hopefully, she was still in town.

Chapter Eighteen

I wolfed down Kat's frittata (no shells, thank goodness!) and then made an excuse to leave, telling her I had an errand to run before my eight PM. shift at the shelter. I could tell from the way she looked at me, she knew something was up but tactfully refrained from pushing me for details. She did make me promise to call her immediately if I needed help, and after I said my goodbyes to her, I got into my car and drove straight to Hat's Off. The millinery store was open from noon to four on Sundays, and it was a little before four when I pulled into the space directly across from the store. Grace looked up at me from her post behind the counter as I pushed through the front door.

"Syd," Grace called out, "What a nice surprise. Come and meet my cousin, MaeAnn."

MaeAnn Topping looked to be a slightly younger version of Grace. Her light brown hair had a few errant streaks of gray in it, and she wore it in the same style as Grace's. She wore glasses too, but hers were wire rimmed with tinted lenses. MaeAnn stepped forward and enveloped me in a bear hug.

"It's so nice to meet you, Sydney," she said. "Grace has told us so much about you and your sister, and the wonderful work you do at the shelter." She closed one eye in a wink. "And, of course, that you are quite the detective too. You solved the murder of that man who owned the art gallery, God rest his soul."

"If you ask me, Syd should have applied for Bennington's job on the force," Grace said with a chuckle. "Although you probably wouldn't want to work that close with your boyfriend, would you, dear?" She turned to her cousin. "Syd is dating one of the homicide detectives. Funny coincidence, they used to date in high school too."

"Oo-oo," squealed MaeAnn. She clasped her hands in front of her. "So you reconnected with an old crush, huh? That's so sweet. I love hearing about high school romances that work out."

I mentally thanked Grace for giving me a good opening, and I returned MaeAnn's wide smile with one of my own. "Speaking of high school, I understand that you went there at the same time as Ulla Townsend."

MaeAnn's smile vanished. The corners of her mouth drooped downward. "Oh . . . *her*. Yes, she was in the same class as me. She was Ulla Beckman back then, though." She looked at me over the rims of her glasses. "Just goes to show you how funny life is, right? Here Ulla returns triumphantly on a publicity tour for her book, and she ends up dead. You just never know." MaeAnn shot me a sharp glance. "Gracie here says it's possible Ulla didn't die a natural death. Are you helping the police investigate, Syd?"

"Of course she is," Grace cut in. "Why, I bet Syd solves it before they do. I bet you've got some idea already, don't you, dear?"

"I bet there are plenty of suspects," MaeAnn put in. "People were surface nice to Ulla, mainly because they feared retaliation. And make no mistake—she did retaliate."

I leaned into MaeAnn and said, "Well, I can tell you this much. Ulla wasn't just here for a book signing."

Both MaeAnn and Grace gasped. "She wasn't?"

I shook my head. "Nope. She was on a mission. She'd turned over a new leaf. She wanted to reconcile with people she'd wronged over the years."

I thought MaeAnn's eyes would bug out of her head. "Really?" Her eyes narrowed a bit, and her chin jutted out. "Are you sure? Because the Ulla Beckman I knew wouldn't give a damn about anyone's feelings but her own."

I tapped on the glass counter with my nail. "Oh, it's true. As a matter of fact, Ulla was seeing a therapist. She was trying to work out some anger issues, hoping to land a contract as spokesperson for a major cosmetics company."

"Ah." MaeAnn's lips curved a bit. "That sounds more like it. There always had to be something in it for her."

I set my cup down and propped my chin in my hand. "I guess Ulla wronged a lot of people, huh?"

"Oh my Gawd, yes!" MaeAnn shot me a double eye

roll. "You could fill Kenan Stadium with all the people that woman wronged! Well, maybe not the entire stadium—but I bet at least half."

"Wow, that's a lot of people. She did mention a few in her book. Like the girl who got itching powder in her Coke."

"Yes, Cathy MacGregor." MaeAnn bobbed her head up and down. "Cathy was only a junior, and Ulla took particular delight in tormenting her."

I tapped my finger against my lips. "There was another incident—Ulla slipped into a party uninvited and put liquor in the punch?"

"Oh, yes. Poor Maggie Shayne. She got in a peck of trouble because it was her party. And that Ulla was such a sneak. No one could ever prove she'd been there, but we all knew she'd done it." She paused. "Grace says that Maggie works at the shelter, so I guess you've heard that story before."

"Actually no. This is the first time."

"Oh. Well, that doesn't surprise me," MaeAnn said. "Maggie never liked to talk about it. Please don't mention I told you."

"I won't," I assured her. "There was someone else too. Another girl Ulla was super-anxious to get hold of, but she didn't seem to be able to connect with her. She had an odd name—Miggs?"

MaeAnn's brows drew together. "You're right, that is an odd name. I don't recall anyone in our class with it."

"Perhaps it could be a nickname of some sort?"

MaeAnn pursed her lips. "A nickname, huh? Well . . . maybe. Can't think of anyone off the top of my head, but . . ." She closed her eyes and I held my breath. I could almost see the wheels turning in her brain. Suddenly her eyes flew open, and she reached out and gave my hand a hard squeeze.

"Of course, it has to be. Madelyn Griggs. Miggs. It fits." MaeAnn let out a long sigh. "I haven't thought about her in years. Not since the accident."

"Accident?"

MaeAnn nodded. "Madelyn was in a car accident our senior year. It was a terrible, terrible incident." She let out a long breath and then continued, "Madelyn was a real nice girl. Pretty. Popular. Ulla was jealous of her, of course. Maddie was always nice to her—Maddie was nice to everyone—but Ulla was her usual rotten self with her. Anyway, Maddie caught a bad cold that she just couldn't seem to shake. She was taking medication for it. One afternoon after Glee Club practice, she seemed a bit out of it. We all tried to talk her into leaving her car and letting one of us take her home, but she insisted she was fine. Long story short, on the way home she lost control and crashed into a tree."

My hand went to my throat. "Oh my goodness. Was she all right?"

MaeAnn shook her head. "She was in the hospital for weeks. Missed the graduation ceremony." She paused and then added, "Later we found out Maddie had Baclofin in her system. Some of the kids had seen Ulla hanging around

Maddie's locker before practice. No one could prove it, but we all figured that Ulla had switched her medication."

I gasped. "That is horrible. She could have killed that girl."

"In essence, she did," MaeAnn said. "The impact of the crash gave Maddie a TBI—traumatic brain injury. She was paralyzed on her left side and blinded in one eye. She had to be put in a care center."

"How terrible," I cried. "And Ulla didn't feel any remorse at the time at all?"

"Ulla's family had moved before anyone knew how serious Madelyn's condition was. Madelyn's sister was especially distraught."

"Sister?" I leaned forward. "Madelyn had a sister?"

"Yes, Laura. I'd almost forgotten about her. She was much younger than us, you see, but she idolized her older sister. Madelyn's accident hit her hard. She wanted her parents to find Ulla and make her pay for what she'd done, but they convinced her no good would come of that." MaeAnn shoved her hands into the pockets of her sweater. "I found out from a friend of mine that Maddie passed a few months ago. When Laura came back to arrange her funeral, she was a wreck. Went on and on about how it wasn't fair for Ulla to have fame and fortune, and her sister's life to have been ruined. My friend thought she seemed slightly unhinged by her sister's death."

"It's understandable," I murmured. "I don't suppose you know where Laura is now?"

MaeAnn put a finger to her lips. "Hmm, let me think. She was some sort of freelancer, that I know. Did something with computers. I thought I heard that she'd taken a job out of the country somewhere—London maybe?"

"So she's not in the United States now?"

MaeAnn's brow furrowed. "Well, now, she could be. It seems to me I did hear somewhere that she'd come back and had taken some sort of job in Charleston . . . dear me, I'm so confused. It's been a long time, you know. I could be wrong on both counts."

I nodded. It was understandable MaeAnn would be hazy with details on Laura. Still, the possibility existed that Laura might be around and might even have taken a job in the same town that Ulla lived and worked in. Coincidence?

I thought not.

I chatted with the women for a few minutes more, then told her goodbye and got back in my car. I drove a few blocks and then pulled over and took out my iPhone. I keyed in "Images—Laura Griggs South Carolina." Some of the photos that appeared I dismissed immediately—they were of women of color. There were a few others, some of a ten-year-old girl that could well have been Madelyn's sister. The images, however, were too grainy to see clearly. I pulled up the white pages site and typed in the same information. One number came up, but when I dialed it, I got a recording that the number had been disconnected. Some more quick Internet searching revealed that Laura Griggs did not have a Facebook, Twitter, or Instagram account. If she was a freelancer, she could be anywhere, but . . . if the last place she'd worked was Charleston, might one of those places have been the CNC studios? And if she'd learned about Ulla's plans to return to Deer Park, there was a good possibility she might have followed the woman here. I called the Deer Park Inn and asked to be connected to Wendy Sweeting's room. She wasn't in, so I left a message inquiring if anyone by the name of Laura Griggs had ever worked at CNC, then hung up. I debated calling Savannah but in the end decided against it.

There was still the issue, though, of Ulla dying of an allergic reaction. Had either Maggie or Laura Griggs been privy to this information? If Laura had made it her life's mission to make Ulla pay for what had happened to her sister, she probably would have worked long and hard to find out Ulla's Achilles' heel. She'd certainly done a good job of disappearing. Something niggled at me, some little detail, but for the life of me I couldn't hone in on it.

I drove home quickly, and the minute I pulled into my driveway, I snatched up my phone again and punched in Will's number. This information was something he should be brought up to speed on. When his voicemail kicked in, I left a message for him to call me, and then I got out of my car and went inside. Toby came over to me and wound himself around my legs. I bent over and patted him behind his ear. "How are you doing Tobes? Kill any more Melvins?"

Toby's whiskers twitched, and he blinked his big eyes

before turning and walking, tail held high, in the other direction. I chuckled and walked over to the counter. My suspect board stared back at me, and I snatched up my Magic Marker. I drew another box and put Laura Griggs's name inside. Underneath it I wrote, *Sister died at Ulla's hand. Revenge?* Then I drew a giant star next to the box. Laura was now my number-one suspect, but I couldn't lose track of the fact that whoever had killed Ulla had to be privy to one important piece of information: her allergy. I jumped as Toby pawed at my leg, and I looked down at him.

"Merow," he said, his tone almost reproachful. His paw waved in the air. "Merow."

"You're right," I said to the cat. "I'm slipping. I never even asked MaeAnn if she knew anything about Ulla's allergies." I glanced at the clock. Since it was still a few minutes before four, there was a chance they might still be at the store. I grabbed my phone, looked up the number for Hat's Off, and dialed it. Grace answered on the first ring and then put MaeAnn on at my request.

"Oh, I'd forgotten all about that," she said when I asked her. "It was an isolated incident. I only knew about it because I was unlucky enough to be standing right outside the biology lab at the time. Ulla was in the lab with two other girls. A bee flew in the window, and she went ballistic. Turns out that she was deathly allergic. She nearly died when she was a kid from a bee sting. Anyway, Ulla lit out of the lab like her pants were on fire. Made us all promise never to breathe a word—or else."

That feeling was back in the pit of my stomach again.
"I'm guessing one of the two girls was Madelyn Griggs?"
"Yup."
"And the other?" I held my breath.
"Maggie Shayne."
Drat.

Chapter Nineteen

I fired up my laptop and googled "bee sting allergy" and found a site that provided the information that, in certain cases, bee venom, also known as apitoxin, can have strong toxic effects on humans. Approximately half of one percent to two percent of the population is hypersensitive to bee stings. In such cases, one sting can cause an allergic reaction that can result in an anaphylactic shock. The blood pressure of the body decreases; rashes appear on the skin; and paleness, a rapid pulse, chills, and cold skin can follow. In more serious cases, there is shortness of breath, tightness of the heart, and faintness, and eventually even death can occur.

Exactly what had happened to Ulla. But how on earth had she gotten stung by a bee? There were no insects flying around that day, let alone bees. The weather had been brisk, not bee weather. Which could only mean one thing: someone knew of her hypersensitivity to bee stings and had somehow given her a dose of bee venom. Which meant, in no uncertain terms, that Ulla had been deliberately murdered. But how had the fatal dose been administered? Toby lofted onto the counter and sat, tail wrapped around forepaws, looking at me with his bright green eyes.

I reached out and gave him a scratch behind one ear. "Maybe it didn't come from an actual sting," I mused. "Maybe the killer somehow managed to slip bee venom into Ulla's water?"

I pulled my phone back out and googled "honey bee venom taste." I tipped the phone so Toby could see the screen. "It says here that honey bee venom is a sharp, clear liquid with a bitter taste. Ulla would surely have noticed it. So, it seems unlikely the fatal dose was administered that way. So then how?"

Toby jumped off the counter and trotted over to the other end of the kitchen, near his fleece bed. He stretched himself across the floor and busied himself with trying to fish something out from underneath the counter. I picked up my phone again and punched in Bart Beckman's number. To my surprise, he answered on the first ring. I identified myself and asked if he'd gotten my previous message.

"Yes, ma'am, I did, but I've been a bit busy deciding my sister's final resting place," he said in a slow Southern drawl. "Her final wish was to be cremated, but the police up your way haven't released her body yet. I've been told it will be within the next two days, though." He paused. "You said you had a few questions about my sister?"

"Yes, I'm—ah—working with Ms. Leila Addams of the

Deer Park Herald on a piece about your sister, and I just need to check a few facts."

"Ah'll be glad to help if ah can, but you should know my sister and I weren't particularly close."

I asked a few simple questions, such as where did Ulla go to school and when did his family move, and then geared myself up for the biggie. "The police communicated the autopsy results to you, correct?"

"Yes, ma'am." He coughed. "I told this to the detective just this morning. I remember the incident clear as a bell. Ulla was out in the garden, playing among the flowers, when she got stung. Man, did she holler! Then she started to swell up jes like a toad—she nearly died. If my daddy hadn't been home and gotten her to the hospital, she surely would have."

"So she's always been allergic to bees? Did she carry an EpiPen?"

"Only allergy she ever had, as far as I know. If there were others, she never let on. Ulla never liked admitting to weakness of any kind." He let out a long sigh. "As for an EpiPen, well, she used to carry one, but my sister wasn't one who believed in conventional medicine. She'd rather just avoid any situation that might put her in contact with bees or any type of insect. For example, she never advertised any type of garden product on *Shopping Your Way* or did any outdoor shows." He cleared his throat before adding, "She was in some experimental group for a while, and she took a series of shots that was supposed to combat the allergy, but obviously they weren't successful."

"One last question: Were you aware that part of the reason your sister came to Deer Park was to get in touch with certain people, people she felt she'd wronged in the past?"

"The last time we spoke, which was a few months ago, she did mention joining some sort of program. My sister was one of the "mean girls" in high school. As a matter of fact, some of the stuff she did was beyond mean. One little prank especially was the reason our daddy moved us away from Deer Park."

"That would have been Madelyn Griggs's accident?"

Silence, and then, "There was never any proof, mind you, that Ulla was responsible for what happened to that poor girl, but she sure hated her. I think my daddy felt Ulla had already been tried and convicted, and he wanted her to have a shot at a decent life. So off we went. It was tough on me, leaving all my friends, but . . ." I could almost see him shrug. "I was the baby. I had no say. Now, if there's nothing else, I have some matters to attend to."

I thanked him and hung up, then took a minute to ponder what I'd just learned. It was apparent to me that Bart Beckman had resented his sister, but had he resented her enough to kill her? He was, for all intents and purposes, aside from a few nominal bequests, her sole heir. More importantly, he knew all about Ulla's allergy. Had he been aware that the experimental shots she'd been taking had failed to work? Charleston wasn't that far away; he could have made the trip here, killed her, and gone back, or he could have partnered with someone. It wasn't out of the realm of possibility. For that matter, it was also possible that Laura Griggs could have done pretty much the same thing. I slid my phone back into my pocket and snatched up my bag.

"Tobes, I'm going out for a while. I'll be back to feed you before I go to the shelter."

No answer. I saw Toby's behind sticking out from underneath the counter and hoped he wasn't snacking on a real mouse under there.

* * *

When I arrived at the police station, Will was in his office, catching up on some paperwork according to Diane, who was manning the front desk. I went back to his office and rapped sharply on the door. "Surprise," I said when he yelled, "Come in!"

He looked tired, but not unhappy to see me. "Hey, what brings you here? Wait—don't tell me you've solved the case?"

I wiggled my finger. "Many a true word spoken in jest, Worthington."

Without any preamble, I flopped into one of the well-worn chairs in front of his desk and wasted no time in bringing him up to date on what I'd learned so far and expounding on my latest theory. When I finished, he was silent, his fingers tented beneath his chin. "Maybe *you* should apply for Bennington's job," he said at last.

The flippant compliment caused my cheeks to flame. "Funny, Grace said pretty much the same thing to me recently," I said. "I'll take a pass on the full-time position, but I don't mind helping out on occasion. You can just call me your private civilian consultant."

" 'Private' being the operative word. Charlie would hit the roof if he knew all this."

The visual of Charlie smacking his head against the roof of the police station almost made me giggle. "So, since Bart already let the cat out of the bag, so to speak, apitoxin is what Ulla died from?"

"It would appear so. The really puzzling part is how she got exposed to it."

"I agree. How did she get stung? There were no bees or insects of any kind at the signing."

"Oh, she wasn't stung." Will lowered his voice. "What I'm going to tell you is confidential and cannot be repeated to anyone—and by anyone, Leila, I mean your sister. Or even Toby."

I smiled at Will's mention of the cat, then made a crossing motion over my heart. I knew certain details in a murder investigation were sometimes kept a deep, dark secret. "I promise."

"Okay. The coroner found traces of apitoxin on Ulla's lips."

"Her lips! But how—wait!" I let out a little gasp as a mental picture suddenly popped up into my mind. "Oh my

246

God," I whispered. I reached out, found his hand, squeezed it. "I think I know how it was done!"

He stared at me. "You do?"

"The lip gloss," I murmured, tamping down the mental image of Ulla's swollen lower lip. "It had to be the lip gloss. I can't believe I didn't put it together sooner."

Will stared at me blankly. "Huh?"

"Haven't you ever seen Kylie Jenner?" I asked in mock horror. "Or more specifically, her lips?"

"Sure I have. I just don't get the connection."

"Well, how do you think her lips got that way?"

"Collagen injections?"

"Maybe, but there's another way. From using certain lip glosses."

He gave his head a quick shake. "You're losing me."

OMG, were men really this obtuse? "Some cosmetics contain bee venom," I said patiently. "It tricks the body into thinking it's been stung, which supposedly stimulates the production of collagen, which strengthens tissue and elastin, which in turn helps the skin remain taut. When you put bee venom in lip gloss, it makes the lips look plumper and fuller, like they've just been stung. Some call it 'pillow lips.' Back when I was in marketing, I remember a friend of mine had a cosmetics account, and bee venom was in one of the lines she was writing copy for." I shook my head. "I can't believe I didn't figure this out before now."

"Wait." Will held up his hand. "Your theory doesn't

make any sense, Syd. If Ulla knew she was allergic to bees, why would she use lip gloss with bee venom in it?"

"That's the whole point—she wouldn't!" I could barely keep the excitement I felt out of my voice. "Someone switched out her lip gloss for one with bee venom in it." I jumped out of the chair and started to pace around Will's tiny office. "It's the only thing that makes sense. She was using a sample Glow lip gloss. The makeup artist tried to put another brand on her, and she went ballistic. She showed hers to me—was very proud of it. She even made a point of saying it only added shine, not fullness. Then she got distracted by the cats. She wanted to be photographed with them, so she put the lip gloss on the table in that utility room, and we went across the hall to the pop-up. When we came back, about fifteen minutes later, her lip gloss was gone."

"Someone had taken it?"

"Yes—no. Maybe. I'm not sure. It ended up being on the floor. Wendy Sweeting found it and handed it to Ulla, but she decided she didn't need a retouch, and she put it in her dress pocket." I snapped my fingers as I thought. "Later, I saw her come out of that utility room again. She said she'd just put on the lip gloss. I noticed a red flush on her neck. About ten minutes later is when she had her attack."

"That would make sense," Will muttered. "According to the coroner, that stuff can act pretty fast." He rose from his chair and also started to pace to and fro behind his desk.

Suddenly I stopped pacing and jabbed my finger in the

air. "Say—what happened to that lip gloss anyway? It should have been in her dress pocket."

"Good point. We took all her personal belongings from the hospital and the bookstore, and we've got them at the precinct evidence locker, awaiting transmittal to her brother back in Charleston along with her body." He leaned across the desk, picked up his phone, and punched in a number. "Hello, who's this? Godrick? Godrick, this is Detective Worthington. Can you check the evidence locker list for Ulla Townsend and see if there's any lip gloss listed among her effects? Yes, you heard right—lip gloss. What does it look like?" He glanced at me helplessly.

"It's a very shiny, dark brown, cylindrical tube," I said. "It's shaped like a giant bullet."

Will repeated my description twice before he said in a testy tone, "Never mind. I'm coming right down."

"Me too," I cried as he barreled out the door. "Unless you're afraid Charlie will catch me down there."

"Charlie's not in the building right now, so it's the perfect time to break some rules," he said with a soft chuckle. I couldn't contain my excitement as I hurried along beside him. I'd always wondered about evidence lockers, and as it turned out, this one was exactly where it is on most crime shows—in the basement of the police station. We rode down in the elevator and emerged into a dimly lit hallway. Then we walked a short distance to where a young officer sat at a large desk in front of a door that bore a sign reading: "LOCKED AREA. AUTHORIZED PERSONNEL ONLY." A big plate glass window occupied one wall. Through it I could see rows and rows of steel shelving, like the ones in the playroom at the café. Will signed in, but when I started to pick up the pen to sign my name, he gently plucked it out of my hand.

"Sorry. I can only bend the rules so far." I shot him a pleading look, but he shook his head firmly. "I can't let you back there. You've heard about chain of custody, right?"

I wrinkled my nose. "It's to establish that the alleged evidence is in fact related to the alleged crime, and not planted to make someone appear guilty."

"Right. And there are strict rules regarding chain of custody as it pertains to evidence. It must be handled in a scrupulously careful manner to ensure there is no tampering or contamination. It most often applies to illegal drugs seized by law enforcement personnel. It's important that an identifiable and responsible person always has physical custody of a piece of evidence. That's why everything is protected in this locked area. Only authorized personnel are permitted back there."

"You mean I can't even watch?" I cried. "That's not fair!"

He leveled me with a rock-hard stare. "You wouldn't want a murderer going free, would you?"

I sighed. "No, of course not."

I crossed over to the wooden bench opposite the desk and sat down. An officer buzzed Will inside the room, then busied himself with paperwork. I drummed my fingers impatiently on the wood and tapped my toe against the cement floor. It seemed as if Will spent an eternity back there, but it was really only about twenty minutes. When he emerged, he was empty-handed and grim-faced. I jumped up as he approached me, and the first thing he did was shake his head.

"I went through everything. No lip gloss."

I frowned. That couldn't be right. "Are you sure? Shiny, brown, shaped like a bullet, yea big?" I widened the space between my thumb and forefinger to demonstrate.

He whipped a notebook out of his jacket pocket and flipped a few pages. "There was nothing in her dress pocket except some tissues. Just to be safe, I examined everything in that flowered tote bag of hers. Two packs of tissues, two combs, a brush, a blush compact, mascara, two small mirrors—but not one tube of lipstick. Excuse me, lip *gloss*."

"That can't be right," I said. "What could have happened to it? I saw her put it in her pocket." My eyes slitted as I thought. "Do you have crime scene photos?"

"Wait here."

He disappeared again, returning in a few minutes with a thick packet. I flipped through them until I came to the ones showing the outline of the body in the restroom. I examined each one carefully. No tube of lip gloss in any of them. "It couldn't have vanished into thin air," I muttered. "There's only one explanation. The killer must have gotten in there and taken it."

"Then the killer must have been very quick and clever, because we gave orders to have that area cordoned off once we heard about her death."

"There was a small window of opportunity, though," I mused. "Right after they took her body out and before Tara clamped down on people milling around back there. That back entrance was still wide open. Anyone could have gotten in. Now why would the killer want to remove the lip gloss?" I pondered this for a few seconds, then snapped my fingers. "The Glow lip gloss had to be switched out with one that had bee venom, and it had to be done so that Ulla wouldn't notice the difference. Not all lip glosses are packaged alike."

"Hmm." Will stroked at his chin. "So, if this was premeditated murder, someone had to buy a lip gloss that was similar in looks and packaging to the Glow product that contained bee venom."

"Exactly." I paused as I remembered something. "Wendy Sweeting was alone in the bathroom with Ulla for a few minutes. If she's the killer, maybe she switched out the lip gloss."

"If she did, that'd be hard to prove now." Will put both hands on my shoulders. "I hope you don't mind if we call it a night. It seems I've got a busy night ahead of me." He paused and then added, "I want to thank you for all your help on this, Syd."

I eyed him. "Really? You're not going to give me a lecture on how I'm not a trained law enforcement official and on the pitfalls of playing Nancy Drew?"

He laughed. "No, I'm not. Not tonight anyway." He

paused before saying, "However, I also want to make something very clear: I appreciate your help, but I don't want you doing anything else, anything that might—well, you know."

"Give Callahan a loophole for arresting me?"

"Can't take you out for a nice dinner if you're behind bars, now can I?" He reached out and touched the tip of my nose with his finger. "Don't worry, Syd. I have a feeling the murderer's almost as good as caught."

It was on the tip of my tongue to ask him what other leads he was planning on pursuing, but truthfully there was a part of me that didn't want to know. He leaned over, gave me a buss on the cheek, and then disappeared back down the hall. I made my way slowly out of the station and back to my car. All the way home I kept turning everything over in my mind. Death by lip gloss. It surely was an ingenious plan. It also practically screamed "woman perpetrator," although I wasn't ready to rule Ken Colgate out entirely.

I pulled up in front of Leila's house and checked my watch. I'd have to get to the shelter soon, but I had time for a quick cup of coffee. I started up the walk, then paused. Had I imagined it, or had that New England aster bush to the left of the back porch moved ever so slightly? Nope, I wasn't mistaken. A few seconds later, a head popped up from behind it.

"Syd!" a familiar voice hissed. "Over here!"

Maggie!

Chapter Twenty

"Maggie. Oh, thank God!" I cried. Relief washed over me, replaced about ten seconds later by anger. I placed my hands on my hips. "Where have you been, and why haven't you returned any of my gazillion texts or calls? And what on earth are you doing hiding in Leila's aster bush?"

"Trying to keep a low profile," she murmured. She motioned for me to come closer. As I drew nearer, I could see that her face was drawn and haggard, and that the sweat-shirt and pants she had on beneath her red jacket looked rumpled, almost as if she'd slept in them. "I only got back a little bit ago," she said.

"Back? Back from where? Where have you been?"

Her brows drew together. "What do you mean, where have I been? I texted you and Kat, didn't I?"

"I only got one text from you, and all it said was that after what happened, you had to leave. Then I went to see your cousin Rhonda, and she said something about a family emergency."

Maggie reached up and lightly massaged the back of her neck with her fingertips. "Sorry. I thought I'd been clearer. Everything was so rushed. I thought I'd copied you on Rhonda's text. I got a call from the nursing home that my Aunt Chloris had fallen. They thought she might have broken her hip, and since I'm listed as her emergency person, they needed my consent in case they had to do surgery. I drove down there, but thank God, it was only a fracture."

I studied her face intently. "And you were so busy at the nursing home, you couldn't find time to return any of my calls? Or send a less cryptic text?"

Maggie licked across her lower lip. "I guess I could have, but . . . like I said, I wanted to keep a low profile."

"Nonexistent is more like it." I looked Maggie square in the eye. "You went to Ulla's signing even though you said you wouldn't touch it with a twenty-foot pole. And don't bother to deny it, because—"

"I'm right in that YouTube video. I know." Maggie lowered her gaze and dug her toe into the ground. "I was there." For a few seconds there was complete and total silence, and then Maggie raised her gaze to meet mine. "I got there just as they were wheeling her out, and I could see she didn't look good. I couldn't stick around because I had to get to the nursing home, but I read what happened online. I knew darn well that if the police started digging into Ulla's past, looking for suspects, that, well . . . it might not look too good for me."

"I'm sorry to break it to you, but the police are already on that angle. Ulla mentions old rivalries in her book, and it would appear the book signing was a cover for her trying to find people she'd wronged and make things right. A sort of rehabilitation program, I guess."

"Or so she said," Maggie muttered.

I could tell that getting any information out of Maggie would be as easy as trying to extract a stubborn wisdom tooth. I planted my hands on my hips and said, "You've got to tell me what happened, Maggie. Why did you go to that event at all after you made such a fuss about not wanting to see Ulla?"

She wrung her hands in front of her and glanced around. "Listen, I'll tell you, but not out here."

"Fine. Let's go inside."

I started to turn to go up the steps, but Maggie grabbed my arm. "Wait. Leila's inside. Jim dropped her off about ten minutes ago. No offense, but she's a reporter, and I do not want to talk in front of her. Not yet."

"Do you want to go back to your place?"

She gave her head a quick shake. "If they've checked into Ulla's past relationships, the police might have it staked out. You never know."

I reached in my coat pocket, and my hand closed around my car keys. "Okay then. I have shelter duty at eight, but I'm sure the animals won't mind if we check in a little early."

"Merow."

We both glanced down. Toby stood there, his tail flicking to and fro. He looked at Maggie, then at me. "Merow."

"How did you get out?" I waggled my finger at him. "Did you sneak out when Leila went in?"

Toby sat back on his haunches and purred.

"He must have missed you," Maggie said.

"Probably. I haven't been around much the past few days." As if in answer, he got up, walked over, and started to rub against my ankles. "Okay, okay. You can come along. Let's get going."

*　　*　　*

Ten minutes later I parked my convertible near the shelter's back door, and we all trooped up the short flight of steps. I put my key in the latch, twisted it, then frowned. "That's odd," I murmured. "It's sticking. It wasn't doing that earlier."

"Probably the humidity," Maggie said, fanning herself. "You know how this North Carolina weather is."

"True." I pushed the door open and pocketed the key. "If it keeps up, I'll have Eddie McGee look at it," I said as we moved inside. Toby turned toward the cattery, no doubt anxious to visit with some of his old friends and maybe make some new ones. I led the way into the breakroom, Maggie right behind me. She sat down at the small table while I opened the rear cabinet and removed a large container of coffee.

Maggie's brow arched. "Out of pods?"

"The Keurig's been acting up. Thank goodness for electric coffeepots. Mocha java?"

"Sounds great."

I put some coffee on to brew. I opened the small refrigerator and found some brownies leftover from yesterday. I put two on a plate and pushed them in front of Maggie. She picked one up and bit into it hungrily.

"Oh, man," she mumbled around bites. "This is so good." The smile she shot me was sheepish. "I'm afraid I haven't eaten much these past two days. Or slept either."

She devoured the first brownie and was halfway through the second one when the coffee was ready. I poured her a large mug, poured coffee into a smaller one for myself, and then sat down across from her, wrapping my hands around my mug. Maggie finished the second brownie and took several sips of her coffee before she pushed her mug off to the side.

"I came to the event," she said softly, "because I'd gotten a call earlier from a woman who said that it was imperative that Ulla speak to me. I started to hang up on her, but she said that Ulla had recently gone through a personal crisis. Part of her therapy was making amends with people she'd wronged, and I was on that list. She said that it was important for Ulla's recovery that she speak to me, tell me how sorry she was for what she'd done in the past. She said that even if I couldn't forgive her, at this juncture in her therapy it was important for Ulla to forgive herself, and apologizing was one way for her to do that."

"Did this woman give a name?"

"No. She just said she was Ulla's personal assistant."

"It must have been Savannah. Go on."

"I listened to what she had to say, and then I told her that I was very sorry, but I didn't think that I could do that. I hung up but then I got to thinking. After all, Ulla had done the shelter a large favor, pinch-hitting for Dudley Simmons like that, even if she did have an underlying motive. And she did agree to have a portion of her sales come to the shelter, so . . ." Maggie's shoulders lifted. "I don't know, I thought maybe by doing this I'd be the bigger person, you know? Anyway, I decided to stop by just for a few minutes before I went to the nursing home. When I saw the crowd, I almost turned around and came back, but then I remembered the back entrance, so I went around the rear. I saw all the cameras, and the people coming in and out of that back door and—I almost left right then."

"But you didn't."

"No," she said with a shake of her head, "I didn't. But in retrospect, maybe I should have."

Maggie picked up her mug and started to drink more coffee. I took a sip from my mug, set it on the counter, then folded my arms and waited for her to continue. At length, she set the mug back down and sighed.

"Where was I? Oh, yeah—I almost chickened out, but

then I figured I'd just go in and get it over with, hear what she had to say. I followed some guys carrying what looked like sound equipment in. There were a ton of people around. I started to lose my nerve, and I ducked into that big room, the one where everybody had put their things, and something brushed against my ankles. I looked down and saw Annie Reilly. She must have figured out how to open the latch on her carrier."

"Yes, we found her loose in there. The lock needs to be fixed. Go on."

"Well, I wasn't sure just what to do, and I was starting to lose my nerve. First I tried to coax Annie back in her carrier, but she went and hid under one of the counters in there, and I figured she was probably scared, that she'd come out when she was good and ready, so I left. I wasn't in the right frame of mind to speak to Ulla anyway, let alone forgive her, and I probably never could—at least that's what I told myself. I went outside and got in my car and then, dammit, I figured that I was being a coward. That the only way to put all this behind me was to face her and have it out, once and for all. Just as I started to go back, the ambulance pulled up. Honest, for a second my heart stopped. I wasn't sure what had happened or what to do. Then some people saw the ambulance, and before I knew it, there was a whole crowd there. I was debating sticking around or leaving, when the door opened and they wheeled Ulla out. I left right after they carted her off." She ducked her head. "You know what was really funny? I felt bad when I saw her on that stretcher. For maybe one or two minutes, I actually regretted not sticking around and speaking to her."

We were both silent for several minutes, and then I reached out and covered Maggie's hand with my own. "Do you want to tell me what happened between the two of you back in high school? What made the two of you hate each other so much?"

Maggie expelled a long breath. "It's a long story—and complicated."

I leaned back and crossed my arms over my chest. "I've got no place special to be."

Maggie gnawed at her lower lip, then held out her mug. "I'm going to need another cup. Too bad you haven't got anything stronger to put in it."

"Actually . . . I might." I scraped back my chair, went over to the cabinet by the sink, and opened the lower right-hand door. I reached inside and pulled out a medium-sized bottle. "Kat got this Bailey's from Mrs. Brandon as a thank-you for her little Chihuahua, Roxie, and she never brought it home. I could whip us up some Irish coffee. I won't tell Kat if you don't."

Maggie made a crossing motion over her heart. "Deal."

I poured hot coffee into two mugs and added a shot of sugar and a shot of Bailey's to both. There was a small can of whipped cream in the fridge because Vi liked that in her coffee instead of regular milk. I added a squirt to both and then brought the mugs back to the table. We each picked up one and clinked them in the air.

"Cheers."

We both took a sip, and Maggie coughed lightly. "You've got a heavy hand with that Bailey's. But it's good."

Maggie set her mug down and rubbed at her eyes with the tips of her fingers. "You know how it is in high school," she began. "I was in with the popular crowd, and Ulla wasn't. She was Ulla Beckman back then, and her hair was frizzy; her clothes were hand-me-downs; and she came from the south side of town. She was easy prey for the in crowd, and, boy, did we let her have it, hammer and tongs. Looking back, though, on some of the things she did to us . . ." Maggie shook her head. "She went above and beyond 'mean.'"

I sipped my laced coffee and leaned back. "How, exactly?"

"Well, she snuck into my sweet sixteen party and slipped a fifth of vodka into the punch."

"That is bad. You could have gotten in a lot of trouble."

"I did. Ulla always made sure there were no witnesses around when she pulled her pranks, and if there were, she threatened them within an inch of their lives. She'd pasted another label over the real one and left the bottle where I'd be sure to pick it up, so my fingerprints were all over it. Of course, I protested my innocence, but I was blamed anyway, and I got suspended for two weeks. At that I was lucky. I think the principal believed me to a point, because I could have been expelled for sure."

I shook my head. "I can see why you'd nurse a grudge."

"She pulled other so-called pranks on kids that she felt had been mean to her. And she didn't just torment the girls in our class—it trickled down to juniors and sophs too. I remember one girl, Cathy MacGregor. She made fun of her all the time, said she was the only girl with worse hair and clothes than her. Cathy was also skinny as a rail and petite. Ulla took delight in bullying her. Once she tripped her during a rainstorm so that all her schoolbooks fell in a puddle. It completely ruined her homework; Cathy got detention for a week. Of course, once Cathy's dad started to rake in the dough, the green-eyed monster took over, and she hated her more than ever. It's a good thing Cathy's dad put her in that fancy private school. Otherwise, who knows? She might have ended up like . . ."

"Like Madelyn Griggs?" I prompted as Maggie fell silent.

"You heard about that?" Maggie shook her head. "Poor Madelyn. She was the sweetest thing. She was frail and prone to colds. Well, Ulla switched her cold medicine with prescription medicine, and it threw Maddie's equilibrium all off. She ended up driving her car right into a tree. Her car was totaled, and she suffered some pretty serious injuries. And, of course, no one could prove Ulla had a damn thing to do with it. I think her father knew, though, because shortly after, the whole family up and moved. Guess he figured he'd better get her out of town before she killed one of us." Her lips twisted into a wry grin. "The ironic thing? Maddie always used to defend Ulla. Said that she'd had a tough life. Can you imagine?"

"Did you ever hear Ulla call Maddie by a nickname? Specifically, Miggs?"

Maggie frowned. "No, but it sounds like something Ulla would do. Why?"

"Because according to her assistant, Ulla was frantic to get in touch with someone she referred to as Miggs."

"It could have been Maddie. Probably was. Of all the people Ulla wronged, she would have wanted to beg her forgiveness the most, especially if she knew Maddie spent the rest of her life as practically a vegetable." She gazed out into space for a few minutes and then murmured, "I wonder what ever happened to her."

"I know. She's dead."

Maggie jerked herself upright. "What?"

"She's dead. She'd been in a convalescent home for several years, and she died a few months ago. Grace Topping's cousin MaeAnn told me."

"MaeAnn. That figures. She was always first with the latest gossip." Maggie flexed her fingers, then clasped them tightly. "I'm sorry to hear Maddie died. She survived the accident, but any semblance of an actual life ended that day. She was a bright girl too. It's such a shame. Such a waste."

"I agree. You know Maddie had a sister, right?"

Maggie nodded. "Yes. Laura. She was only a kid when all this went down."

"Do you think she'd be the type who would want to seek revenge for her sister?"

Maggie's eyes widened. "Why, I honestly don't know. Why do you ask that?"

"Ulla died from an allergic reaction to apitoxin. Whoever killed her had to know about her specific condition. Her allergy to bee venom."

"MaeAnn, Maddie, and I were all in the lab that day the bee flew in. Lord, you would have thought her pants were on fire, she carried on so," Maggie said. "Ulla swore us all to silence but . . . it's possible that Maddie might have mentioned the incident to Laura. They were very close despite the difference in age." She reached up with her fingertips to massage her temple. "I imagine the fact I knew about her allergy puts me on the suspect list, right?"

"Well, that coupled with your history with Ulla and the fact that you snuck into the signing and then vanished right after she collapsed doesn't exactly put you in a favorable light."

Maggie raked both hands through her hair. "I know, I know. In retrospect, taking off like that wasn't too bright, was it?"

"No, it wasn't." On an impulse, I grabbed my phone. "Do you remember what Laura Griggs looked like?"

"I only saw her once. Not bad looking, as I recall. Very thin. Why?"

"Look at these two pictures." I called up images of both Candy Carmichael and Savannah. "Could either of those two be a grown-up Laura?"

Maggie took my phone and squinted at the screen. "Of course, a lot of time has gone by. Either of these girls could

265

be, I guess, but . . ." she pointed to Candy's photo. "If I had to pick one, maybe her. The shape of the face is right, and so is the coloring." She handed me the phone and then glanced at her watch. "It's getting late. What do you think? Should I go down to the station now and see Will, or can it wait until morning? And should I give my lawyer a call?"

"I doubt that you would be charged with anything yet, but it doesn't hurt to talk to your lawyer," I said. "I'm sure that you could do all this in the morning. You should get some rest. Let me just feed the animals, and I'll drive you home."

"I can help. It will probably take my mind off all this." Maggie's hand shot out and covered mine. "If I haven't told you before, let me say now what a good friend you are, Syd McCall."

"Back at ya, Maggie Shayne. You'd do the same for me or Kat, I know."

We linked arms and walked into the cattery. The first thing that caught my eye was Toby, on the far side of the room. He was on his back, trying to chew at something he held between his paws. Something shiny.

I walked over slowly. "Hey, Tobes, what have you got there?" I asked. I knelt and gently pried the object from his paws. Even covered in cat saliva, the bullet-shaped charm on Ulla's necklace shone brightly in the overhead light.

I looked sharply at Toby and dangled the necklace in front of him. "Where did you get this?" I demanded. Toby looked at me, then seemed to shrug. He rolled over on his side and began to purr.

Maggie was beside me, looking anxious. "Is something wrong, Syd?" Her gaze traveled to the necklace, and she gasped. "Goodness, is that what he was playing with? Where did he get it? It looks expensive."

"It's Ulla's. It's been missing." I turned the necklace over in my hand. Sissy had said she'd looked and couldn't find it. Had she somehow missed it? I looked quickly around the room but didn't see anything out of place. I looked back at Toby. "Too bad you can't talk," I murmured, "and tell me just where you found this."

Toby rolled over, blinked, then let out a sleepy yawn.

While Maggie fed the cats, I dialed Will's number. Voice-mail again, darn it! I told him quickly about the necklace and asked him to call me as soon as he got my message. Then I took the necklace back into my office and locked it in my desk drawer.

Between Maggie and me, it didn't take long to finish feeding the animals, so it was just a little past eight when I locked up and we all trooped out to my car. Maggie slid into the passenger seat, and Toby stretched out full length across the back. We drove in silence to Maggie's, the only sound being Toby's contented snoring. I pulled up in front and looked at Maggie.

"First thing tomorrow, you should go to the station. Do you want me to go with you?"

She hesitated, then shook her head. "No. I can do this. After all, I had nothing to do with Ulla's death."

I reached out and squeezed her hand. "I believe you. But if you need anything—anything at all—call me."

I watched as she went up the steps, unlocked the door, and turned on the living room light. I sat in my car for a few minutes, replaying the events of this jam-packed day in my mind. Means, motive, and opportunity. On paper, it appeared Maggie had two of the three. So did a few others. The telltale factor was who had the means? Who could have switched Ulla's lip gloss out for one containing bee venom? If Candy was Laura, she would have it all—means, motive, and opportunity. And her motive would definitely trump Maggie's.

I turned the key in the ignition and was halfway down the block when flashing lights in my rear-view mirror caught my eye. I pulled over and watched as a cop car drew up in front of Maggie's house. When I saw both Charlie Callahan and Will get out and start up the front steps, my heart went down right to my toes. I held my breath and kept watching. A few minutes later they came out, Maggie between them. She got into the back seat of the sedan, and then it pulled away. I ducked my head as the car sailed past me, lights still flashing.

I felt nausea boil up inside my stomach, and I pulled away from the curb, careful to keep a little distance between my car and theirs. I figured the police would hone in on Maggie eventually, but I'd hoped she would have been the one to go to them rather than the other way around. At least it hadn't been Charlie Callahan by himself, I thought. Maggie wouldn't react well to the man's abrasive attitude. When the sedan made a left at the intersection, I turned in the opposite direction, my thoughts in a whirl, certain of only one thing.

I had to find out who murdered Ulla Townsend—and fast. Because if I didn't, there was a very good chance that Maggie might spend the rest of her life in jail for a crime she didn't commit.

Chapter
Twenty-One

I spent a restless night tossing and turning. At one point, I must have knocked Toby off the bed, because I heard a sharp meow and then felt something catapult itself on top of my feet. When I fell asleep at last, it was to dream of Ulla holding a giant necklace and pleading for justice. Ken and Cathy Colgate, Savannah, Candy Carmichael, and Wendy were all clustered around her, laughing. Off to the side stood a shadowy figure. When I glanced its way, it raised a hand and pointed at Ulla. I gasped as I realized that the figure's arm was bony like a skeleton's! I woke in a cold sweat and immediately threw back the covers, grabbed my robe, and headed for the bathroom. Sometimes you really need a cold shower.

Once I'd showered and dressed, I tiptoed downstairs, so as not to wake my roomie, and made myself a quick cup of coffee. One of these days, I was going to write a thank-you note to the person responsible for inventing timers for coffeepots. I put my mug in the sink and dialed Maggie's number. Voicemail. I didn't leave a message—just got in my car and drove straight to the shelter.

"I didn't expect to see you until later," Kat said when I stuck my head in her office. "What's up?"

"Lots." I perched myself on the edge of her desk and brought her up to speed on the events of the evening before. "Maggie never called me, and when I tried her this morning, I got her voicemail."

Kat's eyes popped. "Oh no! You don't think they arrested her, do you?"

"I doubt it. They have no grounds to do so, at least none I'm aware of. I'm assuming they just brought her in for questioning and nothing more, but I'll find out soon enough. I'm going to take that necklace down to Will."

"What necklace?"

We both turned to see Sissy standing in the doorway. She held a tiny calico kitten in her arms. The kitten's claws were stuck in her T-shirt, and Sissy reached up to gently disengage them. She shifted the kitten in her arms. "What necklace?" she repeated.

"Ulla's necklace, the one with the silver bullet charm," I responded. "Toby was playing with it in the cattery last night."

"Huh." The teen looked clearly puzzled. "I went through all of the totes we took to Crowden's, and I swear it wasn't in there."

"I wouldn't worry about it," Kat said. "It might have gotten stuck in one of the zippered compartments, and those totes are pretty old. It might even have gotten stuck in one of the holes in the material."

"Uh-uh." Sissy gave her head a quick shake. "When I said I looked, I mean I *looked*. I dumped everything out, and I felt inside each one of them. Believe me, it wasn't there."

Kat looked at me as if to say, *Another mystery for you to solve, Sherlock.* "Kat's probably right," I told the teen. "I lost a pin once in the lining of my purse. That sucker really got buried in there."

"Yeah, but that bullet charm is big and heavy," Sissy protested. "I think it would be hard to lose."

I shrugged. "There's probably a very simple explanation, but right now I can't think of one." As Sissy turned to go, I called out, "Wait a sec. You went out the back door when your shift was over yesterday, right? Did the lock stick?"

Sissy shook her head. "Nope. The key turned smooth as silk. We just sprayed all the locks with that WD-40 because of the humidity, remember?" She frowned. "Why? Did you have trouble with the lock last night?"

"Just a little. Maybe we didn't give that door lock as good a spray. I'll take care of it later."

"Okay. Oh, I almost forgot." Sissy reached into her pocket and pulled out a small envelope. "I found this lying by the side door. It's addressed to you."

I took the envelope, slit it. Inside was a single sheet of paper. I pulled it out and read the crudely printed message: *U wood do well to mind UR own business.*

"Someone thinks I'm getting close," I said. I passed the note to Sissy and Kat to look at. "I wish I knew what it was I'm getting close to."

Kat looked up from the note with a frown. "I don't like this, Syd. Maybe you should stop looking into Ulla's death."

Both my brows went up. "And give up on proving Maggie's innocence?" I shook my head. "Sorry, Sis. Not a chance. But I'll be careful."

"Yeah, that's what you said last time," Kat grumbled. "Please exercise caution. After all, you're the only sister I've got."

I'd planned on going down to see Will before lunch, but when I called the station, Diane Ryan answered and said that he and Charlie Callahan were out and wouldn't be back until around four. I went to DuBarry's and got takeout for all of us at the shelter, then spent the next several hours catching up on paperwork. Around three o'clock I got a call from Tom Spurlock, the president of Ulla's publishing house. He'd spoken with Ken Colgate, and we weren't to worry. In addition to the sale percentage, Axiom Publishing would be making a very generous donation in Ulla's name to the shelter. The amount he named brought tears to my eyes. I called Ken but got his voicemail. I left a message thanking him and then broke the good news to the others. No doubt we would be getting that alarm system now! Of course, a small celebration ensued, so it was almost six o'clock before I retrieved the necklace and made my way to the police station.

Diane was at the desk, and she greeted me with a wide smile. "Hey, Syd! You're in luck! Will just got out of a meeting with Captain Connolly." She grimaced. "And Callahan. Go right on back."

Will was just settling himself in his chair when I rapped on the door and walked in. As he started to rise, I waved him back down. "Don't get up," I said. "First off, I want to know how it went with Maggie last night."

"I'm shocked you waited this long to inquire," he responded. "I saw you sitting by the curb in your car." He motioned for me to sit and then went on, "We just brought her in for questioning. We advised her that she could have her lawyer present if she wanted, but that if she answered our questions truthfully, that would not be necessary."

"Uh-huh," I grumbled, placing both hands on my hips. "So? What happened?"

"We asked a few questions, she answered them, and then I drove her back home."

"Did Callahan traumatize her? She's not answering her phone."

"That's because she left it here last night. I'll have someone return it to her later. She might be still sleeping. She was pretty beat."

"Well, of course she was," I cried. "She'd just gotten back from a long trek to check on her aunt in the nursing home."

"So she told me."

I frowned. "You sound a bit skeptical."

"I checked with the nursing home. Maggie was there, all right, but . . ."

"But what?" I asked as Will paused. "Something's bothering you, I can tell."

"It's just that when we contacted the nursing home to verify her story, they said that no one there called her. She showed up all on her own."

"No one called . . . you mean there was nothing wrong with her aunt?"

"No, her aunt did take a fall, but it was nothing serious. I checked with three different people there, and there's no record of anyone calling Maggie to notify her of anything."

"Well, maybe no one wrote it down. Maybe you just didn't speak to the right person. Maggie wouldn't lie about that."

"She also said that a woman called her and told her how important it was to Ulla that she speak with her."

"Yes, that would have been Savannah."

Will shook his head. "I questioned Savannah. She was most emphatic in her denial. She's never heard of Maggie Shayne." There was a long pause and then Will added softly, "I'll be honest with you, Syd. Right now, it doesn't look too good for Maggie. She's been caught in two lies; she had definite issues with the deceased; and then there's that You-Tube video."

I bit down hard on my lower lip. "What? That video is—is grainy. I'll agree it does look like Maggie, but it's not all that clear."

"You forget, we at the police department have enhanced technology. It's Maggie, all right."

"Fine, but she didn't lie to you about being there, did she?"

Will picked up a pencil and tapped it on the desk blotter. "Kind of hard to do that when we've got visual proof."

I stamped my foot. "Sometimes you can act just like—just like a cop!" I burst out. "So what—now that you've got Maggie in your crosshairs, that's it? You don't follow up on any more leads? What about Miggs?"

"Who?"

"It's a nickname for one of the people Ulla was desperate to contact. A Madelyn Griggs. But, as it turns out, she's dead. Her sister's not, though." I brought Will up to speed on that issue. "MaeAnn said that Madelyn's sister, Laura, was quite vocal about blaming Ulla for her sister's condition. So, maybe now that she's dead—"

"You think what? That this Laura might have been stalking Ulla, waiting for her chance at revenge?"

"Is that theory so farfetched? Grief can make people do very strange things," I said. "I don't think you can discount the possibility that Laura might have changed her name, her appearance, and maybe gotten a job at CNC to be near Ulla, just waiting for the right moment."

Will looked at me. "It sounds as if you've given that theory a lot of thought."

"I have. Do you know, both Savannah and Candy are

about the right age to be Laura? I showed Maggie their photos, and she thought Candy Carmichael resembled her a bit."

Will shook his head. "That's guesswork, Syd. Maggie would have no way of knowing how much Laura might have changed over the years." He caught both my hands in his. "There's also the possibility Laura Griggs has nothing to do with Ulla's murder at all."

"Maybe," I grumbled. "Revenge is always a powerful motivator, though, and that's certainly the case with Laura. You could at least consider the possibility."

Will stroked his chin for what seemed like an eternity. At last he said, "I'm not saying I agree with your theory, but since you've brought it to my attention, I promise to check it out."

"I guess that's good enough, for now anyway. Now for my other reason for coming here." I opened my bag and pulled out the plastic bag containing the necklace and set it on Will's desk. "I found Toby playing with that in the shelter last night."

Will picked up the bag, turned it over in his hand. "So it was mixed in with your things?"

"That's the odd part. Sissy swears it wasn't, that she went through everything with a fine-tooth comb."

"So what's the other option? That Ulla's killer broke into the shelter and left it as what? A calling card?"

"Don't be ridiculous. No one's broken into the shelter— or have they?" I recounted the incident with the lock, then pulled the second note out of my pocket. "Sissy found this by the side door. Maybe someone did manage to get in. But nothing was taken—at least, nothing anyone noticed." I looked at the necklace, still in Will's hand. "Of course, maybe this was a different kind of thief."

Will saw me looking at the necklace and frowned. "The kind who leaves valuable necklaces, you mean?"

"No, the kind who comes searching for them. Something must have scared him off before he could find it, thank God."

Will sighed. "I'll send someone over to check out the lock, Syd. The shelter doesn't have any sort of alarm system or security cameras?"

I shook my head. "Not in the current budget. We were thinking of installing one, though, with the money from Ulla's event. Provided Ken Colgate keeps his promise." I gestured toward the necklace. "He'll be glad to hear the necklace has been found."

"I'll have it checked for prints before I return it," said Will. "The note too. I'm not too optimistic, though. I've got the idea everybody and his brother has touched this necklace, including your cat." He set the necklace down, got up, and walked around the desk to stand in front of me. "I know you're upset, Syd. Hey, I like Maggie too. And to be honest, I can't see her as a murderer."

"You and I both," I said. "But I bet Charlie Callahan can."

"Charlie doesn't know Maggie like you and I do, so he's going strictly by evidence. There's not enough to arrest Maggie yet."

His tone got softer and he put his arm around my shoulders. "I told you, Syd, I don't think Maggie is a killer, but Connolly will accuse me of not doing my job properly if I don't treat her the same as any other suspect. And like it or not, Maggie is a suspect."

"I don't like it," I burst out. "It's like she's being set up. If it's not by Candy Carmichael, then it's by Savannah or Ken Colgate. One of them is the killer—I just know it."

Will laid his hand on my arm. "It never fails to amaze me how passionate you can get about stuff like this. I promise, I'll check into everything. Now it's time for you to step back and let us do our job."

I gave my head an emphatic shake. "How can I do nothing, Will, when I just know Charlie Callahan is circling, waiting for the opportunity to slap cuffs on Maggie and claim Bennington's job?"

He put his thumb under my chin and tilted my face up to his. "Then how about doing it for me? After all, there's a murderer out there, and if he or she suspects that you might be getting too close to uncovering their identity, you could be next." He pulled me to him and pressed me close against his chest. "I can't do my job effectively if I have to worry about you putting yourself in danger."

"Okay, you win." I mumbled against his jacket. "I won't

do any more investigating." As his eyes narrowed, I held up both hands. "See! No fingers crossed."

Will smiled and kissed my forehead. "That's my girl."

I glanced toward his desk. "How about if I save you a trip and return Maggie's phone? There's no law against that, is there?"

"No." He opened his bottom drawer, scooped out the phone, and handed it to me. He started to say something else, but his desk phone rang just then. I leaned over and gave him a peck on the cheek, then motioned that I was leaving. He seemed torn between stopping me and answering his phone, but in the end duty won, and he scooped up the receiver. "Worthington," he barked.

I left quickly, uncrossing my toes as I hurried out of the station and over to my car. I was just about to head over to Maggie's with her phone, when my own phone buzzed. It was a text from Leila:

Can U stop for toilet paper and paper towels? We're out of both here.

The Redi-Mart was only a few blocks away. I drove there, parked, and went in. The jumbo pack of toilet paper was on sale for $4.99, and so was a large eight-pack of paper towels. I remembered I needed toothpaste, so I picked that up too. As I headed for the checkout, I passed the pet aisle. Jay Johnston was standing in front of the kitty toys, Melvin the Mouse in one hand, a package of three plush balls in the other. On impulse I walked over to him and said, "Looking for a toy for your new kitty? I'd pick Melvin the Mouse if I were you. All the shelter cats love him."

He looked up at me quizzically; then recognition kicked in and he smiled. "Oh, Ms. McCall. Nice to see you again." He tapped Melvin's tail. "So your cats recommend this toy, eh?"

I thought of all the Melvin heads I'd thrown away and couldn't suppress a grin. "Oh yes. Melvin provides hours and hours of fun."

"Well, I think I'll splurge and get both. Susan is just so in love with that cat." With a grin, he tossed both articles into his cart.

"That's good to hear. Who knows? Maybe you'll want to get her a little brother or sister."

He threw up both hands. "Ah, that's all my wife needs to hear. You should see the special meals she makes for that cat. Eats better than both of us."

"I can identify with that." A sudden thought struck me, and as he started to turn away, I laid my hand on his arm. "Mr. Johnston, you said you freelanced at CNC?"

"Yes. It was quite an experience. They offered me a full-time job, but I turned them down. I make good money freelancing, and quite frankly, I've never liked the corporate environment."

"Would you know if a Laura Griggs ever worked there?"

"Laura Griggs, Laura Griggs . . . that name does sound familiar." He took iPhone out of his jacket pocket and started to tap at the screen. "I always keep a ledger of the people I interact with on my different jobs. You never know when you might need a reference. I have a spreadsheet on CNC—ah, here it is!" He scanned it quickly, then said, "Yes, Laura Griggs. She worked in Digital Security."

My heart was pounding so hard in my chest I could barely hear myself speak. "Digital Security? What's that?"

"It's sometimes referred to as physical security. They focus on ways to keep unauthorized personnel from getting into places they shouldn't. Laura was excellent with a computer, and her specialty was, to put it simply, preventing B and E's. She knew how to bypass alarms, secure locks, many times making them computer controlled—that sort of thing."

Something buzzed at the back of my brain, some niggling thought that this all sounded vaguely familiar somehow. "I don't suppose you could tell me what she looked like?"

He gave his head a shake. "I'm terrible at descriptions. Just ask my wife," he chuckled, and then said in a more sober tone, "Why do you want to know about her?"

I shrugged. "No particular reason. Her name was mentioned in connection with Ulla's, that's all."

"Ah, yes. I'd almost forgotten about that. I do remember that Laura was on the security team for Ulla's show, and they transferred her from that to my project, and she was not happy about it. Put up a stink so that they transferred her back, which, to be honest with you, I didn't mind in the least."

"No? Why was that?"

He made a whirring motion on the side of his temple. "I always had the feeling that she was cray-zee. It seemed to me like she was stalking Ulla. She was always skulking around, watching her." He shrugged. "Or maybe it was all part of her job. Who am I to say?"

The words from Ulla's book came crashing back to me. *"It's like she's stalking me, waiting for her opportunity to move in."* I whipped out my iPhone and called up a picture of Candy Carmichael. I handed my phone to Jay. "Is this Laura?" I asked.

Jay took the phone, squinted at the screen, then gave his head an emphatic shake. "Oh, heck no. I recognize this woman. It's Candy Carmichael. Laura doesn't look anything like her. She has very short hair, and her features are more angular. She's very thin too. What some call a boyish build." He started to fumble in his pocket. "Wait a second. I might have a picture of her here." He started tapping at his screen again. "There was some sort of party we were all at, and I was taking candid shots. I got a good one of her, which was a rarity, because she never wanted her photo taken—ah, here it is." He held his phone out to me. "She's the one all the way over to the left. That scowl is because she realized I'd snapped her photo, and there wasn't a darn thing she could do about it."

I took the phone and looked at the screen, and my blood ran cold. Granted, the hair color was different, and the makeup was a bit heavier, but there could be no mistaking those heavy-lidded eyes, that blank stare.

I'd definitely met Laura Griggs, and very recently. Only I'd been introduced to her under a different name. Lois Galveston.

Chapter
Twenty-Two

Jay Johnston made his way toward the checkout, and I tossed my things into an empty cart and beat feet toward the exit. I got in my car and sped home, certain that I'd probably set some sort of speed record and thankful that I wasn't pulled over. I burst through the back door into the kitchen, startling Toby, who was lounging by his food bowl. Leila was cutting up lettuce for a salad at the island counter, and she raised both eyebrows when she saw me. She looked pointedly at my empty hands.

"Don't tell me—the Redi-Mart was out of toilet paper?"

"No, actually it was on sale," I said breathlessly. I shrugged out of my jacket and hung it on the peg by the door. "The line was way too long, and there have been some significant developments in Ulla's case I need to check out."

Leila paused in her chopping and twirled her knife in the air. "What sort of new development? This better be good. We only have one skinny roll of toilet paper left."

"Oh, it's good," I said. "I'm pretty sure my theory about

Laura was correct. I just have the wrong suspect." I proceeded to tell Leila everything that had transpired last night and today, ending with my revelation courtesy of Jay Johnston. When I finished, she let out a low whistle.

"It's kinda scary," she said, "but it makes sense." She tapped the knife handle against her chin. "There were a gazillion people milling around the back that day," she said slowly. "It's possible she could have slipped in and made a switch."

I bobbed my head up and down. "She could even have been the woman in the red tweed coat and pink scarf that Savannah saw, and that I saw arguing with Ulla. She might have known about the rivalry between Ulla and Maggie and planned to incriminate her all along."

"Unhinged sister kills for revenge," Leila murmured. "Makes an interesting front-page headline."

"One thing I don't understand, though, is why she'd break into the shelter. It's the only explanation I can think of for that necklace appearing there. She must have taken it out of Ulla's bag and then dropped it when she was in the shelter—but why? And why was she there in the first place?" I dragged my hand through my hair. "If only I could find that other lip gloss. There's got to be some DNA of hers on it somewhere."

Leila tapped her finger on the counter. "You need to tell Will about this. He can investigate."

"Will's already on my case. I promised him I wouldn't do any more investigating, but if I can put something concrete together, he might end up thanking me."

Leila walked over to the table and picked up her laptop. "Maybe what you need is a distraction. Sometimes when you focus too hard on a problem, you need to just relax and think about something else. Then—voila! The solution comes to you." She booted up the computer and pulled up YouTube. "I think you'll get a kick out of this, you being the intrepid cat lover that you are. I found it today." Leila typed in "Ulla Townsend" and "klepto cat" and hit Enter. A few seconds later, a video popped up on the screen. As Leila hit Play, I gave a little yelp and pointed to the screen. "Am I reading that right? One million hits?"

Leila laughed. "You are, and guess what? That's tame compared to some of the other cat videos on this site. Jim showed me one of a cat stuck in a paper bag that got eleven million hits."

"I guess cats are more popular than Ulla Townsend—or at least they are on YouTube anyway."

I leaned over my friend's shoulder as she started the video. Toby, curious as well, hopped up on the stool next to me and leaned his head over so he could see too. I figured one of the cameramen must have posted it, because it was taken backstage right before Ulla's promo had been filmed. I watched Annie Reilly sit docilely on Ulla's lap for all of five seconds before snaking out a paw and trying to grab the bullet-shaped object dangling from the chain Ulla held in her hand.

"I remember that," I murmured. "Annie Reilly was really attracted to that necklace."

Ulla went into her spiel and held up a purring Annie Reilly. The video ended and I said, "You're right, that was cute." I looked over at Toby, who had stretched up and put both paws on the counter. "What did you think, Tobes?"

Toby lifted his paw and batted the side of the screen. "Hey," I said. "Be careful, Toby. Don't scratch Leila's screen. I can't afford to buy her a new laptop right now."

"Oh, don't worry," Leila laughed. "It's the newspaper's anyway. I'll just requisition a new one." She peered at the screen. "What was he pointing at anyway?"

"I think it was this one." I pointed to the next video, entitled "Klepto Cat Antics" and said, "Maybe we should play it."

Leila clicked on that video, and a big Himalayan cat appeared on the screen. There was a large leather bag on a nearby chair. Quick as a flash, the cat hopped up on the chair and swiped its paw inside the bag. A moment later, it had a shiny necklace clasped between its paws. The cat ran across the room, dragging the necklace and, with its nose, edged up the cushion on its little bed. Then she shoved the necklace underneath the cushion, patted it with her paw, and turned to face the camera.

"Good job, Klepto Kris," said a disembodied voice, presumably the owner's. "Maybe we'll make *America's Got Talent* yet." The cat looked supremely pleased with herself as the video cut off.

"Wow," said Leila. "Was that for real? Someone was

training their cat to be a pickpocket so they could get on *America's Got Talent?*"

I shook my head. "It takes all kinds."

Toby swiveled his head to look at me. "Merow," he said. His paw shot out and tapped at that video again.

Leila chuckled. "Maybe Toby wants to get on *AGT* too, Syd," she suggested.

I reached out and gave the cat a pat on the head. "Is that what you want, Toby? Or did you have another reason for wanting me to watch that?"

Toby blinked twice. "Merow."

I paused, remembering. "Vi said that Annie got into everything," I said slowly. "And she got loose that day in the storage room because the lock is broken on her carrier." I slid off the stool and started to pace. "Ulla threw that necklace into the tote bag. She tossed it in the corner so that it was open. You could see inside."

Leila watched me, her eyes slitted. "I know you're going somewhere with all this. I just can't figure out where yet."

I closed my eyes. "The top of the Glow tube is bullet-shaped, just like that charm. The Walnut Meadows lip gloss matches Glow in shape and color, and even the base is the same. All the killer had to do was switch out the covers. The killer had to be somewhere close, because he or she retrieved the lip gloss after Ulla used it. It wasn't in the crime scene photos or anywhere back there. What if the killer got the gloss, but before they could switch it back they got greedy and wanted that necklace? What if while they were retrieving the necklace, they accidentally dropped the lip gloss into the tote, and then heard someone coming, so they took off before they could get the gloss back. And what if Annie Reilly, who was loose, saw all this and decided that a bullet-shaped cover was just as good as a bullet-shaped necklace! After all, the cover was very glossy—I saw it."

Leila was staring at me, her mouth open. "You think the cat took the murder weapon?"

"Annie really liked that necklace. With it gone, what's the next best thing? The tube itself. According to Vi, she's just as good a klepto as that cat in the video!" I started to pace faster. "The killer figures that the lip gloss must be mixed in with our stuff, so they broke in here to look for it. Maybe a police car came by—they do patrol the area quite frequently—and the intruder panics and somehow loses the necklace. The clasp was loose after all. In any event, I think the tainted lip gloss is still at the shelter."

"Because the killer didn't have time to get it?"

"No—because the killer was looking in the wrong place for it." I hurried over to the door and snatched my jacket off the peg. "I have to go to the shelter right now."

"Wait." Leila shot out her hand and closed her fingers around my wrist. "Shouldn't you call Will?"

I shook my head emphatically. "No. I could be wrong. My theory could be all wet. I wouldn't want to send him out on a wild goose chase. But if I can produce the murder weapon, it's a whole other ball game. Just say a prayer that the killer doesn't decide to pay the shelter another visit right now."

"I can't talk you out of this, can I? Well, then, fine." Leila snatched her jacket from the peg. "I'm going with you. If Ulla's killer is lurking around, at least you won't be alone."

* * *

I parked my convertible around the block from the shelter, and Leila and I cut through the parking lot over to the rear entrance. As I swung open the door, I said, "Maybe you should stay out here—you know, as a lookout."

"Fine. I'll wait behind those bushes. If I see anything or anyone suspicious, I'll whistle once. If I see Will or Callahan coming, I'll whistle twice."

"Okay. I shouldn't be too long."

I left my bestie and went inside. I didn't want to switch on any lights and call undue attention to the fact that someone was in the shelter after hours, so I pulled out my phone and turned on my flashlight app. The pencil-thin beam afforded me enough light to see my way around, so I headed straight for the cattery. Annie's cage was the last one, tucked in the far corner. I walked over and shone my light inside. Annie was awake, and her bright blue eyes regarded me curiously as I approached.

"Hello, Annie Reilly," I said. "I'm curious, girl. Where did Vi put your carrier? I'd like to know just what you might have hidden there." I remembered Vi saying that she was going to put the carrier off to the side. I swung my light around the cattery but didn't see anything against any of the walls. I moved the light around the room again, and off in the far corner saw two stacked carriers. I walked over to them while Annie Reilly let out a plaintive "merow" behind me. The top carrier was blue; the bottom one, pink. I was sure the pink one was the one with the broken lock, and a swift glance told me I was right. I moved the blue one off to the side, picked up the pink one, and carried it over to the long table that was in front of Annie's cage. I set it down, opened the door wide, and let my fingers roam over the thin carpet that we used to cover the bottom of the carriers. As Annie meowed again, I walked over to her cage and stuck my fingers through the bars. Annie's pink tongue darted out to lick my fingertips.

"Good girl," I crooned at the cat. "What treasures have you got hidden in your carrier, Annie? Did you see something shiny and bullet-shaped you thought you simply must have?"

The cat cocked her head at me, almost as if she understood what I was saying. I went back to the carrier and felt along the edge of the carpet. I paused as my fingers touched a slightly raised portion of rug. I pulled it back. There lay a catnip Melvin the Mouse, a small ball . . . and a cylindrical object that looked amazingly like the Glow sample I'd seen Ulla with.

"Bingo," I whispered. I started to slide my hand through the bars of the cage and then stopped. Had I heard a bird call? I listened a moment, but nothing was repeated, so I thrust my hand into my pocket, pulled out a Kleenex, and then very gently removed the lip gloss tube from the carrier. My hand shook as I held it up.

"This is it," I said. "This is what killed Ulla, I know it! The killer got spooked and dropped it in the tote bag, and you got it out."

"Very good, Sydney," said a raspy voice behind me. "That's exactly what happened."

I whirled and saw Lois Galveston née Laura Griggs standing in the doorway of the cat room. The gun she held in her hand was pointed directly at my heart.

Chapter Twenty-Three

Laura Griggs moved toward me, her lips curved downward in a sneer. "Thanks for finding it for me," she said. "I saw you talking to that Johnston guy at the Redi-Mart. I was in the next aisle over, and I listened to your conversation. Since you're such a master sleuth, I knew it would only be a matter of time before you put two and two together." She held out her other hand and wiggled her fingers at the lip gloss. "I'll take that off your hands now."

Although my heart was beating so hard I thought it was going to fall out of my chest, I managed to make my tone remain calm as I said, "You don't want to do this, Laura. You don't want to kill me."

Laura shrugged. "You're right, I don't. I like you, Sydney. You're bold and fearless, and you've got a quick mind. I had an idea you might figure everything out, but I didn't count on you putting all the pieces of the puzzle together before I got out of town."

"You left me those notes, didn't you? In my jacket at Antonio's, and at the shelter?"

"Yes. They were meant as friendly warnings. Like I said before, I like you." She let out a slow breath. "You fooled me, Sydney. You were far smarter than I gave you credit for, and now you have to pay the price." She paused. "You and your friend, the reporter."

The birdcall I thought I'd heard earlier came to my mind, and I gasped. "What did you do to Leila?"

"She's just taking a little nap, for now. But unfortunately, I'll have to dispose of her too, right after I take care of you. Can't leave too much of a trail, you know?" She waved the gun at me. "Take your cell phone out of your pocket. I know you've got one; you wouldn't have come here without it. Take it out and put it down on the floor where I can see it, then step away from it."

I hesitated, then pulled my phone out of my pocket and set it down on the floor. I took a step back and raised my chin defiantly. "What? Are you going to try and frame our murders on Maggie too?"

Laura barked out a laugh. "I hadn't thought about that, but it's not a bad idea. I can have you make a call, get her down here, then make it look as if she killed you two, thinking you were intruders. When she realized what she'd done, she took her own life. It's worth considering."

Laura's eyes glittered, and I truly feared she'd lost her mind. Talking to her might be my only hope—maybe one of those patrol cars would come by and decide to investigate. I jammed my hands into my pockets. "You sound like you've thought that out pretty good. Not as good as you thought out killing Ulla, though." I paused. "You did kill her, right?"

"Of course I killed Ulla!" Laura's lips thinned and she made a derisive snort. "I'm not sorry for it either. Madelyn would never have approved of my plan for revenge, but once she died, I knew it was time Ulla paid the piper for all her sins, not just what she did to my sister. Once I heard she planned to stop here at Deer Park on her book tour, I knew it would be the perfect place to end her life."

"Rather an ingenious method—death by lip gloss. You knew about her allergy."

Laura's lips curved into a semblance of a smile. "My sister told me all about what happened that day in the lab. She swore me to secrecy; she was so afraid of that witch! Switching out the lip glosses was the easy part. They always put samples together so carelessly. Finding just the right one was more challenging. There aren't too many lip glosses that have bee venom in them. I was fortunate to find one that looked almost exactly like the Glow sample. Walnut Meadow Gloss." She barked out a laugh. "A fitting end, if you ask me. She was such a vain creature. Fitting payback for all the lives she ruined."

I spoke slowly and softly as I started to back up, little by little, toward the desk in the corner of the room. "I can understand how you feel. It was a horrible thing, what she did to your sister."

" 'Horrible' isn't a strong enough word," Laura spit out. "Ulla was so insecure; she was always pulling these pranks on those girls. Only trouble was, some of her pranks were downright evil, like putting alcohol in the punch at Maggie Shayne's party. My sister told me about that too. That's why I figured Maggie would be the perfect person to set up."

I felt anger well up inside me, so much so that I forgot to lower my voice. "Why would you want to do that? Maggie never did a thing to you!"

Laura stared at me, wide-eyed. "She never did anything nice for my sister either. Never even visited her in the hospital, and she professed to be her friend. Maggie didn't fight back with Ulla either. She just ignored everything she did. She deserves to take the rap for her death. I'd seen her around in that coat and scarf. It wasn't hard to find duplicates. I got the ratty coat at the thrift shop, and there were a ton of those scarves at King's. When I went around the back of the store, I stashed my coat in the bushes and slipped those on."

"It must have been pretty easy for you to slip back there unnoticed and switch out the lip gloss," I said.

Laura nodded. "Darn easy. That security was horrible. I walked right in behind some of those lighting guys and hid. When everyone went to see the cats, I switched the lip gloss. Then after Ulla collapsed, in the confusion I saw a chance to slip in, grab the lip gloss, and get out. I forgot to switch it back with the Glow one, though. My mistake."

Keep her talking, my brain screamed. *That patrol car should pass by soon.* "You made another mistake too. You wanted Ulla's necklace."

"I happened to pass by her office the day the Glow people gave it to her. You could see in her eyes how much it meant to her, how much she coveted it. I felt that was the least she owed me. I'd overheard Savannah on the phone, calling for a repair on it, so I figured it was stashed somewhere. I almost missed it because the tote was on your end of the room, but thank goodness I remembered Ulla had a flowered tote. Just as I lifted it out of the bag, though, I heard someone coming. I panicked and in my haste, the Walnut Meadows gloss fell inside the bag. I figured I'd just come back for it later, but when I did, the gloss was gone. I never thought the cat might have taken it, but I did think that maybe it rolled out of the bag and got mixed up with your stuff."

"That's why you broke in the other night. To look for it. And that's when you lost the necklace?"

"I thought I'd fixed the clasp, but it was still too loose. It fell off and rolled across the floor. I didn't have a chance to hunt for it because that damn patrol car was too close."

"The police have it. Your fingerprints will be on it."

"Yeah, along with tons of others. You and your friend won't be around to tell any tales, and by the time the police figure everything out, I'll be long gone."

I took another step backward. "You know, it's still not

too late for you, Laura. Your sister's accident and eventual death took a large toll on you. You and your sister were very close, weren't you? I'm sure with a good lawyer—"

Her eyes widened, and she broke in, saying, "Are you suggesting that I plead insanity?" Her fingers tightened on the barrel of the gun. "Hell, I'm not insane. I've never been saner in my life. What was insane is the way Ulla Townsend, or Beckman as she was called in those days, was allowed to get away with murder. Because, in a sense, she did murder my sister. Maddie's life stopped the day she was injured in that accident. I wouldn't call what she went through after that living—not by a long shot."

"Ulla must have felt the same way. Savannah told me she was desperately trying to get in touch with a woman she called Miggs. She had no idea Maddie had died."

"Hah! I watched her carefully when I worked at that studio in Charleston. She started going to a therapist to work out her anger issues, but it had nothing to do with wanting to make things right. Heck no. Do you know what was behind all that? Getting that damn Glow contract, that's what!"

I took another two steps backward and felt the rim of the desk hit against my butt. "Really?"

"Yep. She'd heard that someone at Glow thought that she was too confrontational to be a spokeswoman for their product, so she went to that therapist, Dr. Gray. When I found that out, I made an appointment too, under an assumed name, of course. I managed to strike up an acquaintance with Gray's assistant, and one night when Gray was out of town, we had ourselves a little wine party in the office." She let out a low chuckle. "That gal has zero tolerance for booze. When she was worshipping the porcelain god in the bathroom, I found Ulla's file and snapped photos of the contents. It was quite revealing."

I stole a quick glance at my wristwatch. "In what way?"

"Ulla's therapist told her that all her past indiscretions from her youth were the reason for her pent-up rage, and if she could make good with the people she'd wronged, why, it could be a real turning point for her. She was so desperate to make those Glow people like her, she'd have jumped off a bridge if she thought it would help." Abruptly she waved the gun in the air. "I think we've done enough talking. Give me that lip gloss."

It's now or never, I thought, and focused my gaze on a point over Laura's left shoulder. "Oh my God!" I cried.

Laura turned her head to see what had attracted my attention, and I took advantage of the momentary distraction to hurl myself over the desk. Laura's head snapped around, and I heard her say angrily, "Nice try, but you're forgetting I'm the one with the gun. Now come out from behind that desk and give me that lip gloss, or—"

The rest of what she was about to say was cut off as I sprang upward, Vi's can of White Rain hairspray clutched in my hand. Before Laura could react, I raised the can and sprayed her full in the face. She dropped the gun and scrubbed her hands across her face with an agonized wail. I leapt over the desk and made a beeline for the gun. My fingers closed over the butt of the handle just as Laura whirled about and rammed herself into my back. We both went down, legs flailing. I tried to reach for the gun, but she grabbed my arm and held on tight. Her eyes were red and watery, her face a mask of rage.

"You little interfering witch," she rasped. "It's going to give me great pleasure to rid the world of you." Her fingers tightened on my arm, twisted it. "Give me that lip gloss!"

In answer, I brought up my knee and hit her square in the stomach. She fell back with a grunt. I tried to get to my feet, but she reached out and grabbed the edge of my jacket and pulled me down. She shoved me back against the desk and pushed to her feet, grabbing the gun as she did so. She backed up against the door and leaned there, then raised the gun and pointed it at me. "Okay, I'm through being nice," she growled. "The lip gloss."

I shook my head. "You're going to have to shoot me before I'll give that up."

Her lips curved into a sneer. "If you insist—oh!"

A shadow loomed up in the doorway behind Laura, a shadow who moved quickly. Will grabbed the wrist that held the gun with one hand and clamped the other around the barrel, snapping it out of her grasp before she could react. "Well, well," Will said. "What have we here?" He pushed Laura over to the side, and another policeman appeared from the hallway. He took Laura away from Will and handcuffed her wrists behind her back.

"Take her out and read her her rights," Will said. He still held Laura's gun in one hand. As the policeman led Laura out, Will walked over to the desk, set the gun down, and then turned to me. "So this is what you call not doing any investigating?"

"Sorry," I mumbled. "I figured out what happened to the poisoned lip gloss. Leila said that I should call you, but I wanted to get proof first." I sucked in my breath. "Oh my gosh, Leila! Laura said she knocked her out!"

"She's fine now. Leila saw someone in the shadows when you went in, and she dialed nine-one-one just before Laura knocked her out. Dispatch alerted me." He folded his arms across his chest. "What were you saying about the lip gloss?"

I reached into my jacket pocket and pulled out the shiny brown cylinder. "Leila and I watched a video of a klepto cat on YouTube, and it struck me that Annie Reilly had the same tendencies. Annie especially liked the bullet-shaped charm on Ulla's necklace, and since the lip gloss cover is shiny and the same shape—"

"You thought maybe it appealed to her. Not bad," Will said. He reached out and took the tube of gloss from me. "Of course now it's got both your prints and the cat's, but maybe we can still get DNA off the tube."

"And if that fails, we have Laura's confession." I walked over to where my cell phone still lay on the floor and scooped it up. "I set it to record when she told me to put it down, and hopefully it did." I hit the button, and Laura's voice echoed clearly through the room. *"Of course I killed Ulla."*

Will's brows lifted and he let out a deep chuckle. "Can't beat that," he said.

Chapter
Twenty-Four

It was Friday afternoon, a little after four, and Kat, Maggie, Leila, Will, and I were all gathered at Dayna's café for a little impromptu celebration of the successful closing of the case and exonerating Maggie of murder. Dayna had baked her specialty, a rich carrot cake, for the occasion. I'd just finished my slice and was reaching for a second when Leila asked, "So, what's going to happen to Laura?"

"Well, she'll be arraigned," Will said. "I'm sure she'll take Syd's advice and hire a good lawyer, but even with an insanity plea, I rather think she'll end up serving time. Thanks to Syd, I had a nice little recording to play for the DA. She sure sounded like she knew full well what she was doing. The DA thinks we've got a good case, and she can't wait to throw the book at her."

Dayna emerged from the kitchen, a steaming coffeepot in hand. "Oh, she knew what she was doing all right," she said. "Hell-bent on revenge maybe, but crazy? Like a fox."

Maggie sighed. "I'm not sure whether to hate Laura or

to feel sorry for her. In a way, she was a victim of Ulla's machinations too."

"Yep." Will held out his mug for a refill. "She did come slightly unhinged after her sister's death. Oh, and I found out Laura had another reason besides revenge for leaving her job at the cable station. They were giving all the employees psych evaluations, and guess who the examining doctor was?"

Leila and I both said it together. "Not Dr. Gray?"

"The very same. Even though she'd worn a wig and used a phony name, she was still afraid that Dr. Gray would recognize her, and if that happened, well, her career there would be over anyway."

"Not to mention she probably would have failed a psych evaluation," Maggie observed.

"Amen to that." Leila touched the sore spot on the side of her head where Laura had clocked her with the gun butt. "I agree with Dayna's assessment. She's crazy like a fox, and I hope they throw away the key in her case."

"I guess all the CNC people are finally headed back to Charleston now?" Kat asked.

"Oh, yes, and according to Wendy Sweeting, 'not a moment too soon,'" Will said with a chuckle. "I can't say I'm sorry to see them go either."

"I bet Tara's glad," I remarked. "She mentioned Wendy was starting to get on her nerves. I wonder what will happen to Ken and Savannah's book and movie deal now?"

"I was curious about that myself," Leila admitted, "so

I put out some feelers. From what my source was able to piece together, Ken promised to get Ulla the Glow deal in exchange for Ulla's signing the book rights back to Savannah. At the same time, though, he was undercutting Ulla with the Glow people, making a pitch for Candy to become the spokeswoman. He was doing some pretty fancy juggling."

"And he wasn't afraid of Ulla's wrath?" Dayna asked.

"Guess not," Leila said with a shrug. "I guess he figured he'd be making enough from the combo book and movie deal with Savannah, to tell Ulla to take a hike. My source said he was getting pretty sick of her high-handed ways."

"What a rat!" Kat cried. "Ken wasn't above double-crossing anyone, was he?"

"Nope. Of course once Ulla died, he threw his hat full force in the ring for Candy Carmichael for Glow. I do have to say, though, one person he never tried to cheat was Savannah."

"Because he needed her," Maggie put in. "I hear she's a very talented writer."

"I'll reserve judgment on that till after I read the book," I said with a chuckle. "I imagine it's full steam ahead for both projects."

"Yes, but I bet Ken won't see very much of the profits if Cathy has anything to say about it," Leila said. "I heard she's taking him back to court and demanding a slice of that pie—a very large slice."

"Well, I hope she gets it, and more," declared Dayna. "And what about Miss Candy Carmichael? Did she end up with the Glow deal?"

"Actually, no," Leila said. She reached up to twist an auburn curl around her finger. "After all this drama, Miss Candy decided she'd had enough of Ken Colgate, Glow, and CNC. She turned down the Glow deal, and I understand she quit CNC. Not to worry, though. My source told me she got a sweet deal with a major network retailer. Candy will be back, selling products, but to a much wider audience."

"And I bet she got a sweet raise too," I said with a sigh. "Some people just step in it. So, who ended up as the Glow spokesperson? Please don't tell me Savannah."

"Oh, no. Savannah's too busy plotting out her next novel. I heard they were thinking of approaching Sofia Vergara."

A plaintive "merow" sounded from underneath the table, and Toby stuck his head out. I reached down to give him a pat. "Gossip aside, we should all be thanking Toby. If he hadn't directed my attention to the video of the klepto cat, I might not have figured it all out."

"Oh, you would have," Maggie said. She covered my hand with hers. "You've got a real flair for detection, Syd."

"I agree," Leila added. "You're a junior Nancy Drew."

"Fine." I wrinkled my nose at her. "Then you have to be either my Bess Marvin or my George Fayne. I'll let you pick."

"Hmm." Leila scratched her head as she pondered my question. Finally she said, "I'll take George. She's more daring."

Will's phone rang, and he excused himself to take the call. Leila leaned over and hissed in my ear, "If I'm George, then does that mean Will's your Ned Nickerson?" she said with an impish grin. "Or do you have someone else in mind for that role?"

"Merow" sounded loudly from underneath the table.

I started to laugh. "I think you just got your answer."

Kat rapped on the table. "Before Maggie and I leave to check on that new litter of kittens, I wanted to impart some really good news. Vi called a little while ago. It seems that video of Annie Reilly piqued a lot of people's interest. We've got ten applications for adoption for her so far, and there are more coming."

We all applauded. "Thank goodness Annie's story has a happy ending," I said. "I felt bad that out of all the cats at the event that day, she was the only one not adopted. Now she's got more applicants for a 'furever' home than we can count."

"And I'll be going over each one very carefully to ensure that Annie gets in the best home possible," Kat said. "Thank God for YouTube videos. Sometimes they do come in handy."

As Kat and Maggie rose, I pushed back my own chair. "I'll come with—" I began, but Maggie held up her hand.

"You most certainly will not. You will stay here and

enjoy your moment. And," she added, "no one deserves it more."

I grinned at the two of them. "Okay, fine. But if you need help with the kitties or going over those applications for Annie, call."

Kat glanced over toward the corner where Will stood and wiggled both eyebrows. "You do the same," she said with a chuckle.

Leila glanced at her watch, then jumped up. "I've got to get going too."

"What's this? Everyone's leaving me?" I made a face and tugged at my pal's jacket. "Where are you going?"

"Home to change. Jim's picking me up in an hour. We're going to try out that new Thai restaurant in Berwick."

I stared at her. "You can eat Thai food after two large slices of carrot cake?"

Leila patted her slim stomach. "Honey, I can eat Thai food anytime! It's my favorite. You're welcome to join us—and Will too, of course." She looked over at him significantly and then shifted her gaze back to me. "You never answered my question, you know."

"What question was that?"

Her Gucci-shod foot tapped impatiently on the parquet floor. "Oh, you know, but in case you've forgotten, I'll repeat it. Has Will's kissing technique improved since high school?" Thank God, her phone buzzed just then, because I hadn't the faintest idea how to answer. She dug through her purse for her phone, looked at the screen, and let out

a gasp. "Heck! He's going to be early! I've got to leave now."
She tossed the phone back in her bag and started for the
door. "Tonight, Nancy Drew. I want my answer. If you're not
up, I'm waking you."

The door banged shut, and I looked up to see Will standing over me. "I've got good news and bad news," he said.
"Which do you want first?"

I sighed. "Let's have the good news."

"Okay. Callahan gave his notice."

I almost fell out of my chair. "What? He did? When?
Where's he going?"

"One at a time," Will said, and chuckled. "He gave it to
Connolly about an hour ago. Turns out that he met with
some of the Macon PD brass the other night. His uncle set
it up."

I recalled the incident at Antonio's and shook my head.
"His uncle didn't trust Connolly to give him the job,
huh?"

"Guess not. Anyway, they made him an offer he simply
couldn't refuse, quote unquote, and he's headed back to
Georgia even as we speak."

"Tsk-tsk," I said. "What is it with the Deer Park PD? They
can't seem to hold onto their senior homicide detectives."

Will's grin broadened. "Oh, I think they'll be able to
hold onto their newest one."

I stared at him. "So that means you got Bennington's
slot?"

"Yep. Whether it was by default or not, I don't know, and I don't care."

"That's terrific!" My smile morphed into a puzzled frown. "That's two pieces of *good* news though, right? You said you had good news and bad news?"

"The bad news is part of the good news. Connolly wants me to consult with another homicide detective on a case in Flemington. Tonight. So—"

"Friday night dinner's on hold—again." I sighed. "It's okay, Will. I understand." My eyes sparkled with mischief as I added, "I'll find something else to occupy my time."

He arched an eyebrow. "Just as long as the 'something else' doesn't involve a dead body, I'm okay with that." He reached out and took both my hands in his. He looked deeply into my eyes as he said, "You like to take chances, Syd, but one of these days I might not get there in time to protect you."

"Merow," came from underneath the table.

"See, even your cat agrees," Will said with a laugh.

"Hey, it didn't turn out so bad," I protested. "I got you a taped confession, didn't I?"

He released my hands and moved his up to rest on my shoulders. "You do know that you could have gotten yourself killed with that little stunt. If Leila hadn't had the presence of mind to make that call before she got knocked out, and if I hadn't gotten there in time, and if that can of hairspray hadn't been in the desk drawer, and if—"

"Way too many 'ifs' for my taste," I muttered. "But you're right. I—or you—*we* could die tomorrow, and if we do, then we'll never know. Leila will never know."

"Know what?" he asked.

"The answer to her question. This." I reached out, pulled Will's face down to mine, and kissed him—hard—right on the lips.

Soft fur brushed my ankles. "Mer-OW-OW-OW," Toby said.

I hardly heard him. Because Will was kissing me back.

Acknowledgments

Once again I have to thank my wonderful agent, Josh Getzler, for making sure that my stories continue to get told and for putting up with all my comments and questions, even when they come at five-thirty AM in the morning. I would also like to thank Matt Martz, Jenny Chen, and the entire editorial staff at Crooked Lane for taking what I thought was a good story and making it even better.

My thanks to Ken and Kathy Colgate for lending their names to characters in this book. Ken, you finally got your wish. I know my dear friend, the late MaryLou Ricciardi, would have been so proud. Thanks also to Tara Pitsenberger and Donna Blondell, who also lent their names to characters in this book, as well as Amanda Winfield, Doris Sharp (aka Dayna Harper) and Laurie Rubin. What are friends for?

More thanks go out to Vi Kizis, always my muse and my Phoenix contact. The Pet Rescue series would not be the same without the character of Vi. A special shout-out goes to Susan Johnston and her beautiful Maine Coon, Princess Fuzzypants, ROCCO's Facebook friends. How could I not

Acknowledgments

put a cat that beautiful in this series? Check out her Facebook page if you don't believe me!

As always, my thanks go out to the legion of authors interviewed on ROCCO's blog. I am so grateful to have met all of you. And of course to my fur babies, ROCCO and Maxx, without whom I would not have had my two series. Finally a shout-out to all the animal rescue groups and animal shelters everywhere. What you do for homeless animals is incredible, and I salute each and every one of you.